The Marriage Proposal

The Romano Family Trilogy - Book 2

Debra A. Daly

iUniverse, Inc.
Bloomington

The Marriage Proposal
The Romano Family Trilogy - Book 2

iUniverse books may be ordered through booksellers or by contacting:

iUniverse
1663 Liberty Drive
Bloomington, IN 47403
www.iuniverse.com
1-800-Authors (1-800-288-4677)

Because of the dynamic nature of the Internet, any web addresses or links contained in this book may have changed since publication and may no longer be valid. The views expressed in this work are solely those of the author and do not necessarily reflect the views of the publisher, and the publisher hereby disclaims any responsibility for them.

Any people and/or image depicted in stock imagery provided by FOTOLIA.com are models, and such images are being used for illustrative purposes only.
Certain stock imagery © FOTOLIA.com.

ISBN: 978-1-4759-4954-4 (sc)
ISBN: 978-1-4759-4955-1 (ebk)

Library of Congress Control Number: 2012916751

Printed in the United States of America

iUniverse rev. date: 09/19/2012

This book is dedicated to my husband

The man who makes my heart soar

I love you always . . .

Chapter One
My best friend's wedding . . .

Rebecca McFarlan circled around the dance floor at her best friend's outdoor wedding advancing on her target. It was a quiet and precise maneuver she learned at the New York State Police Academy five years earlier. The goal was to approach your subject without drawing any unwarranted attention. *This is as good a time as any,* Rebecca thought.

Rebecca needed a husband and, by God, she needed one fast! *So what if it's at my best friend's wedding! So what if the guy I'm gonna ask to marry me is the best man and the brother of the groom! So what if I can hardly stand the man!*

Bottom line, she needed a successful, preferably male collaborator and Anthony Romano fit the bill to perfection. He was the only man she could think of who wouldn't further complicate her already complicated life. Out of all the men she knew, and heaven knew she knew plenty; Anthony was the most logical choice. He would have enough common decency not to attack her every night of the week until her mission was complete and he would have enough integrity to uphold his end of the bargain. In a nutshell, he was "textbook husband material."

Rebecca felt that if she asked him, he would solve her problem then move on. No one would get hurt and no one would be the wiser. When she didn't need his husbandry services anymore, she would file for divorce and explain to her family and friends that, *Hey it just didn't work out!*

"There he is . . . it's now or never!" Rebecca declared. She took a deep breath while circling the dance floor waving to this relative or smiling at that one, quietly and very strategically working her way around until she stood directly in front of her target, Anthony Romano. Rebecca silently studied the man before her. *Damn, he's hot!*

Anthony Romano was leaning against a tree looking a little dangerous in his jet-black tuxedo that matched his jet-black sunglasses. At six foot-one, Anthony Romano was tall, but shorter than most of the other men in his family, Rebecca mentally noted.

She visually studied the extremely wealthy, international executive whose day job was to run a multi-billion dollar corporation.

Rebecca suspected that women made drooling fools of themselves whenever they were around him and that kind of attention could definitely over-inflate a man's ego. As she stepped closer, his head was bowed in what appeared to be an act of contemplation. His blonde-white hair was tousling about from the wind that swept up from the river below. His light hair was in stark contrast to his raven-black wedding attire, which he donned with perfection. The man was obviously in phenomenal shape. "Hi!" Rebecca spoke loudly to announce her presence, since Anthony hadn't noticed her standing there for several minutes. It seemed he was far away in his own thoughts.

"Hello Rebecca," Anthony moodily replied.

Watching him pull himself out of a somewhat meditative state, Rebecca got a good look at his purpling eye at the side of his face not covered by his sunglasses. "Ouch, that looks worse now than it did during the ceremony!" Rebecca moved in closer to survey the damage.

"Thanks!" Anthony snorted.

Rebecca knew there had been some kind of altercation when Jack, the groom, came home and obviously from the black eye Anthony was sporting, a few punches had been thrown. But since the Romano men were one tight-lipped clique, Rebecca's odds were not greatly in her favor of discovering who rewarded Anthony his shiner. All she knew was that Anthony took a hit. For whom or by whom, she had no idea.

"So what happened?" Rebecca asked hoping to draw Anthony into a conversation. Every other time she asked that question to anyone else while on the job, the flood gates generally opened and within minutes she would be tubing through a river of information. However, Anthony completely ignored the question and looked away from her towards the river.

Rebecca stared off too. It really was a lovely day. The outdoor, riverfront wedding ceremony was a large celebration yet intimate with a hint of humor, because her best friend was more than a little pregnant. Off in the distance music played and people were dancing, eating and laughing. Children ran about the large expanse of property and horses neighed and galloped about in the corral, while the little ones were given rides around the ring. The dogs begged for food from some of the older relatives, who simply couldn't resist feeding them. Some of the guests were fishing off the dock and others took off their shoes and rolled up their pants or hiked up their dresses to dip their toes along the littoral. Boats bobbed in the blue, brilliant waters and everything seemed right with the world—except in Rebecca's world. It felt like nothing was right in her world.

Anthony watched Rebecca scan the area, seeming to study the people. He knew that the only reason why she was speaking to him at all was because he was the best man and she, the maid-of-honor. Not to mention that soon they would both be godparents to Francesca and his brother's baby.

When she walked down the aisle during the wedding procession, Anthony felt his heart crash into his ribs in a chaotic pinball response, painfully reminding him that she would never be his. The damn shame was that she was perfect for him. He didn't know how he knew that, he just did! She was the perfect height, with the most perfect curves and she even had the most perfect profession. She was a psychologist and, Lord knew, he and his family needed a good psychologist. She was exactly what he wanted in a woman.

"Excuse me," Anthony mumbled, pushing away from the tree. He didn't need to spend one more minute near a woman he could never have. Okay, it probably didn't help his chances when he blurted out to Rebecca, not long after they first met, that he intended to make her his wife. *Yeah, that really didn't go over very well!* He quite possibly made the biggest mistake of his life that day and he didn't need reminding of that now. He felt so sad for himself, yet overjoyed for his brother. It was a mixed bag of emotions that Anthony was physically struggling with on his brother's wedding day. It seemed the Romano men were the kind of men who could never find true love, made simply impossible, because they were so rich. Anthony had watched his many cousins search for that special someone who wasn't after their money, but their efforts were always fruitless. Jack beat the odds and found Francesca who was kind, gentle and patient. Today, it became obvious to Anthony that his brother's bride was one of a kind. *Man*, Anthony thought to himself, *I need to get a life!* Raking a hand through his hair, Anthony started to walk away from Rebecca.

"Where are you going?" Rebecca asked nervously.

"Why should it matter to you where I go?" Anthony bristled.

"Oh," Rebecca immediately recoiled, but remembered young Trevor, the homeless child she desperately wanted to adopt and pushed ahead instead. "I have to ask you something." Rebecca spoke quickly, realizing that she sounded uneasy. She knew the instant Anthony detected her tenseness, when one of his eyebrows lifted from behind his dark sunglasses. *It must be instinctive for a high-powered businessman like Anthony Romano to identify uneasiness . . .*

Anthony folded his arms over his chest. Lowering his head while looking over the tops of his sunglasses, his one eye practically closed with the black eye he was sporting, he shrugged. "What might that be?"

"What might what be?" Rebecca asked.

"What in God's name, woman, do you need to ask me?" Anthony countered quietly.

"Right . . ." Rebecca swayed slightly in her maid-of-honor dress that revealed sun-kissed shoulders and voluptuous breasts that rose and fell with each deep breath she took. "Well I have a little problem . . ." Rebecca held up her hand and pinched her thumb and index finger together to emphasize her point. Anthony appeared to be in full agreement with her statement and his head nodding certainly worked wonders to piss her off, feeling her calm, passive disposition slip into an aggressive one in a split second. "Forget it! I don't know what I was thinking! You would've never agreed to it anyway." Rebecca turned to leave.

Anthony caught her arm and gently pulled her back. "Try me," Anthony suggested struggling to concentrate on the conversation, because Rebecca was robbing him of his abilities to control his own cursed body. *She can try everything and anything she wants with me*, Anthony considered as his mind began to conjure up fantasies of her.

"Well I guess I'll just come right out and say it." Rebecca started to wring her hands and sway slightly.

At this point, it was noticeable to Anthony that Rebecca appeared to be uneasy. *This must be something embarrassing,* Anthony started guessing. His curiosity was certainly heightened now. "You can ask me anything." Anthony took her lovely hand into his to reassure her and to stop her from turning her hands to a frightening shade of purple. "We are family now." Rebecca took a deep breath in before she popped the question. "Will you marry me?"

Anthony shook his head knowing that he must have misunderstood her or he needed to lay off the wine for the rest of the reception. "I'm sorry?" Anthony questioned leaning in closer.

"It will only be temporary," Rebecca assured.

"Temporarily married?" Anthony puzzled.

"Yes," Rebecca nodded her head to affirm with a hopeful smile.

"Temporarily . . . ?" Anthony asked again.

"Yes," Rebecca nodded again to verify.

"Is this some kind of a joke?" Anthony dropped her hand.

"No it's not. I'm serious."

Anthony nodded while looking around wondering who was up to this prank. *She couldn't possibly be serious?* "Why do you want to 'temporarily' marry me?" Anthony held up his fingers to lay invisible quotation marks on the word "temporarily."

"Because I want to adopt a child . . ." Rebecca looked away, because her eyes started to well up. Anytime she spoke about Trevor, a large lump formed in her throat and tears stung the backs of her eyes making it impossible for her to speak or see clearly.

Anthony couldn't bear to see that anguished look upon her face. "Come here," Anthony pulled her in close while she cried softly. He circled his arm around her lovely shoulders and walked her over to a bench. "Here take this and dry your eyes, darling." Anthony handed her a clean, white handkerchief.

Rebecca took it and wasn't the slightest surprised that Anthony had a clean white handkerchief, because he was a gentleman. "Thank you," Rebecca said as she sniffed and dabbed at each eye. "My face must be a mess."

"No." Anthony thought she was stunning, with mahogany eyes that appeared golden in the bright light of day and a flawless complexion that reminded him of the finest Lotus Ware. Her hair was swept up with delicate tendrils of deep, shiny chestnut framing her face and neck giving her a dreamy appearance. *No darling*, Anthony thought, *your face takes my breath away*. Clearing his thoughts, Anthony began to speak to her quietly. "You are a very successful woman, Rebecca. There should be no reason why you cannot adopt this young boy yourself."

"Successful, single women have a thirty percent success rate of adopting a child. But successful, married couples have an almost one hundred percent success rate of adopting."

"Are you on some kind of list?" Anthony found these adoption statistics fascinating, as he removed his sunglasses.

"Yes. Trevor is the son of a woman who was a prostitute with a serious drug addiction. Trevor's mother was an indigent patient of mine who was mandated by the Court for a fixed number of sessions at the mental health clinic after she completed her drug rehab."

"Was . . ." Anthony was feeling ill over the matter already.

"Actually she never made it." Rebecca corrected as she watched Anthony shake his head. "Kelly was assigned to me at the mental health clinic, because a neighbor had complained to the State that her son was going to school, doing the food shopping, cooking, you name it, all on his own! When it came time for one of her male callers, Trevor would go to his neighbor's apartment even though he told his mother he was going to the movies." Rebecca took a deep shaky breath before she continued. "Once Children's Services got wind of this situation, they put Trevor in a foster home and his mother went straight to detox. I met Trevor briefly before he went with his foster family. His mother, Kelly, broke out the first night she was there and when she got home, she literally got the beating of her life. We're assuming from her pimp." Rebecca grimly continued. "Personally, I believe he served her up the cocktail of crystallized poison, which ultimately killed her."

Anthony looked away for a moment.

"As far as my part as the social worker, the case is over. The coroner's report was submitted to us and the Court. According to the coroner's report, she was severely beaten and died from both her injuries and a drug overdose. Case closed." Rebecca stopped for a moment trying to manage her emotions. "That was two months ago and Trevor has already been in three foster homes so far." Rebecca started sobbing uncontrollably again. "I don't know why I feel this way about Trevor . . ." Rebecca hiccupped from crying so hard. "I can't bear to see another child slip through the cracks."

"Don't cry, darling. I'll do whatever you need me to do to make certain that this young boy is secure with you forever." Anthony held her hand and gently swept his thumb over her knuckles.

Rebecca nodded and cried softly, because she was so grateful for the opportunity Anthony was giving both her and Trevor. She reached up and gently kissed his cheek under his bruised eye, tenderly. "Thank you. I don't think I can ever thank you enough."

Anthony simply nodded and patted her hand softly.

Chapter Two
Avoiding all the fanfare . . .

Getting married was complicated enough when you were in love and a Romano. But when you were getting married for some other reason, one that wasn't disclosed to the corporate attorneys, it was pure hell! There was a two hundred page Prenuptial Agreement that had to be reviewed, refined and re-edited, and if Anthony had to read the document one more time from cover to cover, he was certain he was going to lose his mind.

"I am NOT reading this document again," Anthony quietly emphasized to a table of four in-house attorneys who all looked surprised. Anthony stood up and tossed the telephone book-sized Prenup onto the high-gloss, African, black wood tabletop with a thud, causing the attorneys to flinch.

"Mr. Romano, please . . ." the roundest attorney pleaded.

"No. No more drafts. It is simple." Anthony paused, raking a hand through his blonde, straight hair. "I am marrying Rebecca McFarlan and we are immediately adopting a child. For how long, is anyone's guess? The one-year, two-year, three-year and twenty-year terms of marriage are to be removed, which I stated nearly SEVEN drafts ago, or I am hiring new attorneys to handle this matter," Anthony broke off in order to give the thin attorney with glasses an opportunity to jot down notes on a yellow legal pad. "The boy, together with Ms. McFarlan, will be taken care of according to my first draft's revisions with absolutely no alterations, additions, addendums, or attachments."

While Anthony's frustration grew, the level of his voice lowered until it was barely above a whisper. The longer this prenuptial process took, the further it delayed the wedding ceremony, which ultimately delayed the adoption hearing, which meant more time Trevor would be spending with another foster family who might or might not be taking care of him properly. And now, the notion of that reality was starting to eat at him.

"Mr. Romano, if we could please review page one hundred and fifty-seven?" the thin attorney with the tiny glasses asked politely.

"No. Reduce the document to twenty-five pages, then we will not have to review page one hundred and fifty-seven." Anthony stated firmly, yet softly, while still standing, because as far as he was concerned the meeting was over.

"But that would be impossible! The introduction of the assets of Romano Enterprises is more than one hundred pages." the oldest attorney argued.

"I am confident you will get that accomplished in . . ." Anthony stopped to look at his watch. ". . . one hour."

The look of horror on the attorneys' faces was rather comical, Anthony concluded, but he wouldn't dare laugh at them. Rather, he watched as the four gathered up their papers and scurried from the room, three-piece suits and all, each saying nothing to the other or to Anthony, silently closing the door behind them. The attorneys began to argue in the hall for several minutes then all grew quiet.

Anthony took this opportunity to compose himself. He was getting married to the woman he loved, but his love was never going to be received or returned. He was going to be a father to a child he never met, yet this young boy would soon be his legal heir. Anthony shook his head. *Talk about life throwing you a curve ball!*

Anthony's next meeting was with the attorneys who would be handling the adoption proceedings. Apparently they already had a closed-door meeting with the judge in chambers from the Family Court and things should be moving both swiftly and quietly, but the marriage had to take place first, *obviously!*

Anthony picked up his cell phone and slid through the screens to check for calls or missed messages. But there was nothing. *Should I call my future wife?* Anthony silently questioned himself. *This is crazy!* He was afraid to call his soon-to-be-bride!! It was no wonder the corporate attorneys were looking at him crossly. He was marrying a woman he didn't even feel comfortable telephoning. While Anthony raked a hand through his white-blonde hair, his cell phone began to vibrate. It startled him, causing him to drop the device onto the floor. Still vibrating, he found it under his desk and slid the screen to engage the call.

"Hello?"

"Hi, it's Rebecca."

"Hi." Anthony started to get up from under his desk and proceeded to bash his head somewhat forcibly on the underside of the solid mahogany wood. "Good Lord!" he shouted.

"What? If you want to call everything off, I'll understand . . ." Rebecca responded quickly.

Since their agreement, Anthony and Rebecca had been secretly meeting at Romano Enterprises in an effort to formalize their arrangement. "No, no, of course not. I bumped my head. That's all." Anthony quickly calmed his nervous bride's jumpy fears.

"Are you okay?" Rebecca giggled.

"Yes." Anthony started to laugh as he rubbed the spot, feeling slightly embarrassed. He found Rebecca's laughter uplifting and contagious. "I just met with the attorneys. This Prenuptial Agreement is such a grueling process. Wait until you get the opportunity to read it. I am contemplating scratching my eyes out so that I won't have to read it again." Anthony listened as her giggling stopped.

Rebecca spoke in a serious tone. "I'm not going to read it, Anthony. I'm just going to sign it."

"What? Why? Of course you have to read it. You should bring it to your attorney . . ." Anthony started to insist, but Rebecca cut him off.

"The fact that you are helping me adopt Trevor is good enough for me."

"Rebecca, there is more to it than that." Anthony wanted to tell her that they belonged together, that they were meant for each other, but it was either too soon or too late for that—he wasn't sure.

"Not for me there isn't. I would never have been able to do this without you and for that I will be eternally grateful."

"Maybe we should get together for dinner and try to tie up the last of these loose ends?"

"That's probably a good idea," Rebecca agreed.

"How about you come over to my apartment—our apartment," Anthony corrected. "Carlo could bring you over after work." Anthony suggested. He knew she was angry with the fact that she was being followed around by a bodyguard. In fact, now that she was marrying a Romano, there would be additional bodyguards put in place, which would probably piss her off even more. Anthony smiled broadly, keeping that bit of information to himself.

"Right . . . Carlo. The man is definitely starting to grow on me." Rebecca joked.

Anthony laughed. *She had better get used to it,* he thought silently, *because once she becomes Mrs. Anthony Romano and Trevor becomes a Romano, both directly in line to receive enormous fortunes, they were both going to be watched and followed all the days of their lives, regardless of the outcome of this marriage.* "We can have a bite to eat and iron out some of these details. Plus, we also need to get ready for our interview with Children's Services."

"You're right. Well, I'm free tonight. That is, if you are?"

"Yes."

"How about, say seven, if that works for you?"

"Perfect." Anthony looked at the mounds of paperwork on his desk and inwardly grunted. Lately, it seemed, he wasn't able to accomplish a single task ever since this bouncy, brunette bounded into his life.

"Okay, I'll see you at seven." Rebecca whispered before she ended the call.

Once Anthony did the same, he quickly called his housekeeper Sofia and hoped she could pull something together for dinner at the last minute.

"You're sure it's not too late?"

"Of course not." Sofia answered. "I have a chicken prepared and will put it in the oven before your guest arrives."

"You're the best Sofia! I really appreciate all your hard work and wonderful cooking."

"You're welcome."

Over the last few months Sofia noticed a change in Anthony Romano's eating patterns. She prepared dinner for him usually five times a week, but, lately, he would pick at the meals she fixed for him. After some thought, she calculated that he hadn't eaten a decent dinner in at least the last two months. At first, she thought it was her cooking. Then she heard him talking to himself about a woman named Rebecca. Then she heard him on the phone with someone talking about this woman named Rebecca.

So apparently this Rebecca had her boss all twisted up in knots, which made her smile. She didn't care for the women who went faint around her boss. *It was pathetic!*

Anthony made it a point to get to the apartment at least a half an hour before Rebecca was to arrive. Going through his usual bachelor routine, he put his keys in a brass tray that rested on an ebony walnut table that appeared to be sawed in half, that leaned up against the wall in his foyer. He placed his briefcase on the floor near one of the chairs that flanked this exquisite antique. He leafed through the mail then placed it in a neat pile on the table.

Sofia poked her head out of the kitchen to greet her employer. "Good evening."

"Good evening Sofia." Anthony smiled broadly, remembering the time she called him a 'very old soul,' because of all the formalities and gentlemanly qualities he naturally displayed. Qualities, she told him, which were long lost on today's man. "It smells delicious in here."

"I'm glad to hear you say that, because for the last eight weeks you have been picking at my dinners like a hummingbird." Sofia tossed the tiny red potatoes about in the roasting pan before placing them on a large platter around the chicken.

"A hummingbird?" Anthony questioned with a raised eyebrow. "That could be considered an insult."

Sofia turned and raised a lovely, dark, dueling eyebrow at him. "Yes it could be."

"I've been working late and when I get home, I'm not prepared to sit down to such a big meal. It's a decidedly legitimate claim."

"Who decided that?"

Anthony raised his eyebrow and thought it best to bridle his tongue.

"Exactly . . . but tonight you are home early, you have company coming and hopefully that will encourage your appetite!"

Sofia is so sweet, Anthony thought. There was no other way to describe her.

"I set the dining room table for two," Sofia started. "Now if you want me to stay and serve that will be no problem . . ."

Anthony immediately cut her off. "NO . . . I mean . . . no, that will not be necessary," Anthony lowered his voice.

"I guess the only thing left to do is for you to pick the wine."

"That's fine. I'll take care of that."

"Okay, so I have everything right here in the warming drawer, but you will need oven mitts, because the platter is *mucho caliente!*" Sofia spoke in her native Spanish tongue. Since Anthony was fluent in Spanish, along with many other languages, he understood exactly what she said. Anthony watched Sofia pull open the draw to reveal a perfectly golden, basted chicken with roasted mini-red potatoes and bright, green beans surrounding it. Anthony nodded. *"Muy bien."*

"Mira . . . here is dessert." Sofia opened the freezer and lifted out two frosted glasses.

"Mmm . . . what's that?"

"Mousse . . . chocolate of course," Sofia smiled knowing that this dessert would tempt any woman.

"Of course," Anthony smiled that engaging smile that would make any girl swoon. Sofia placed the frosty treats into the refrigerator, because the mousse had already set. "Alright then . . . everything is ready."

"Thanks again."

"Mr. Romano, it's my job."

"Yes, I know, but thank you." Even though they were relatively close in age and Anthony insisted more times than he could count that she call him by his first name, she never did. She always kept their relationship strictly employer-employee.

"You're welcome. I'll see you tomorrow. Have a wonderful evening." Sofia left the apartment and went to the elevator. As she reached the lobby and circumnavigated through the revolving door, Rebecca was walking in. Sofia couldn't help but wonder if that was Anthony's dinner companion.

In the apartment, Anthony had already taken out a bottle from his *Chateau Pichon* collection and opened it so it could breathe. He focused on the dining room table setting and noticed that Sofia opted for creamy linen placemats and napkins rather than a tablecloth, which Anthony appreciated, because it kept the dinner less formal and a little more intimate. He was tempted to move the place settings onto the kitchen island, because he thought that might put Rebecca further at ease. While he considered what to do, the doorbell chimed, causing him to nearly jump right out of his suit.

Man, I'm a nervous wreck! I have got to calm down! He scolded himself, quickly eating up the distance to the front door shaking out his hands. Suddenly, he realized he was still wearing his suit jacket. Hastily he pulled it off, as well as the tie and unbuttoned the top button on his shirt. He draped both over one of the chairs that flanked the antique table in the foyer before he answered the door.

When Anthony pulled the front door open, in that moment, he knew that this was the woman he couldn't live without—Rebecca.

"Hi," Anthony whispered softly, suppressing his urge to pull her into his embrace.

"Hi." Rebecca responded softly.

"Please come in." Anthony stepped aside to let Rebecca enter. She was wearing a lightweight tan suit with a silky, pink blouse underneath the jacket. He closed the door behind her and touched her shoulders, causing her to jump from his unexpected touch. "I just want to take your jacket."

"Oh . . . right . . . my jacket." *You'd better calm down,* Rebecca silently chided herself. Rebecca placed her oversized purse on the floor, slid out of her jacket and handed it to Anthony.

Anthony painstakingly hung her jacket in the closet, taking defined and deliberate steps to slow his racing heart, but it wasn't working. When he turned to face her, Anthony was certain that Rebecca could see his heart pounding violently in his chest.

Rebecca took a deep breath to try and catch her own traitorous heart rate. This was the first time she was in Anthony's apartment and she was having difficulty taking in all of the obviously priceless furnishings and paintings.

Anthony took a moment to take in this beautiful woman before him. She wore a long strand of fake pearls and fake pearl earrings. Straightaway, he decided to give her a proper set of pearls as a wedding gift. His mother had been haranguing him about a proper wedding gift for his bride for weeks and threatened that it had better be exceptional. Anthony was stunned with the number of times his mother called him just to remind him of the wedding gift for his bride alone. When he text-messaged his brother to complain about their mother, Jack wasn't the least bit sympathetic. His message was clear. "Didn't you see what they put me through before my wedding? I don't want to hear it!"

"Okay," Anthony started rubbing his hands together. When Rebecca stared at him rubbing his hands, he quickly stopped. "Dinner is all set. I thought we could eat first then go over some of the details later?"

Rebecca nodded. She looked down at the dark hardwood floors that were accented with a lovely, creamy yellow oriental rug. There was an unusual table propped up against the wall that appeared to have been sawn in half, flanked by two chairs. A mirror hung above the table. A pair of sconces, which resembled a candle with crystals dangling from the bottom, framed either side of the mirror. Above was a very large chandelier which lit the area with soft light that sparkled through the crystals. It was beautiful. There were many oil paintings in the foyer. *Probably very expensive*, Rebecca tacitly surmised.

Anthony turned back to see Rebecca's surprised expression. "Maybe I should show you around first?" And when Rebecca nodded, Anthony led the way out of the foyer. "This is the formal dining room and living room."

The apartment opened up into a huge, formal living room with a fireplace and a banquet-sized formal dining room. In the living room, a grand piano sat in the corner and appeared small, simply because the space was so voluminous.

"Do you play?" Rebecca asked motioning her head toward the piano.

"A little," Anthony answered her quickly. "And the kitchen is here to your right."

The immense kitchen was wrapped in glossy, white cabinetry with white-and-gray veined Carrara countertops and backsplashes. Oiled, black soapstone was the material that covered the island. A miniature crystal chandelier graced the area above the sink, as well as three more that hung over the island. It was stunning!

The apartment invited you in with dark hardwood floors, which were partially covered by exquisite area rugs that drew your eye out to the impressive view of the city beyond. It was getting dark and the lights were coming on in the neighboring buildings, as far as the eye could see. The view was breathtaking!

Rebecca nodded, nearly dumbstruck. She couldn't believe someone lived here or that anyone actually lived like this. "You live here by yourself?" Rebecca asked trying to sound as though she wasn't gob-smacked. *This apartment has to be easily the size of a city block,* she surmised.

"Yes. I really bought it as an investment, because I used to travel so much for RE."

"RE?" Rebecca questioned, too flabbergasted to process the initials in her mind.

"Romano Enterprises," Anthony clarified suddenly wondering if all of this was getting to her as much as it was getting to him.

"Oh," Rebecca knocked her forehead with the heel of her hand. "How often do you travel for work?"

"Before I became president, I traveled probably three-quarters of the year as a buyer for Romano Enterprises."

"That much!" Rebecca commented shockingly. "That seems like an awfully long time to be away from your family and friends."

"I suppose. But now with the day-to-day operations that come with the title of president, travel has been delegated to other employees at the company. I will be traveling once or twice a year in the foreseeable future. We have a woman leading the team of buyers right now and she is bringing a softer side to the company. Sales are up, so her eye must be better than mine was." Anthony shrugged. "So let me show you the rest of the place, because next week you will be living here."

Next week, Rebecca swallowed audibly. *Is it really only a week away?* She quietly followed Anthony as he continued the grand tour. Grand was an understatement. Rebecca could not believe that she was going to be living in such an amazing place. It was a penthouse palace without the ostentatious glam and glitz, but, funny enough, everything sparkled in the way of old money.

Rebecca asked if she could use the powder room and Anthony pointed toward the door. Once inside the bathroom, Rebecca mouthed the words *OH MY GOD* soundlessly to her reflection in the mirror over the sink, cupping her flushed cheeks. She could not believe this. Her entire apartment could, without a doubt, fit into his living room alone. She turned on the water and shook her head. *How is Trevor going to adjust to this? How am I going to adjust to this? This was class, elegance and status all rolled up into one. It is almost too much.* Rebecca started to analyze the situation. *We are expecting a young boy to fall in love with us then we are going to tell him that we are splitting up. He is going to have to move out of this amazing apartment and into my measly one.* Suddenly, she felt a vein pulsing wildly in her neck. She tried to calm herself down by washing her hands. She dried them, wondering if she should discuss this with Anthony tonight.

When she exited the bathroom, she followed a noise finding Anthony washing his hands in the kitchen sink. He turned around and smiled at her while he dried his hands on a dishtowel. *Gosh, he really is very handsome,* Rebecca wordlessly admitted to herself. There was absolutely no way around it. Rebecca watched as Anthony tied an apron around his waist, donned oven mitts and pulled a platter of food from a drawer below the stove. Closing the drawer with his hip, he motioned with his head for Rebecca to follow him into the dining room.

Anthony placed the food on a large trivet in the center of the high-glossed wood table. He came around to where Rebecca was standing and pulled out a chair for her.

"Thank you." Rebecca was very unaccustomed to all this male courtesy. Since she went through the Police Academy, men treated her like one of the boys. In her line of work, stopping to pull a chair out for a woman was frowned upon at the station.

"You're welcome."

Rebecca watched while he served and poured the wine, noticing that his hand was trembling. She quietly waited until Anthony sat down, placed his napkin on his lap and began to eat. They ate, or maybe not ate would be a better way to describe the meal and after a few minutes of pushing her food around, Anthony looked up and spoke softly. "I brought the Prenuptial Agreement home with me tonight so that you can take it home. You should bring it to your attorney and review it with him or her."

"Anthony, I already told you that I'm not going to read it." Rebecca watched his face. Studying facial expressions was her business and she knew he was about to object, so she quickly proceeded. "That may sound reckless, but the only thing I need to know is that when we get this marriage annulled, you will give me full custody of Trevor."

"Yes, that is all in the agreement. I will not be filing for any custody rights under any circumstances other than death."

"Thank you. This must seem cold to you . . ." Rebecca looked down. She didn't have the backbone to look him in the eye.

"No. You have a thought process and I have already accepted that. I'm only doing what is good for the boy." Anthony pushed his food around in his plate. He never seemed hungry anymore. "I'll get the paperwork." Anthony rose, very calmly placing his napkin next to his plate. "Okay here it is. Let me show you the part about custody . . ."

"That won't be necessary. Do you have a pen?"

"Ahhh . . . yeah . . . let me get one." Anthony returned with a fine, Montblanc pen. "Here." Anthony handed her his pen.

"Thanks." Rebecca flipped to the back of the document, shocked that it was so short. She was expecting an enormous document, but it was a fraction of what she anticipated. She signed her name and handed the whole thing back to Anthony.

"When are you going to move over your belongings?"

"Belongings?" Rebecca asked with her eyes wide.

"Yes."

"Why?" Rebecca snapped.

"If Children's Services finds out that you are still keeping your own apartment . . . I mean . . . I'm not sure, but I think that could be a real problem for us."

"Do you know how hard it's going to be for me to find another affordable apartment in this city?" Rebecca was feeling anxious and she knew her voice revealed that anxiety.

"Yes I do. So I've taken care of that on page . . ." Anthony paused to flip to the specific page he was referring. "Here it is, on page twelve."

Rebecca was surprised. "Really?"

"Yes. It is right here," Anthony pointed to the spot in the agreement and began to read it out loud. "Anthony Romano will provide similar or greater housing than is currently provided by said Anthony Romano to Rebecca McFarlan or Rebecca Romano and Trevor Michaels or Trevor Romano for as long as they both shall live. Anthony Romano will provide an allowance per month . . ." Anthony trailed off. "I wasn't sure if you or Trevor wanted to take my last name."

Rebecca's mouth fell open. "For as long as we both live? Whaaat?"

"Yes. It is right here," Anthony pointed to the paragraph he just read.

Rebecca ran her eyes over the words and was taken aback. "Anthony, that isn't your responsibility!"

"Of course it is! I'm making a commitment, even though we aren't actually making a commitment to each other." Anthony shrugged. "I'm making a commitment to provide for you and Trevor."

"But what will your future wife think?"

"You are my future wife!" Anthony stated succinctly, his eyes studying hers.

"I'm serious . . ." Rebecca countered.

"So am I. Besides, lots of people today have baggage. I guess I will be joining the masses."

"This really isn't necessary," Rebecca said, pointing to the paragraph. "I think you should revise this portion about me."

Anthony shook his head in a clear sign of objection. "I am not taking this back to the corporate attorneys to change this. It is a benefit to you and Trevor, as well. If you think something in the document is unfair, then I will take it back to them, but both you and Trevor will be provided for including . . ." Anthony paused to find the section. ". . . the college of his choice and to the degree(s)/ or any level(s) of education he so chooses," Anthony read aloud pointing to the section for her to review.

"That is very generous of you."

"What else am I going to do with all this money?" Anthony gathered the plates.

Apparently they both had the same appetite—*none.* Rebecca noticed.

"Sofia made dessert."

"Who's Sofia?" Rebecca asked curiously.

"She's our housekeeper and cook." Anthony called from the kitchen.

"I really shouldn't . . ." Rebecca wanted to run for her life at that particular moment.

"It's chocolate!" Anthony tempted from the kitchen.

"Chocolate . . ." Rebecca murmured.

"Yes." Anthony walked back into the dining room with two frosty glasses filled with the chocolaty delight, topped with homemade whipped cream and garnished with tiny green mint leaves.

"That looks lethal!"

"Sofia is a really good cook although she hasn't had any formal training. Not yet. I'm trying to convince her to start classes in the spring."

"Mmm, it's delicious." Rebecca rolled her eyes.

Anthony smiled and took a spoonful, nodding. "It is good. It's only a matter of time before she wakes up and decides to open her own restaurant."

"Then what will you do?"

"I don't know what the future has in store for me. I'm simply going to take it one day at a time."

Rebecca could hear the honesty in his response. "Makes sense," she accepted. Although she was enjoying dessert, Rebecca stopped halfway down the dessert glass. It was one of many ways she controlled her portions whenever she was out. When she looked over at Anthony he was watching her.

"Maybe we should discuss the move?" he suggested.

Rebecca looked around and knew that she didn't even want to bring any of her cheap, particle-board furniture to Anthony's. Her stuff wouldn't hold a candle to all of Anthony's fine furnishings. And besides, there was simply no room for her things. "If I could just bring my treadmill and I would need an area to do my work and sleep."

"Sleep?" Anthony asked in shock.

"I'm not sleeping with you." Rebecca made it clear, lowering her tone.

"But Children's Services will be doing impromptu visits according to their report. If we are not sharing a bedroom, they will know."

"I am NOT sleeping with you!" Rebecca was adamant.

"Rebecca, I promise you that I will not touch you. I will not lay a finger on you. This arrangement is for one reason and one reason only and that is to give a little boy a different path, a fresh start."

"Well, we don't have to sleep in the same room until we are well into the process." Rebecca huffed.

"I suppose, but if they ask me if you sleep on the right side of the bed or the left and we don't share a bed, we are going to have a problem."

Rebecca pursed her lips and started to bite her fingernail. "Okay, I can see where that could become a problem. I suppose it will be a way for us to learn about all those little idiosyncrasies."

"Exactly . . . here . . ." Anthony got up and held out his hand, hiding his surprise when she placed her hand into his extended one. Deliberately concealing his surprised reaction, Anthony walked her down the hallway that branched off from the main part of the apartment toward the left. There were two bedrooms and two full bathrooms on this side of the apartment. "We could make this Trevor's room and we can turn this into your workout room and home office. What do you think?"

"What are you going to do with all of this furniture?" Rebecca questioned, unsure.

"I can store it here or at one of my warehouses. It's no problem."

"Okay. I think that could work."

"Great." Anthony looked down at their locked hands and it suddenly reminded him of something he wanted to give her. "I almost forgot." Anthony led her back down the hallway through the middle of the apartment and down a hallway that branched off to the right. Anthony pointed out an office and a family room with a full bath, but once he entered the master bedroom suite, Rebecca immediately recoiled, pulling her hand out of his.

Anthony said nothing as she drew back, going into the bedroom alone. He walked over to a large highboy with many drawers. He opened the very top drawer and removed the box before pushing the drawer closed. Rebecca was still standing at the entrance to the bedroom when he handed her a little, white velvet box. "Will you marry me?" Anthony asked, shrugging his shoulders.

"Let's not forget who asked who first . . ." she joked.

"Open it." Anthony commanded softly.

Rebecca lifted the lid revealing a pink, multi-facetted stone that was secured by a dark gold ring, in an intricate, feminine pattern. Her mouth fell open as she breathed . . . "My goodness. I can't possibly accept this . . ." Rebecca mumbled. She could see that it was an antique of some kind and probably worth a small fortune, making her feel as though she were about to hyperventilate.

"You have to. We're getting hitched and we need to do everything by the book."

"I can't! I couldn't . . . it looks expensive . . . really, really expensive." Rebecca's eyes were wide with shock.

"It is a pink diamond. It is very rare and, yes, very expensive, but it's insured. Besides, Children's Services will know that I can well afford an expensive engagement ring for my fiancée since my accountant faxed over my last three years of financial statements to verify my ability to afford to adopt a child. If you don't wear an engagement ring, this might cause them to doubt our intentions and disrupt our plans."

Anthony took the ring from the box. He studied it and thought it suited her. The pretty pink stone and the curves on the setting reminded him of her. Her perfectly pink complexion and soft curves. Moreover, it had another meaning he hoped to share with her one day, but not today. "If you're not pleased with it, you can pick out whatever you like," Anthony spoke very softly, slipping the ring onto her finger.

"Not pleased? It's magnificent! I promise to return it when this . . . situation is over," she stuttered.

"It's in the Prenuptial Agreement that any gift you receive from me or my family is yours. You can sell it later and buy yourself . . . something." Anthony shrugged hoping he was pulling off his casual act. He started back down the hall, toward the dining room, but when he turned around, Rebecca was heading for the foyer. Anthony turned around and followed her. "Would you like a brandy?"

"No, it's late. Thanks for dinner . . . and the ring." Rebecca knew that sounded lame. "I have to get into work early tomorrow."

"Of course." Anthony agreed pleasantly.

"So I will see you next Friday for the marriage certificate appointment?" Rebecca wasn't sure if he would show.

"Yes. I'll be there." Anthony guaranteed.

"I have a lot of packing to do."

"Why not let the men from my warehouse help you with that? They are very familiar with how to pack and move furniture. Just pack your personal items and leave the rest for my men."

"Are you sure?"

"Absolutely," Anthony confirmed. "I'll call Carlo and tell him what to do."

"Okay." Rebecca was thankful for the help. Between working at the mental health clinic, working her undercover police post, getting married, moving and adopting a child all at the same time, she was about ready for a rubber room!

Anthony took her tan jacket from the closet and helped her into it. She smelled wonderful and when her soft chestnut curls brushed along his knuckles, he wanted to take a fistful and pull her toward him. He quickly removed his hands from her shoulders, watching her retrieve her purse.

"Thanks."

Anthony smiled politely. He pulled open the apartment door and walked her down the hall to the elevator. While they waited for the elevator, neither one spoke a word. Anthony shoved his hands deep in his pockets and was rocking back and forth on his heels with his head lowered. The doors silently opened and Rebecca walked into the elevator turning to face him. When she reached to depress the lobby button, Anthony placed his hands over the doors to stop them from closing. "Rebecca, I understand that this arrangement is meant for one purpose, but I cannot be humiliated by my wife."

Rebecca unblinkingly stood still while he continued.

"The press will have a field day with infidelity and that is something I will not be able to tolerate, because it could impact my business." It was a topic that was clearly defined in the Prenuptial Agreement and Anthony made certain that it was put in place.

Rebecca studied him. He could see that she wasn't expecting this discussion.

"I will be faithful to you, because you will be my lawfully wedded wife and I expect the same in return. I know this period of celibacy will be difficult for us, but I hope that we can both show the other respect until we have the final documentation in our hands saying that Trevor belongs to us, as well as the divorce decree. Deal?" Anthony asked, sticking out his hand for Rebecca to shake.

"Deal." Rebecca put her hand into Anthony's firm, solid grasp while she studied his stormy-eyed stare, which clearly meant business.

"Goodnight," Anthony murmured, pulling back his hand, watching the doors glide silently closed.

"Goodnight," Rebecca said, as the doors closed silently. Suddenly, she started to cry and couldn't seem to stop herself. It was an uncontrollable and all-consuming cry, as she buried her face in the corner of the elevator while it made its descent.

Anthony could hear her sobs drifting up the elevator shaft into the hallway where he stood. He placed his hands on the elevator doors and hung his head. It felt as though it took all of his strength to pull himself out of the dark place he felt himself rapidly descending into. He pulled out his cell phone and sent Carlo, her bodyguard, a text message that Rebecca was on her way down.

Raking his hand through his blonde hair, he reminded himself that this arrangement was to elevate a child and for that reason and for no other, he felt his plan was justified—that alone should be his driving force. With a knot the size of a Winston in his throat, he went back into his apartment. Closing the door quietly, he locked it and set the alarm. He walked soundlessly into the dining room and took out a bottle of Macallan Scotch. Pulling a Waterford tumbler from the glass cabinet, he studied the intricate cut-crystal pattern for a moment then proceeded to fill it nearly to the top with the amber liquid. He downed the entire glass. Deciding that refilling the glass would only delay the result he was hoping to achieve, he took the entire bottle into the living room. He sat at the grand piano, in a room that was hardly ever used in his apartment, drinking directly from the bottle until the liquor began to numb his senses while his fingers lightly stroked the keys. With little food in his stomach, the Macallan performed like magic. In no time, it was lights out slumped over the piano.

Chapter Three
Wedding jitters . . .

With the Prenuptial Agreement behind them and the wedding plans in front of them, Rebecca insisted that they keep it as simple as possible, despite Anthony's struggles with his family's pressures to have a normal 'Romano' family-style wedding, which was anything but normal.

Making arrangements for an extravagant wedding, Rebecca reasoned, when they weren't going to be staying married for very long, was being deceitful and unfair to their families and friends, and Anthony agreed. With everything that was happening in her life, Rebecca had a perpetual headache that began at dawn and lasted well after dusk. And each morning when she woke, the migraine was still there, throbbing.

It was Friday and most of Rebecca's belongings were packed, organized and ready to be moved tomorrow. Some personal effects and a few other items, like her police uniforms and gear, she would take over herself tonight after work. With her lease expiring on Saturday, she would be living at Anthony's starting tonight and the wedding was the following Friday. Besides not advising her day-job boss at her undercover post, she still hadn't told her real boss at her real job. The thought of telling Captain Rice that she was getting married to a very visible public figure, moving and, oh yeah, adopting a child was nearly causing her to break out in hives. She couldn't even seem to find the right time to tell her own parents or brother that she was marrying Anthony Romano. It was going to be a hard sell and she wasn't up to the fight. The notion of explaining this to everyone was stressing her out, because she would have to admit to marrying a man under false pretenses to trick a State Agency into letting her adopt a child. *Ugh*, Rebecca thought, *that is so not going to sit well with my family or my Captain.*

They had already gone to the doctor for their blood tests. The last thing they needed to do was to pick up the marriage certificate paperwork from the Health Department in the City Clerk's office, in person. When you resided in the city itself, you had to show proper identification to even get the marriage certificate paperwork. So the plan was to meet at the Hall of Records during Rebecca's lunch break, grab the paperwork and be out of there in five minutes. And since the Health Department was located between where they both worked, they agreed they would meet up right outside the front of the building at a quarter past twelve.

As she quickly made her way to the Hall of Records, Rebecca spotted Anthony standing in front of the building. He was wearing black sunglasses and a dark gray suit that was custom-made for him. To Rebecca, Anthony always appeared well put together and that detailed attention to his appearance made him look very powerful.

Anthony looked up from his cell phone to see Rebecca running down the street. She was wearing a tight, black pencil skirt and a dark, navy blue satin-type blouse with no jacket, much thanks to the perfectly gorgeous Indian summer weather they were experiencing. Anthony watched Rebecca, who appeared flushed, as if she had been running for most of the trek. Her dark stockings and extremely high heels she wore were, in Anthony's opinion, HOT! Not hot to the touch, but hot to look at! He couldn't help but smile at the image bounding toward him. He was surprised she hadn't twisted her ankle running here in those things. She abruptly stopped directly in front of him while she slung a gigantic purse over her shoulder nearly taking out the man who was walking up behind her, unaware.

"Sorry." Rebecca said to the man who strategically dodged her purse.

"Hi." Anthony caught her by the arm, because she looked as though she were about to topple over.

"Hi." Rebecca placed her hand on her chest, trying to catch her breath, clutching her enormous bag which held her 40-caliber Sig service weapon. "Sorry I'm late, but we had a patient attack one of the psychologists today." It was difficult to tackle someone in a pencil skirt, so she opted to hit him over the head with the heavy duty stapler. *Worked like a charm . . .*

"Tell me you have security at the clinic . . ." Anthony demanded as he removed his sunglasses to reveal his concern.

"Okay, but I would be lying." Rebecca shrugged.

Anthony could feel his blood pressure rise, but made a mental note that he would take care of that very shortly. When he pulled open the heavy wooden door for Rebecca, flashbulbs started to burst in an array of blinding lights.

"Oh no!" Rebecca panicked, turned and slammed right back into Anthony, trying to run from the building.

"Someone tipped off the press," he whispered into her ear. It was so obvious, because there were far too many reporters and paparazzi all waiting inside. It was a surprise attack. "It's fine." Anthony circled Rebecca's shoulders and began to plow through the throng. "Keep your head down," he quietly instructed.

The reporters shouted questions, calling them by their first names to draw their attention.

Rebecca wasn't wearing sunglasses and the flashes forced her to keep her eyes focused on the floor. She raised her left hand to shield her face and eyes from the flashes of the cameras. The photographers devoured the fact that she was revealing to them her engagement ring.

As they walked briskly down the hall, strangely, Rebecca's thoughts refocused on Anthony, rather than the confusion. He felt solid. His large hand shielded her shoulder away from the madness making her feel warm and secure. *Funny*, she thought, *but I never noticed how rock-hard he is.*

They wormed their way through the throng of reporters and photographers, quickly entering a corridor that deliberately declared "No Press Past This Point." Anthony found the door to the Health Department's offices and held it open for Rebecca to walk through first.

"Good afternoon, Mr. Romano," a very portly, poorly dressed Health Department official announced loudly and somewhat cynically from behind a counter. She loved the rules that were in place at the city's Health Department. The clerk met many, many famous and important people personally, because they had to come to her office with proper identification in order for them to receive their marriage certificate paperwork.

"Good afternoon," Anthony, always the gentleman, responded kindly, removing his black sunglasses and sliding them into his outside breast pocket.

"What can I do for *YOU* today?" the obnoxious clerk taunted.

"You know damn well why we are here!" Rebecca shouted, with one hand on her hip, the other pointing at the clerk's plump face.

The tone of Rebecca's voice shocked Anthony as he cleared his throat to get her attention, but she wasn't having it. It was obvious to both Anthony and Rebecca that this tub-of-lard leaked to the press that they would be here today, at precisely this time.

Anthony quickly stopped her. Taking her hand in his, Anthony rephrased Rebecca's answer with one that was laced with charm. "Yes," Anthony peered into Rebecca's face, a clear warning. "Thank you for asking. We are here to pick up our marriage certificate paperwork."

"So, you're getting married," the clerk snickered, with long wiry, gray hairs that stuck out of her chin here and there, all while sneering at Rebecca.

"Why . . . I am gonna . . ." Rebecca started to advance on the woman with wide eyes.

"Yes, as a matter-of-fact we are. Right, darling?" Anthony smiled that one and only killer-Romano smile, while trying to strategically restrain his future bride, completely shocked by her strength. "Thank you so much for asking!" Anthony answered pleasantly, but could swear he saw smoke spewing out of Rebecca's ears from the corner of his eye.

The clerk waddled toward a shelf that had numerous cubbies and pulled the necessary paperwork from several cubbies and stapled the paperwork together, but not quite getting it into a nice, neat packet. She barked, "Identification," then proceeded to pick at something between her front teeth with her pen.

Anthony and Rebecca released their hands and each one pulled out their own documentation.

"You look like you weigh more than a hundred and twenty-five pounds," the clerk jeered at Rebecca as she studied her ID.

"That's it!!!" Rebecca shouted slamming her enormous purse onto the counter. She was tempted to pull out her duty weapon and jab it into one of the triple chins that sagged around the clerk's neck.

Anthony quickly pulled Rebecca back against him, placing his arm around her shoulders, holding her fast to him and smiling. The woman continued to pick at something between her teeth, letting everyone know exactly who was in charge.

She filled in some of the blank spots on the forms, all while taking her damn sweet time. "Sign here and here." She slammed the pen down on the counter separating them.

Anthony wordlessly removed his Montblanc pen from his inside jacket pocket signing as instructed. He handed his pen to Rebecca who signed directly beneath his name in two spots.

The clerk waddled over to a desk, stamped and sealed the signatures and handed them the packet with their original identification documents. "Give this to whoever is performing the ceremony and they will know what to do with it."

"Thank you so much. You've been very helpful . . . let's go darling." Anthony gracefully took the paperwork and yanked Rebecca from the office before she drew this woman's blood.

"Stop pulling my arm! And don't call me 'darling' again . . . I hate it!" Rebecca snapped pulling back.

"What's wrong with you?" Anthony hissed, turning around to face her. Since he was so much taller he bent his knees so that he could glare into hers eyes at her level.

"She was nasty . . ." Rebecca curled her lip.

"So?"

"Sooooo, I didn't like that!" Rebecca crossed her arms and turned her face away from him.

"When did you become the manners police?" Anthony asked placing his thumb and index finger under her chin pulling her face back so that he could study her eyes.

Rebecca audibly gulped at the word 'police.'

"What if she held up this paperwork because of your attitude?" Anthony asked waving the forms in the air.

"She wouldn't dare!" Rebecca declared through clenched teeth, literally fit to be tied. Besides the obvious fact that now she would *have* to call her supervisor and tell him about the press, who just might completely blow three years of undercover work. *Son of a bitch!*

"If she held up this paperwork, it could have delayed everything." Anthony continued waving the paperwork back and forth quickly.

Rebecca exhaled loudly. "I think that woman should be fired! I don't treat anyone that is assigned to me at the clinic with such contempt. 'You don't look like you weigh a hundred and twenty-five pounds',," Rebecca mimicked the woman. "I'll put money on it that that cow weighs over two hundred and fifty pounds."

Anthony started directing Rebecca down the hallway in the opposite direction they came from. "Who cares?"

"Where are we going?"

"We're not going out the way we came in." Anthony pulled out his phone sending a text message to Paul. He needed a decoy. He told Paul in his message to bring a limo out in front of the Hall of Records and to smile for the cameras. He told him that they were taking the subway and that he would contact him later, but to let Carlo know.

Rebecca was once again getting pulled along behind Anthony, but since she was usually the drag-gor and not the drag-gee, she yanked back letting him know how much she didn't like it. "Well you don't have to drag me by my arm anymore. I am more than capable of keeping up with you!" she shouted.

Anthony glared at her again from his full height, watching her raise an intimidating eyebrow to him. The woman was such a handful, Anthony smiled inwardly, and that was another thing he loved about her. "I want to put as much distance between you and that clerk." Anthony pointed to Rebecca's face with a very large, long index finger. "I don't want to have to tear you off of her and have that kind of unsavory news hit the press before we've had our adoption hearing." Anthony seethed, watching Rebecca raise her eyebrow again and purse her lips. "Regardless of whom is right, in the big picture, does it really matter?" Anthony could see that she was mentally processing a perfectly legitimate response and decided to shut her down—"Don't answer that question!"

"Fine." Rebecca closed her mouth and headed for the stairwell and away from Anthony.

Anthony knew she got the point. "And what's with those shoes?" Anthony shot her heels an absurd look, electing to once again drag her along behind him. Oddly enough, it was fun manhandling her a bit. She needed someone to push back.

"What's wrong with my shoes?" Rebecca asked looking down at her little imitation black peep-toe stilettos, all while desperately trying to keep up with Anthony and his elongated strides.

"And why would you possibly need a handbag that size?" Anthony asked while increasing his pace. He knew it was a fake and hoped the press didn't notice.

"This is smaller than what I normally carry." Rebecca stuck her tongue out at him when he turned away from her.

"Stop that," Anthony scolded, stopping to look back at her with dark, gray eyes.

"Stop what?" Rebecca asked sweetly, blinking her eyelashes quickly.

Anthony smiled. "Come on. I don't want the press to get wind of our direction." Taking her hand into his, he led her up the stairwell, down the hall, then down the opposite stairwell.

They made their way out of the building, down an alleyway and quickly found their way to the subway. Anthony held onto her in the subway as they rode the short distance down two stops away from the Health Department building. They exited the subway and climbed the stairs, with Rebecca still struggling to keep up with Anthony's enormous strides.

"So I guess I'll see you tonight?" Anthony wanted to sound confident, but instead, his statement came out more in the form of a question.

"I hope so . . . otherwise I'm gonna be homeless." Rebecca pulled her cuff back slightly and looked at her watch. "Geez, it's already one-thirty! I have to get back to work."

Anthony spotted Carlo, Rebecca's bodyguard, down the street. "What time do you usually get home?" Anthony wanted to be there the minute she did so that he could spend as much time with her as possible.

"Usually I get home by seven, but because I took longer for lunch I will have to work later tonight." Rebecca started to walk away from Anthony and towards her office. "I'll text you when I'm on my way," she called over her shoulder.

Anthony found that to be encouraging—very encouraging.

That evening, as soon as Anthony entered the apartment, he was instantly greeted with the scents of an Italian delight. "Wow! It smells great in here," Anthony exclaimed from the foyer.

"Flattery will get you everywhere," Sofia called back from the kitchen.

Anthony walked into the kitchen to see Sofia busy at the stove stirring a pot. Anthony told Sofia about Rebecca McFarlan. He told her that he was going to marry Ms. McFarlan and that tonight she would start living at the apartment. Anthony could tell that Sofia was stunned with his latest personal developments, but accepted it without question. She seemed excited about the news and insisted that the apartment was in need of some *real* cleaning. The apartment was actually spotless and nearly dust free, but still Sofia insisted that all the carpets, drapery and upholstery be cleaned professionally and scheduled the window washer only that day to make certain the windows gleamed.

Anthony came up to the stove and peeked over her shoulder, "Spaghetti and meatballs!" *Anyone who doesn't like this dish should have their head examined*, Anthony decided silently. His cell phone vibrated in his pocket with a text message from Rebecca saying she was "on her way."

"I was going to wait until . . . ah . . . Ms. McFarlan gets here then put on the pasta."

"I can do that," Anthony said eagerly.

"Are you trying to get rid of me?" Sofia turned to look at Anthony.

"Is it that obvious?"

"Yes." Sofia smiled. "Nervous?"

"Of course I'm nervous—I'm getting married! All men get nervous before they get married." Anthony didn't want to look into Sofia's dark eyes, which reminded him of his father's. Doing anything to dodge those black bullets, he went over to the refrigerator and pulled out some leftover red wine that would be perfect for this dish. When he finally turned around, Anthony caught her stare.

Sofia arched a dark eyebrow while studying him. "Let's review."

Anthony raised an eyebrow in challenge, silently thinking *seriously?* Anthony was inwardly pleased that she was getting cheeky with him. It was showing him that she was growing more confident and sure of herself. *It took a long time to get to this point,* Anthony recalled when he first met Sofia, who was a scarred and broken teenager.

"Here is the pasta water. I already salted it. All you need to do is boil it and cook the pasta."

"Boil and cook," Anthony was verbally taking notes. Cooking was definitely not his strong suit.

"You cannot overcook it!"

"Overcook what?" Anthony asked.

"The pasta!" Sofia exclaimed emotively before mumbling a well-coined phrase in her native tongue.

"Right, the pasta." Anthony tapped his temple.

"You need to take it out while there is still a bite!"

"Woman, I'm Sicilian. Do you really think I don't know when pasta is *al dente*?"

Sofia raised her usual telling eyebrow to him. The man didn't know a frying pan from a ladle, but she opted to refrain from responding. When she got the last of her things together and was about to leave the apartment, the doorbell rang. With her coat on, Sofia pulled open the door to see the woman who was about to become her new "Mrs." Boss.

"Hi. You must be Ms. McFarlan." Sofia stood to the side to let her in.

"Please, call me Rebecca." Rebecca walked into the foyer avoiding the temptation to stare at the angry scars that ran down one side of Sofia's face. Pulling a huge piece of luggage behind her that was missing a wheel Rebecca slung her huge purse back in an effort to reposition it on her shoulder, which began to knock over the priceless items from the expensive table in the foyer.

Anthony caught the vase before it pitched forward.

"Nice save." Rebecca smiled over her shoulder at him.

"Sofia, this is my future wife, Rebecca." Anthony made the introduction, replacing the incalculable Roman vase back onto the table, making a mental note that he had better childproof and Rebecca-proof the apartment, and soon.

Rebecca turned and shook hands with Sofia.

"Rebecca, this is Sofia. She does the cooking, cleaning, you name it," Anthony continued.

"I've heard so many nice things about you." Sofia nodded before glaring at Anthony, because that statement couldn't be further from the truth.

"Same here." Rebecca looked from Sofia to Anthony.

They all stood in the foyer looking at one another, smiling. The thick silence was actually a little awkward.

Sofia realized she was the unwanted party in the trio and decided to make her exit. "I'll see you on Monday."

"Right, Monday." Anthony was standing with his hands deep in his pockets, nodding.

"Nice meeting you." Rebecca raised her hand in a wave, wishing Sofia would stay to make this transition a little easier.

"Nice meeting you too." Sofia left quietly closing the door softly behind her. She went to the elevator and thought it odd that they were getting married and didn't touch each other or kiss each other 'hello.' *Strange*, Sofia thought silently, *very strange*, as she rode the elevator down pondering those thoughts.

Inside the apartment, Anthony and Rebecca stared at each other unmoving. He almost couldn't believe that she was there—and with her luggage. Anthony decided he had better make the first move before she changed her mind. "Here, let me take that."

Rebecca handed him her dilapidated piece of luggage and knew it looked pitiful, but it was better than the garbage bag she was contemplating.

Anthony smiled, taking her luggage. He decided he would order Rebecca a full set before their honeymoon. He was sure that the Italian designer they dealt with regularly could get him what was needed before their trip. He started to walk then turned to Rebecca. "Where should I put your things?"

Rebecca bit at her fingernail, not sure what to say. She just shrugged.

"Since we are supposed to act like husband and wife, we should probably put these things in the master bedroom."

Rebecca shook her head. "We aren't married yet."

"Good point. How about we put your belongings in your office workout space . . . for now?"

"I think that would be fine . . . for now." Rebecca gulped, knowing full well that in a week they would be living together as husband and wife . . . and that meant sharing the same bed.

Anthony raked his hand through his hair and carried her sorry-excuse for a piece of luggage down the hall. They started to walk past Trevor's future bedroom and Rebecca stopped on a dime.

"You put little boy furniture in here," Rebecca declared in surprise, extremely delighted. She wanted to hug him, but squashed the feeling quickly. The new bedding had a print of the latest action figure.

Anthony watched her soften. He had taken a poll at work and according to the results; the action hero that was depicted on his future son's bedding was the most popular and appropriate for a young boy's room. Ergo, the bedding had a creature so far removed from Anthony's knowledge that he actually purchased the DVD to see what it was all about.

"He's going to love this." Rebecca whispered touching the bedding.

"Good." Anthony commented from the doorway, surprised by how serene Rebecca's face looked as she studied the furnishings.

Anthony had filled the room with juvenile furniture that was perfect for an eight-year-old. He also had a new laptop perfectly positioned on the new desk, with a lamp and next to the lamp was a cell phone. "A cell phone . . . seriously?" Rebecca questioned in shock. She wasn't happy to see that.

"He is about to become the son of a Romano. It is important that Trevor be able to contact us. Plus it has a GPS device in it so we will know where he is, at all times, which could be important."

Rebecca remembered how her best friend, Frankie, was abducted and the thought of that happening to Trevor sent a chill right down her spine, causing her to openly shiver.

Anthony walked in and tried to calm her fears. "He will be guarded by many highly qualified men both when we are with him and when we are not with him."

"If something happened to him, I don't think I could live with myself." Rebecca put her hand to her forehead.

"Shhh, darling, nothing is going to happen to him." Anthony came up behind her and rubbed his hand up and down her back still clad in the silky, blue blouse she wore today. "In fact, even *you* will start to see additional men in the coming days."

"Me?" Rebecca turned to look at Anthony directly, watching him nod.

"Unfortunately, the Romano wealth comes with a price. One of the prices is the extreme lack of privacy, which you saw today, firsthand. But the greatest price is that people want to extort and hurt us." Anthony dropped his hand, because even slightly touching her was causing his body to react powerfully. Anthony turned out of the room leading Rebecca down to the next bedroom.

Rebecca followed Anthony into the next room which was her room. He placed her luggage on top of a bench that was at the foot of a single bed. He added a lovely antique desk which dated back to the early 1800s with a uniquely, delicately upholstered chair. He had a laptop placed in the center of her desk with wireless internet already set up.

"I left space for your treadmill over here by the window and I mounted a TV above so that you could watch something when you work out," Anthony pointed to the TV and shrugged. "When it comes tomorrow, we can always move things around to your liking."

"Aaaaaaa, my treadmill fell apart when the guys came this afternoon. Carlo called me to tell me, and these were his exact words, 'She's broke'," Rebecca started to giggle. "I guess I wore old Betsy out."

"Betsy?" Anthony thought that was strange and his expression showed it.

"Since I spent so much time with her, I thought it only right that I should name my treadmill. Besides, she was way cheaper than any gym membership, so she deserved respect." Rebecca started to giggle again.

Anthony chuckled as well and decided he would take care of the treadmill replacement after dinner. "Do you want to change before we eat?"

"Absolutely. I hate staying in my work clothes a minute longer than I have to."

"Alright I will meet you in the kitchen in . . ." Anthony stopped to check his watch, ". . . ten minutes."

"It's a date." No sooner did the words leave her mouth before she wanted to take them back. "I mean, okay." Rebecca blushed, turned and opened her bag. When Anthony closed the door behind him, Rebecca silently scolded herself. *It's a date? What a really, really stupid thing to say! I have got to be more careful with what comes out of my mouth, especially around Anthony, now more than ever.*

Anthony jogged to the kitchen igniting the pilot to begin the pot to boil. He moved to the other side of the apartment, peeling off his suit jacket and tie along the way. He took off the rest of his clothing once he was inside the closet, then went into the bathroom dropping the laundry in the basket and observed his partial erection. Not only was it uncomfortable, but he was too large to be able to hide it from Rebecca forever. He washed up at the sink then crossed a small hallway in the master bedroom suite to go back into the closet.

The closet was professionally organized by his brother, Jack, who had chosen deeply rich walnut woods to match the antique bedroom furniture. In the center of the closet was a stand-alone cabinet, about counter height, that dated back centuries, in the same walnut woods. One large continuous original piece of white marble graced the top of this unique lowboy for hundreds of years. The nearly white Carrara was original to the antique, which fascinated Anthony every time he looked at it, because it survived hundreds of years and traveled thousands of miles. He had completely emptied out the cabinet and assumed that Rebecca could use it for her fold-wear items. He also cleared out more than half of the hanging portion and left that space open for Rebecca as well. He hadn't realized how much clothing he had that he rarely wore and was glad to give it away.

Anthony pulled out a pair of blue jeans and a black, short-sleeved T-shirt. He sat down on a lovely high back chair that was placed in the closet for this simple purpose. It was covered in the same dark paisley fabrics as in the master bedroom's bedding. He pulled off his black dress socks and put on a pair of short, white sport socks, slapped his thighs and went back into the bathroom to dump his socks in the hamper. He washed his hands and raked his damp fingertips through his hair so that the stray strands stayed off his forehead. He looked at his reflection in the mirror and saw a trim man with blonde hair and gray-blue eyes. Although he was fair, his eyebrows and eyelashes were darker, which intensified the gray in his eyes. His face, with its sharp angles and square chin, resembled his mother's side of the family. He was hoping that Rebecca would see something, anything, in him that she might be attracted to. He didn't care for his own looks. The only thing he cared about was if Rebecca found him appealing.

He exited the master suite past the bed, which he was fairly certain he would be sharing with no one at all tonight and headed toward the kitchen. At that same moment, Rebecca came from the opposite direction.

"Perfect timing." Anthony shoved his hands deep into his front pockets taking in the beauty before him. She wore black yoga pants that dragged along the Oriental rug, a white tank top and a matching black yoga jacket that remained unzipped. His body reacted well before his mind could register the feedback, which was pulsing toward something that was strictly off limits!

Rebecca looked at Anthony wearing his tight black T-shirt and jeans, which were cut very low, nearly falling off his narrow hips. Rebecca only saw Anthony a couple of times out of a suit, so this casual look always caught her off-guard. "You actually look like a regular human being in street clothes."

"Thank you." Anthony was not going to engage in any of her bantering. If she wanted to verbally box with someone, she was going to have to find someone else to do it with tonight. "You look great."

"Thanks." Rebecca got the hint and tried to mind her manners.

"You're welcome." Anthony removed two wineglasses from one of the high gloss white kitchen cabinets. He placed the glasses on the black soapstone countertop, which was oiled to highlight the magnificent veins in the stone.

"This kitchen is gorgeous." Rebecca commented, watching Anthony open the bottle of wine.

"My brother renovated this space. Actually, Jack renovated the entire apartment."

"He does amazing work."

Anthony nodded in agreement. "Wine?"

"Yes. Thanks."

Anthony poured the wine and handed Rebecca a large-bowled glass filled halfway with the fine *Gamay Noir*. Anthony raised his glass and tapped it with hers. *"Salute,"* Anthony said.

Although Rebecca had heard the term before, she didn't have a clue what it meant, but assumed it meant cheers. She took a sip and was surprised with the quality, how it filled her senses with a fragrant richness and boldness.

The pot quickly reached a rolling boil, because Sofia and Jack talked Anthony into getting all commercial-grade appliances that were supposed to cut preparation time in half and they were right, as usual. Anthony dropped the pasta into the water and stirred it. He took a sip of his wine and turned to light the flame under the pot that was filled with the sauce and meatballs.

"How about I set the table . . . island?" Rebecca suggested.

"Sure." Anthony answered. "The dinner plates are over there in that cabinet just above the dishwasher and the salad plates are right above the dinner plates."

"Okay." Rebecca went around the island and took out two dinner plates. She stood up on tiptoes just managing to reach the salad plates. "Got it," Rebecca declared.

Anthony smiled and continued to stir the pot with the sauce. The pasta looked ready so he took the wooden spoon and scooped out a piece to taste it. "Perfect." He scooped the pasta out of the water and directly into the pot with the sauce and meatballs. After grabbing two potholders, he brought the huge pot over to the island, setting it down next to their plates.

Rebecca found the salad in the refrigerator and the dressing was right next to it clearly marked "Dressing!" She poured the creamy dressing over the salad and tossed it while Anthony served up the pasta and meatballs.

"One, two or three?" Anthony asked, holding a meatball above the pot ready to place it into her plate.

"One is fine. Thank you." Rebecca answered while she put a little salad into the salad plates. She placed the salad next to their dinner plates and sat down on one of the six chairs that were around the island, taking another sip of her wine.

Anthony walked over to a wall of ovens, opened a drawer and pulled out a long, foil-wrapped object. "Garlic bread," he announced.

"We'll both have to eat it. That's the rule when garlic is around."

"Okay," Anthony smiled, then his face changed quickly when he hot-potatoed the object to the island.

"Hot?" Rebecca giggled.

"Very!" Anthony dropped it onto the island and quickly pulled back the foil. Instantly, the room filled with the aroma of warm bread, garlic and butter.

"Do you eat like this every night?" Rebecca was growing concerned, because if he had one of those 'I can eat whatever I want and never gain any weight metabolisms,' she was going to hit him in the side of his head with her dinner plate.

"I usually get home too late to eat like this." Anthony sat down and sipped his wine. He grated some cheese on his pasta and motioned to Rebecca. She nodded, so he did the honors. He placed a piece of garlic bread on her plate and a piece on his plate, as well.

"What time do you usually get home?" Rebecca started to twirl her pasta and watched Anthony fetch two soup spoons from the cutlery drawer.

"Try this," Anthony suggested and began to twirl the pasta using the spoon.

"Okay," Rebecca tried and tried again and after a few tries found it helpful. "It works!"

Anthony smiled. "I usually get home at nine."

"Nine! Gosh, that's late."

"I guess that will change once Trevor moves in."

"Can you do that?"

"Of course I can. I'm the president."

"That doesn't sound very convincing." Rebecca shook her head quickly.

"I know. I will probably have to bring work home if I come home early, but we should try to eat dinner together as a family. Trevor should experience that. Some of my fondest and most dreaded moments occurred at the dinner table."

"Give me an example." Rebecca twirled and placed a scoop of pasta into her mouth.

"Most dreaded had to be when I failed my math test in fifth grade and I hid it in my book bag. I think that's what we called it then, not a backpack. Anyway, I lied to my parents and said that the teacher was absent and we didn't get the results back. When we sat down for dinner the phone rang. It was the neighbor popping her top, because her son, who was in my class, failed the math test. My mother looked at me with death in her eyes." Anthony shuddered, causing Rebecca to laugh. "When my neighbor asked what my score was, my mother said we had just sat down to dinner and she would call her back later. I didn't eat a single bite. That meal was bad! Not because the food was bad, but for the simple fact that I was too worried about the consequences—not because I failed the test, but because I lied."

"Interesting . . . and your fondest memory?" Rebecca cut her meatball in quarters and popped a section into her mouth closing her eyes. "This is delicious! Wow, Sofia can really cook!"

"I know . . ." Anthony twirled his pasta using his spoon and placed a forkful of pasta into his mouth. This had to be his first real bite of food in days. He was way too wound up with Rebecca moving in, his parents calling him incessantly and the lawyers badgering him with the fact that there were too many loopholes in the Prenup.

Rebecca motioned with her fork for Anthony to continue with his story.

"Right, fondest. That was when my father handed me the keys to my first car at dinner. A Corvette! I was thrilled to pieces."

Thrilled to pieces? Rebecca thought. *Who speaks like that? I know! Someone with wealth. Someone with class. Someone with great intellect.*

"My father bought one for me and one for my brother, Jack. Jack got a red one and I got a blue one. I still have it. It's in the parking garage. I put it in the Prenuptial that it is to be transferred to Trevor on his seventeenth birthday."

"Why?" Rebecca asked in shock.

"Because I want Trevor to have it," Anthony eyeballed Rebecca quizzically. "He's going to be my son in a few weeks."

"Yes." Rebecca answered astounded by that statement. Anthony made it sound perfectly natural that he should leave his prized Corvette to a total stranger. *Was he really that giving?* Rebecca wondered silently. "Now tell me about your family." Rebecca was enjoying listening to Anthony's tone of voice, something she really never paid attention to before. It was deep, smooth and calming. "Start with Jack. What was it like to have a brother like Jack Romano?"

"Jack got into trouble—a lot!"

"And here I thought you were the troublemaker. You know what they say—you've got to watch the quiet ones." Rebecca bit into her garlic bread and closed her eyes proclaiming, "I can't!"

"You *can't* what?" Anthony had no idea what she was talking about.

"I can't eat like this every night of the week. I will look like a . . . a big, big-busted troll."

So utterly surprised by her comment, Anthony laughed loudly. It actually felt good to laugh so hard. "You forgot sexy!"

"I'm serious!" Rebecca sneered at the garlic bread menacingly. This little piece of dough was going to cost her hours on her treadmill.

"Alright, we'll speak to Sofia about lighter meals during the week and maybe heartier meals on the weekends?"

"That could work." Rebecca motioned with her last bite of garlic bread for Anthony to continue with his story.

"Let me see. Where was I? Jack. Well there is no other way to say it. Jack was in trouble all the time and when he wasn't getting into trouble on his own, he was helping me to stay out of trouble, which ultimately got him into trouble. It was pretty much a vicious cycle for him."

"An example," Rebecca prompted before devouring her final piece of garlic bread.

"Uhmm," Anthony thought. "I know. One time he took my father's car for a joyride."

"What's so bad about that?"

"If I remember correctly, he was thirteen years old, he did not have a driver's license and he got a speeding ticket and two other moving violations."

"How did that go down?"

"Oh it went down alright. My parents sent him down to Sicily for the rest of the summer."

"Good answer. Ship him off to distant relatives."

"I think that's when he fell in love with architecture."

"Something positive out of something negative. I like that!"

"Yeah," Anthony agreed. *Maybe something positive will come out of this situation . . .*

They ate and drank their red wine. The conversation stayed light and simple while they cleaned up together after dinner.

Anthony did the dishes and the pots which caused Rebecca's mouth to hang open in shock. She had no idea that Anthony was so domesticated. He most definitely did not look the type. Never-a-hair-out-of-place Anthony Romano put the leftovers into containers and into the refrigerator.

"Coffee and dessert?" Anthony asked.

"Are you completely out of your mind?" Rebecca growled. "That meal was like five thousand calories!" Rebecca glared openly with her hands sitting firmly on her trim waist.

Anthony had no idea she was so concerned about her food consumption. He held up his hands and asked, "How about a movie then?"

"Better."

"More wine?" Anthony asked. He had the second bottle already breathing on the counter.

"I could be persuaded." Rebecca was secretly hoping the wine would put her to sleep. She felt wired and on edge.

Anthony picked up the bottle of wine in one hand and his glass in the other. Walking out of the kitchen, he hit the overhead light switches with his elbow, turning off all the chandeliers and the many tiny pot lights, but left the backsplash lights on. Rebecca followed him, her wineglass in hand, down the hall and into the family room. He placed the bottle of wine and his wineglass on the coffee table, which was a large, old, wooden red door covered with a piece of glass. A large flat screen TV sat opposite the couch between cabinets that flanked it from floor to ceiling. A stone fireplace graced the adjacent wall. Anthony opened the far left cabinet and waved his hand over the hundreds and hundreds of movies.

"Geez, what a collection." Rebecca stared in wonder taking a sip of her wine.

"I have it broken down. Horror right here, comedy over here, movie classics right here, TV classics there, X-Rated here, XX-Rated and NRs way up there, so Trevor will not be able to see them."

Rebecca shot him her wide eyes in warning.

"Yes dear, they will be removed permanently." Anthony smiled inwardly enjoying the idea that his future wife was about to launch a fit.

"Good," Rebecca was dying to see what type of double x-rated and un-rated movies he viewed. She would have to inspect that section later, before they were removed.

"And romance comedy right there," Anthony pointed to his left.

Rebecca looked at the cabinet and in that instant she realized how organized everything was in the apartment. His apartment was arranged in a highly compartmentalized way right down to the DVDs and inviting total strangers into his space to live with him for an undetermined period of time was probably going to be a challenge for him. Rebecca handed Anthony a comedy and watched him glide it into the machine. They both sat at either end of the couch and while the upcoming snippets were running, Anthony filled each glass with a little more wine.

"Comfortable?" Anthony asked.

"Is it alright if I use that afghan?"

"Of course. This is your home now." Anthony got up and handed her the afghan.

"Not until after the official wedding . . ."

"Wrong . . ." Anthony stated before he sat down, taking a long drink from his glass of wine. "It is your home right now. Besides, the Prenup states that from the moment we were engaged, which was technically at Francesca and Jack's wedding."

"Oh." Rebecca was shocked that he had attached a hard date to their engagement.

The movie was underway and they both sat back and drank their wine, with Anthony occasionally refilling their glasses, intently watching the movie. Eventually they both fell asleep on the couch with Anthony waking first. He blinked several times and watched an image circle around in a random pattern across the flat screen. At first, his mind forgot that Rebecca was there until he turned to see her softly snoring, her legs curled to one side and her head resting on the arm of the couch. He turned everything off then gently nudged her. She didn't wake. He tried again and she still didn't wake. He peeled off the afghan, gently swept her up into his arms and quietly walked her to the other side of the apartment. He entered her bedroom and tenderly laid her onto her bed. He pulled the covers out from underneath her and covered her, pressing a kiss to her forehead which was furrowed with what appeared to be deep unconscious thoughts. He stood over her for some time and regarded the woman who was about to become his wife in name alone. That was going to *suck*, because all he wanted to do was love her. He turned, raked his hand through his fine, blonde hair and walked from her room softly closing the door behind him. He went back into the family room and gathered the wineglasses and bottle. He went into the kitchen, re-corked the wine and set the glasses into the stainless steel sink. He went to the front door, secured the additional locks and set the alarm.

Anthony's apartment was actually a combination of three apartments, encompassing the entire western half of the seventeenth floor. There was a second door just through the laundry room on Rebecca's side of the apartment in case of a fire and a third door through the additional laundry room that was located off the master bedroom suite entrance. The alarm covered all the doors, windows and two balconies—the first of which was located off the living room and the second which was off the master bedroom.

Anthony left a few lights on in the apartment in case Rebecca woke up in the middle of the night and needed to find her way around. The apartment had additional nightlights that came on automatically in the hallways spreading soft pools of light along the passageways. Anthony started toward his bedroom when he heard Rebecca's door open. She softly padded out and whispered, "Goodnight."

"Goodnight darling." Anthony spoke in a soft deep tone watching as she turned to walk back into her room. He inhaled and exhaled deeply, then went to his room closing the door silently. He undressed, washed up and pulled on a pair of pajama bottoms. He climbed into bed, but couldn't fall asleep for what seemed like the entire night.

Very early the next morning, the apartment's burglar alarm started BLARING!!! The loud shrieking sound propelled Anthony out of his bed, out of his room and down the hall.

Rebecca was standing in her tank top and yoga bottoms with her hands covering her ears. "My God! What is that?" she shouted over the alarm.

"That's the burglar alarm." Anthony shouted back.
"No! Really?" Rebecca shouted sarcastically, placing her hands firmly on her hips. Rebecca figured he was like everyone else with a house alarm. They had them, but never used them until they got robbed.

It was then that the house phone began to ring which was immediately followed by his cell phone that began to dance on the foyer table. Anthony went over to one of the keypads in the apartment and quickly punched in the code, then picked up his cell phone. "Hello?"

The person on the other end of the phone asked for the password and Anthony revealed the coded word. He apologized for the inconvenience and said that his fiancée accidentally set off the alarm. Once he ended the call, the houseline stopped ringing as well. All was quiet again as he walked back over to where Rebecca was standing.

"Sorry! I should have shown you that last night."

"Ya think?" Rebecca shouted then lowered her voice. "That thing nearly scared me half to death!" Rebecca was standing there still trying to catch her breath. When the alarm went off, she grabbed her gun and was about to apprehend the intruder. Thank God she remembered what she was doing and hid the gun. As that thought passed, she slowly took in the sight before her. Anthony was standing there in only his pajama bottoms which hung very low on his hips. His bare upper half was an image right out of a fitness magazine. He was cut, defined and, simply put, perfection. Every muscle, every detail was delineated and pronounced. It startled Rebecca so much so that she started gulping for air.

Anthony watched Rebecca struggle for her next breath. "Are you alright?" he began to reach for her.

"I'm fine." Rebecca pulled back looking away from his body. She quickly darted back into her bedroom pushing the door closed behind her. Leaning against her bedroom door she whispered to herself, "Saying NO to 'that body' is going to be hard." *Poor choice of words*, Rebecca thought. "That body is . . . ridiculous! Who has a body like that?" Rebecca began to pace her room mumbling. "The man must workout like a maniac!" Rebecca dropped down onto her bed and tried to regain her composure.

Anthony went back into his bedroom and pulled on a T-shirt. He worked his way back to the kitchen and started the coffee. While the coffee brewed, he opened the apartment door and got the paper. When he unraveled the paper, right there on the front page was a picture of Anthony and Rebecca at the Hall of Records building. You couldn't see her face, because her hand was covering it. He walked back into the kitchen, tossed the paper onto the island and poured himself a cup of coffee, black. He went back into the foyer looking for his reading glasses, which annoyed the living daylights out of him. When he found them, he retraced his way back into the kitchen, donned his eyeglasses that he never needed before he became president of Romano Enterprises and began to read the newspaper.

Rebecca came into the kitchen and looked at him, "Eyeglasses?"

"Only since I became president of Romano Enterprises." Anthony shrugged. "Too much small print on a daily basis." Anthony recited the exact explanation the eye doctor gave him six months earlier. He then shook the paper until it was fully opened. "The mugs are in the cabinet over the coffee pot."

"Thanks."

"I'm sorry about the alarm." Anthony lowered the paper.

"I opened the window because, I don't know, I just always open my bedroom window in the morning."

"That's fine, but you are going to have to remember to turn off the alarm."

Rebecca poured her coffee and sipped the hot brew, thinking *duh!*

"There's milk in the refrigerator."

"No thanks. I drink it black."

Anthony waved for her to come over into the hall. He wanted to show her how the alarm pad worked.

Rebecca watched and listened to Anthony pretending to be new at this how-to-set-a-house-alarm business. *If he only knew that I'm a cop*, Rebecca thought biting the inside of her cheek to stop herself from laughing out loud.

"Here is one of the keypads right outside your bedroom door. The code is 007 and the password is—eagle. Here, let me show you.

When this is red, it means it's activated; when this button is green, it means it is not activated, but you should keep it on all the time."

"Green is activated?" Rebecca asked dim wittingly, playing her act to perfection. The only thing she could think about was the image burned into her mind's eye forever—a shirtless Anthony.

"Green is not activated." Anthony stated calmly. "Red is activated."

"That is so stupid! Green means go!! Why would green mean not on?" Rebecca questioned before storming away from the keypad like a helpless twit.

Anthony followed behind her. "It's easy to remember. Just think of the color red—red is hot!"

Rebecca looked at him and pursed her lips. *Hot*, she thought silently, *like your body*.

Anthony recently learned that when she pursed her lips exactly like that, it seemed to mean that she was in the mental process of relenting. Suddenly, he followed her eyes to the newspaper that lay open on the island.

"WHAT IS THAT?!" Rebecca shouted in exasperation, pointing to the paper.

"Yeah, I was going to wait until you had your first cup of coffee."

"Oh . . . My . . . God! Is that us . . . on the front page of the paper?" Rebecca's hand flew to her open mouth to cover her gasp. In that instant, she was certain that her cover must be blown. Her superior officer nearly caused her ears to fall off her head when she told him her current state of affairs and about the press. This was going to send him through the roof!

"Yes." Anthony opened the paper to show Rebecca that there were indeed several pictures of them on the front page, but oddly enough, her face was always obscured.

"Oh my God! I haven't even told my parents," Rebecca blurted out, then gasped.

Anthony's head snapped back. "YOU DIDN'T TELL YOUR PARENTS THAT WE'RE GETTING MARRIED!?" he shouted. "Did you want to keep this a secret?"

"I . . . well . . . I mean . . . I told Frankie, but really no one else, not yet." Rebecca stammered while wringing her hands. She told her superior officer, because of what happened at the Hall of

Records yesterday. And she told Frankie, her best friend, who was married to Anthony's brother. *It was a start, right?*

"You didn't plan on inviting your parents to our wedding?" he asked.

Rebecca could see that he was openly shocked. "I was . . ." Rebecca didn't have an answer, so she snapped her mouth shut.

"I guess you should start making some phone calls, because you cannot keep this a secret. We're getting married in a week and adopting a child as soon as possible after that. We have to stay married for at least one year after the adoption is approved. You were there at that meeting when the lawyers told us that the adoption could be reversed if we stayed married for anything less than one year!" Anthony couldn't believe it. *Did she really want to keep the child from his future grandparents?*

"Yes. I was there. I heard them."

"Listen, I know you hate me . . ."

"I don't hate you." Rebecca cut him off knowing she didn't sound very convincing.

"Why else would you keep this a secret from your parents?" Anthony asked, but rather than wait for her to answer him, he took his coffee and started to walk out of the kitchen.

"Anthony . . . I know this looks bad." Rebecca quickly followed after him, grappling for the right words.

"I can tell you how it looks from where I'm standing. It looks ungrateful." Anthony took a deep breath in and out. He signed up for this and that was a decision he was going to live with. In a softer voice he continued, "I am opening my life up to you, Rebecca, so that you can adopt a child. In fact, I have turned my life upside down and inside out. I had the corporate attorneys pulling their hair pieces from their sutured scalps for weeks to protect a stranger in a Prenuptial Agreement rather than their own client! I will not even get into what my parents have to say about this . . . this arrangement."

"Anthony, please . . ." Rebecca was still having trouble formulating into words what she wanted to say.

"Did you want to keep Trevor a secret from his grandparents?" he had to know. When she didn't respond he plowed ahead. "I thought you wanted him to have a stable life!" Anthony was growing more concerned, yet his voice became softer and lower by the minute. As soon as the words 'stable life' exited his mouth he knew that the boy would never know the meaning of that and that reality hit Anthony hard and straight to the heart. Trevor would still be subjected to a dysfunctional situation.

"Yes. No. I mean, of course not. I want him to know his grandparents." Rebecca felt flustered and confused.

"I'm sorry that I'm such an embarrassment to you that you would not even tell your own parents you are marrying me."

"I . . ." Rebecca fumbled for the words, but Anthony turned away apparently unwilling to wait while she groped for her next sentence. She watched as he went down the hall to his bedroom, silently closing the door behind him. "Great . . . just great," Rebecca put her hands on her head. She felt like her skull was about to explode. Suddenly she heard a sound coming from the foyer. Her cell phone was vibrating in her purse. Digging around in the oversized plastic purse, Rebecca studied the device then looked heavenward. *It's my mother.* Rebecca slid the screen on the phone to engage the call. "Hi Mom!"

Veronica McFarlan was a lovely woman. She had recently turned sixty years old and had a very fulfilling and reasonably comfortable life. She was blessed with a loving husband, a beautiful son, Stephen and, of course, her daughter. "Rebecca?"

"Yeah, I'm getting married."

"In one week!" Veronica tried to conceal her crushed emotions.

Rebecca heard the hurt in her mother's voice. "I'm sorry. I was going to call you guys, but I've been really busy."

All of a sudden the phone went dead. Her mother ended the call. Rebecca put her hand to her forehead. She managed to piss off a number of people so far this morning, in spite of the fact that she hadn't even showered or left the apartment. Then the phone started to vibrate again and when she looked down she noticed that the phone number was from one of her co-workers. Rebecca let that call go to voicemail. She saw that she had several text messages and one was from Mitchell. "Why the hell am I reading about your impending nuptials to Romano in the newspaper? This could jeopardize our mission!" Rebecca erased the messages immediately.

Walking back into the kitchen, she picked up her mug of coffee which sat next to the source of all of her aggravation. Working her way around the island, she went back into her bedroom. She figured she would shower while Anthony, hopefully, cooled off. She went into her private bath and started the shower. By the time she got out, she had eight new voicemails—one was from her brother and there were three new text messages. "Ugh! This is going to be one long day."

Rebecca put on a pair of dark jeans and dried her hair with a diffuser. She slipped on a lightweight black sweater and applied her makeup. Not much today. Powder for a foundation, eyeliner, mascara and a little blush was enough. She found her lip balm and applied the light pink shade.

She looked at herself in the mirror and thought she had better talk to her fiancé, because not speaking was going to be a problem during the wedding ceremony. While she began to tidy up the bathroom, she thought about her parents and remembered that they had met Anthony last Thanksgiving and of course at the wedding. So he wasn't a total stranger to them. She walked back into her bedroom and started to tidy that room up as well. She made her bed, put her laundry in the laundry basket that was in her bathroom and made a mental note to talk to Sofia about her wash. Occasionally she quietly opened her bedroom door a crack to peek out. *No sign of him!* "Crap!" Rebecca grumbled quietly.

When she was done straightening out her room, she opened her door and padded barefoot down the hall towards Anthony's side of the apartment. Anthony was standing by the window in the family room with his cell phone to his ear. He turned and saw her standing in the doorway.

"I'll come back." Rebecca whispered, turning to leave.

Anthony motioned for her to stay. "I was listening to my voicemails. Some friends of mine read the paper and called to congratulate us."

"That's nice. My mother just hung up on me."

Anthony pushed his phone into the front pocket of his jeans, standing silent.

"Anthony I'm sorry. Really I am! I'm grateful, very grateful. Trevor is the luckiest boy alive. He will have Anthony Romano as a father."

Rebecca took a deep breath. "What I did was foolish! It was foolish of me to wait this long to tell everyone and I know it must seem like a slap in the face to you." Rebecca took a deep breath. "I know that your attorneys are probably costing you a small fortune to make it possible for me, for us, to adopt Trevor. I am thankful—truly. I just don't want you to . . . you know . . . think that this is going to be anything more than what we originally discussed." Rebecca was waving her hand between her and Anthony.

"That's up to you Rebecca." Anthony took a subtle step forward.

Rebecca decided to divert the conversation. "My parents are pissed. You are pissed. I haven't listened to my brother's voicemail, but I would venture to say that he's probably pissed too. And look at that," Rebecca facetiously looked at her wristwatch. "It isn't even eleven o'clock yet!"

"I'm not pissed . . ." Anthony stepped closer looking down at the brunette bombshell that smelled serenely of lavender, but was anything but serene. To him, she was a bundle of dynamite sticks decorated with enticing fuses.

Rebecca looked down at her feet. Her toes were polished in the same vibrant color that matched her nails. Anthony's feet were bare too. The first thought that popped into her head when she studied them was they looked manly. When she looked back up, she could see the gray in his eyes deepen and she studied each eye for several minutes.

"I think you should call your parents and brother and ask them to dinner tonight. You can explain everything to them then."

"You mean tell them the truth!" Rebecca was speaking in a nervous high-pitched tone. She watched Anthony fold his arms across his chest, and after this morning's alarm fiasco, she knew exactly what that chest consisted of and fought with the images that spun in her head, making her feel dizzy. "I haven't even told YOU the truth!" Rebecca poked her finger at Anthony without touching him. "Well, not everything, anyway." Rebecca whispered as she began to wring her hands.

Anthony was fairly certain he didn't like the sound of that. He also knew that when she wrung her hands like that, it was never a good sign. "The movers will be here at one and your new treadmill will be here then too. So you have a few hours to explain everything to me."

"You got me a new treadmill?" Rebecca asked in her sweetest voice hoping to change the subject again.

"Yes and nice try. Very smooth segue. Start talking darling. But first, I think I'm going to need another cup of coffee or maybe a drink!" Anthony walked from the den toward the kitchen, raking his hand through his hair. Once in the kitchen, he started a fresh pot of coffee.

While the machine did its thing, Rebecca started to speak. "Let's see. Where should I start?"

"How about at the beginning . . ."

Rebecca was standing in the kitchen looking directly at Anthony. "Is this floor heated? It is so warm on my toes," Rebecca was looking for a diversionary tactic, because any one would do at the moment.

"Yes. The whole apartment has heated floors," Anthony placed his hands on his hips and studied her.

"Alright, alright, I was adopted. Okay? Now you know!" Rebecca raised her hands and dropped them with a slap to the sides of her thighs.

Anthony was shocked. He was marrying this woman and had no idea that she was a child who was given up for adoption. That statement alone made so many things clearer to him. "Go on," Anthony encouraged, removing the shocked expression from his face as he poured himself a fresh cup of coffee. After that statement, he realized that they had a lot of work to do before the family court proceedings. They were going to have to start talking and sharing this kind of information that people in love share—and fast!

"Uhmm, well, after my mother had my brother, Stephen, the doctors screwed up something during the birth. They sent my mother home and she started hemorrhaging. It was really bad and she spent close to a month in the hospital. She nearly died. Scar tissue and a whole bunch of medical terms later, no more kids!" Rebecca decided she needed another cup of coffee, too.

"That is horrible," Anthony leaned against the counter.

Rebecca got a mug and filled it with fresh coffee. "She was shattered. My father and mother wanted more children, but weren't capable of having anymore. That is when they decided to adopt me!"

"Do you know who your birth parents are?"

"Yes and no. My mother is, was, a stripper. And I don't know who my father is."

"Your mother is a stripper!" Anthony exclaimed. He could see the corporate attorneys going into cardiac arrest when they heard this story.

"Well, not anymore. She's in her late fifties so her body is not in stripper form, if you know what I mean. She's a bartender down in the village."

"Are you in contact with her?"

"No. I only found her a few years ago. My job gives me access to most of that kind of information." *My police job that is,* Rebecca thought. *Should I tell him I'm a cop?* She questioned herself silently. "That's one of the perks of working for the city. I looked her up, went to the bar one night and ordered a drink. She didn't know who the hell I was—just some chick who wanted a drink." Rebecca took a sip of her coffee and realized that her head was pounding. "Where do you keep the aspirin?"

"In my bathroom." Anthony walked out of the kitchen raking a hand through his hair. If either of her birth parents found out she was marrying a Romano, they were going to come out of the woodwork—and for all the wrong reasons. Anthony wasn't sure why it happened like that, but it just did. People can be greedy and naturally take before they give. He went into the bathroom and grabbed the bottle from the cabinet. He turned and nearly ran Rebecca over. Reaching for her arm so that she didn't fall backwards, he handed her the aspirin bottle. "Here you go."

"Thanks."

"You're welcome. I think we should contact the attorneys on Monday and advise them of this situation."

"That would probably be best."

Anthony sensed that she was still holding something back. "Is there anything else you want to tell me?"

Rebecca watched his gray-blue eyes study hers with nearly laser precision. A weaker woman would have been seared. "I don't think so?" Rebecca felt her palms start to sweat. *Maybe he already knows I'm a cop, but he's waiting for me to tell him . . .*

ugh! Rebecca didn't know what to do or say. All she knew is that she had no idea how long she was going to be able to hide from Anthony the fact that she was a cop working undercover as a social worker.

"Alright." Anthony accepted her answer, but something deep inside him didn't believe she was telling him the whole truth. "First though, you need to call your parents and brother and tell them that we are taking them to dinner tonight. That is where we are going to beg them for their forgiveness and swear to them that we are never going to let anything like this ever happen again."

"Can't you do that?" Rebecca pleaded.

Anthony crossed his arms over his chest in that *Mr. Clean* likeness, shaking his head with an emphatic *NO!*

"But you're so diplomatic and no one would ever yell at you."

Anthony's eyes flew open wide. "You're joking, right? My father would have been at my front door first thing this morning if he read the paper and found out I was getting married and didn't tell him. My family is one of those 'in your face' kind of families." Anthony turned her shoulders and paraded her out of his bathroom and bedroom, "Make the call."

As Anthony walked away he continued to talk to himself. "My father would have cursed and raged in Italian for nearly an hour. He would have listened to an apology for maybe a minute or two then he would have thrown in some guilt-riddled phrases in French, then finished up with one of his long English tirade conclusions." Anthony pulled out his cell phone and calmly made reservations for four at a discreet, yet casual, restaurant not far from the apartment then he continued to talk to himself. "Of course, my mother would have chimed in." Anthony openly shivered. To him, nothing was worse than having his mother haranguing and harassing him. As he finished that thought, the doorbell rang. He peered through the peephole to see the doorman standing there. "Yes?" Anthony asked the doorman who was holding a box.

"Mr. Romano, I have a package for . . . Mrs. Romano-to-be," the doorman had no idea what to call her since they weren't officially married according to the newspaper he read this morning.

"Thank you," Anthony replied politely, taking the package.

"Also, Mr. Romano, the press was starting to set up camp at the front entrance to the building."

"Perfect." Anthony laughed.

"Good news though . . . sir. The press got a hot tip that Mrs. Moore is staying at the Plaza, because she is calling her marriage quits! So the press has left for now."

"Good news for me, but unfortunate news for Mr. Moore." After giving the doorman a tip, Anthony took the package into the kitchen and placed it on the island.

"Okay, we are on for dinner tonight. They are all coming here first, if you don't mind."

"Of course I don't mind. This is your home now." Anthony stated firmly with an expression of exasperation, because she wasn't accepting the fact that this was her home too.

"What's that?"

"It's for you from my mother." Anthony slid the box to the side of the island where Rebecca was standing.

Rebecca pulled and tugged, pretending to be unable to open it. She didn't want him to know that she could tear a telephone book into halves. Cops needed strong hands. She lifted her best helpless gaze to Anthony and he fell for it. He walked to her side and opened the box. Rebecca pulled out a large, red box tied with a white satin ribbon and bow. She untied the ribbon and lifted the lid. Inside was "the real" designer handbag in the same exact color and style as the fake Rebecca wore yesterday. "How did she know . . . ? Oh boy, this is a real . . . wow!" Rebecca was speechless while she looked over the original handbag that retailed for more than two thousand dollars.

"She probably read the paper where they talked about your knock-off attire."

"NO! Oh no . . . that is so mean! Where is that?"

Anthony pointed to the section in the paper.

"No wonder the stars hate the press." Rebecca put the bag down on the island placing her hands on her hips.

"It won't be long before you do too." Anthony took the box and placed it by the front door. As he walked back into the kitchen, he opened his wallet and handed Rebecca his credit card.

"What's this for?"

"I think you might want to start buying some *new* things." Anthony emphasized the word 'new.'

"That's insulting." Rebecca threw the card back onto the island.

"Let me read for you what the press wrote about the skirt you wore yesterday. Here it is. 'The future Mrs. Romano was wearing a thrift-store pencil skirt that was pilled like only rayon can. The miracle fabric . . .' do you want me to read on?"

"NO!" Rebecca lowered her eyebrows. It felt like someone was beating her brains from inside her head.

"The press can be relentless. Anyway, do you really want to be named as one of the city's worst dressed residents?"

Rebecca placed her hands on her hips again getting ready to take a stand. "Why should I care what a bunch of nothing-better-do-with-their-lives gossip columnists have to say about my clothes?"

"The answer is simple . . ." Anthony folded his arms over his chest again, ". . . because it would be very bad for business."

"How does my handbag and skirt hurt your business?" Now Rebecca was getting annoyed.

"Because WE, darling . . ." Anthony pointed his index finger between her and himself, ". . . are in the business of authenticity!"

Rebecca raised her eyebrows and pursed her lips.

Anthony was going to teach this woman a thing or two before the day was through, even if it meant cramming it down her lovely throat.

Rebecca opened her mouth then closed it. Snatching the credit card from the counter, she went to her room. She turned on her laptop, went online and began to search the net for one of the finest stores in the city. The prices for designer jeans, T's, dresses and skirts were crazy. Rebecca was experiencing some real sticker shock and she wasn't even paying for it! She knew she needed daywear, eveningwear, athletic-wear, swimwear and lingerie.

"Seriously," she mumbled to no one. Her order totaled close to five thousand dollars and she hardly bought anything. Before she hit the accept button, she pulled out her cell phone and text messaged Anthony the price for the clothes she was about to purchase. A few seconds later Anthony was standing in her bedroom doorway.

"Seriously . . ." Anthony sounded annoyed.

"I know! These prices are insane!" Rebecca got up and pointed to her laptop.

Anthony could care less what she bought and how much it cost. "I don't care about the prices. What I care about is that you are text messaging me in our own home!"

"Oh right . . . sorry." Rebecca looked genuinely sorry, but Anthony let her have it.

"You need to start communicating. This is obviously a problem area for you and you need to start working on it before an eight-year-old sees this type of behavior."

"Yes of course. You're right." Rebecca pursed her lips. She watched Anthony go over to the computer and lean down. *He smells good*, Rebecca instantly noticed. It reminded her of citrus and wood and his scent was starting to make her mouth water.

Anthony looked at the shopping cart, as his eyes quickly noticed some lingerie purchases, which nearly caused his heart to stop. The fact that he loved her and wanted her was making it nearly impossible to remain detached.

Rebecca watched as he moved the arrow over to the 'confirm' key to complete the transaction. "Thank you."

"You're welcome."

"I think I've had enough shopping for today. I will order more things tomorrow." Rebecca stood standing in front of Anthony as the sun was shining into her bedroom, causing her curls to appear silky. He ached to touch her hair, to touch her, as he raked his hand through his hair. They had hours before their dinner plans and they needed to fill that time with something other than staring at each other.

Rebecca felt the tension between them as well; whether it was sexual or not, she didn't want to think about it. "What do you normally do on Saturdays?"

"Run."

"The press . . ." Rebecca tried to reveal her concern. She didn't want them looking at her sweat outfits, which were also curbside finds.

"They left. The doorman told me they were chasing a better story."

"You mean to tell me that there is a better story than my tasteless, knock-off wardrobe?" Rebecca used humor to break the electrical current in the room.

"Apparently . . ." Anthony started to turn to leave her room.

"What about the movers?" Rebecca wondered.

"I can call Carlo and tell him what to do. If you don't want to go with me, I'll understand." Anthony needed to get out of the apartment for awhile. Maybe he needed to put a little space between himself and Rebecca.

"I'll go with you!"

"How far do you run?" Anthony turned back, because he didn't want to start his run and hear about how she broke her fingernail midway through and would need to go home. He needed to release some of his pent-up energy or whatever it was he was feeling. Before he started working out regularly, he had no idea how much it changed his life. He felt better and he even believed that his mind was sharper.

"About five miles." Rebecca started to bite her fingernail.

"Mile time?" Anthony wanted to run not walk.

"About nine minutes . . ." Rebecca lied. She could do a mile in seven minutes easily. When she was at the police academy she broke the record. She would have to play the part of barely being able to keep up. Not telling Anthony that she was a cop was important to the success of her mission. She would handle explaining everything to Anthony after she nabbed the biggest sex trafficker on the east coast.

"Be ready in ten minutes." Anthony turned and left her side of the apartment and went back to his side. When he closed the master bedroom door he was grinning from ear to ear. *Welcome to the life of the rich and famous*, Anthony laughed quietly. *Everyone thinks it is so easy, so easy, to have everyone watching for your slightest misstep.* He changed and was waiting in the kitchen in five minutes.

Rebecca pulled the door open to her bedroom in a flurry and ran down the hall to the kitchen.

"Ready?"

"Yup." Rebecca was actually looking forward to going, as she zipped up her sweat jacket. But first she grabbed her new bag off the island and went into the foyer. She transferred the contents of her old bag into the new designer-labeled bag and handed Anthony the decoy. Rebecca walked out of the apartment feeling a whole lot better already.

Holding the old knock-off purse, Anthony picked up the box and set the alarm before he closed and locked the door. Apparently security was a high priority for Anthony and Rebecca respected that. He walked past the elevator and opened a door marked "Disposal." He put the box down a chute marked "Recyclables" and the purse down the chute marked "Incinerator."

"Destroying the evidence," Rebecca joked.

"Absolutely! I don't want my bride-to-be to have any undue stress before our big day." Anthony stated sincerely.

"Then maybe you should explain to me why we're going to dinner with my parents and brother tonight?"

"In order to clean up your mess, darling." Anthony took hold of her beautiful, strong shoulders and turned her about. He knew her shoulders were both lovely and muscular, because of the off-the-shoulder dress she wore at his brother and sister-in-law's wedding. He took her hand and she didn't object as they walked to the elevator. She was wearing his ring and that made him happy. Actually, that made him very, very happy.

Anthony lived only steps from the park and he held Rebecca's hand until they reached the entrance. Once they entered the park, they both took some time to stretch, then started to run. They began slowly at first then picked up the pace. Anthony was impressed that for such a short woman, she could keep up with his elongated strides. They did a little more than five miles and that was good enough, even though Anthony preferred to do ten miles on the weekends. When they winded their way back to the entrance, they stopped at a vendor in the park who sold water and Anthony got them each a bottle. They walked around a little and drank their water.

"That felt good." Anthony said between deep breaths and gulps of his water.

"Yeah, but that was faster than what I normally do." Rebecca lied, as she calculated the time per mile on her watch. "Seven-and-a-half-minute mile."

Anthony nodded "I usually do ten eight-minute miles." "Whoa!" That reminded Rebecca of her days at the academy. Anthony would've made a fine cadet. "That's not going to happen with me by your side."

"Why?" Anthony found her declaration curious, because she certainly kept pace with him, studying the flushed beauty before him.

Rebecca pointed to her breasts "It gets a little uncomfortable with these things bouncing around after five miles."

"Oh." Anthony never considered that a woman's breasts could be such an impediment. He took her hand in his and walked back toward the apartment. As they walked through the lobby, the doorman had another package for Rebecca. Anthony carried the large box and once inside the apartment, Anthony pulled the edges for her. Rebecca opened the lid and found an inscribed garment bag from the department store she ordered from this morning. Rebecca lifted the bag out of the box and unzipped it, revealing several of the items she purchased earlier.

"These are some of the things I ordered this morning!" Rebecca was genuinely surprised, but Anthony didn't look surprised at all.

"Maybe you should try on your purchases. If you need tailoring, we can do that today and have them cleaned and pressed before this evening, just in case the press comes back."

Rebecca was shocked. She was actually speechless. Probably for the first time in her life! "Is the press going to be constantly looking at me and examining my wardrobe?"

Anthony shrugged.

They decided to make a light lunch and while they were preparing it, Rebecca asked, "This restaurant that we're going to tonight, is it fancy-casual or casual-casual?"

"Very casual." Anthony answered. "I'll clean up lunch so you can go try on your things. Anything that doesn't need altering leave in the kitchen for dry cleaning. I'll call Paul to pick them up and you will have them back before we go to dinner."

Rebecca didn't argue. She took her new things into her bedroom and tried on each and every item. The clothes were lovely and the feel of silk and cotton as opposed to rayon and polyester was in a word—divine. She bought several cashmere sweaters and they were the softest things she had ever felt against her skin in her life. She was audibly *ooohhhing* and *aaahhhing*, as she ran her hands up and down the sleeves. She also ordered several pairs of shoes and it was so nice to be able to order her small foot size, instead of searching store after store and never finding any shoes. She even made sure to get a pair of ankle high boots.

Rebecca pulled on the pair of two-hundred dollar dark wash boot-cut jeans and the black ankle high leather boots topped with a black cashmere sweater that had a deep V neck, but not so deep that people would be gawking at her cleavage. Although she had basically the same thing on this morning, this outfit without a doubt looked richer and fit better while she studied her reflection in the large cheval mirror. Rebecca gathered up all her new things and left them on the kitchen island. She didn't see Anthony, so she went back into her bedroom and decided she would take a bath and soak before they went to dinner. She ran the tub and noticed that it was jetted and squealed with delight. She put lavender salts into the warm water and stripped off her clothes. She placed her engagement ring in a crystal dish that rested on the white marble counter near the clear vessel sink. She studied her figure in the mirror, which was the polar opposite of what was popular today. She had way too many curves and large breasts. Even though she exercised regularly and wasn't flabby, curves were definitely not the rage. She shrugged an 'oh well' and stepped into the hot water. She sank down into the lavender scented water and started the jets, letting the pulsating water do its magic.

On the other side of the apartment, Anthony sent her clothes out to be cleaned and pressed. He showered, shaved and dressed for dinner in half an hour. So what does a man do when he's waiting for his female partner to get ready? He paces, of course. Except Anthony was pacing like a starving wolf along the edge of a pen filled with lambs. He decided to move his pacing into the living room, because he was convinced that he was wearing out the carpet in the den. Anthony could have gone into his office to catch up on some of his paperwork, but he didn't want to work. He wanted to be with Rebecca. He could hear her running the tub in her bathroom. Although the apartment was very quiet with extra sound-deadening techniques that were installed when the apartments were renovated into one penthouse, when you lived alone you noticed every new noise that was not usual.

Rebecca took her time and enjoyed her soak. Nearly an hour later, she was toweling off and creaming her still-warm skin with a thick lavender jam. She pulled on a white imitation silk robe, which she knew she would have to replace with the real thing before the honeymoon. In fact, her mind made a mental checklist of all the things she was going to have to order before the honeymoon. Anthony warned her that there would be other people on the ship that would be doing their wash and she needed to make sure that she didn't give the stewards anything to write home about. He also told her that they were going somewhere tropical. They had to go on a honeymoon to keep up with the deception with Children's Services. It would definitely draw negative attention to their adoption case if they didn't go on one.

Rebecca dried her hair and applied her make-up. She opened her door slightly and found the freshly pressed clothes hanging on the doorknob to her bedroom. She took the clothes then closed the door. She pulled off her robe and pulled on her undergarments. Since her breasts were large, actually very large, she always bought the best bras for herself for years. She put on a navy-blue lacey bra and matching panties. She removed her new jeans and sweater from the packaging and quickly dressed. She pulled on a pair of trouser socks and her new boots. She went over to the cheval mirror and looked at her reflection knowing that something was missing. Quickly she ran back into her bathroom and put on her engagement ring.

She cleaned everything up and hung up all her new clothes in her closet. Everything was pressed and on beautiful, dark wooden hangers from the cleaners, something she had never seen before. Her room was filled with the boxes Carlo and his men had packed for her marked 'bring to Anthony's.' Most of it was clothes and shoes and all of it was cheap, except for a few items that she felt confident would pass the 'press test.' In less than fifteen minutes, she pulled the worthless things from the boxes and started to make a pile on her bed. After she went through all the boxes, she filled them back up with the unwanted items. She opened her bedroom door and was going to drag them out when she saw him standing at the end of her hallway looking a-m-a-z-i-n-g! She swore he looked younger, fitter and more handsome than just an hour before.

"Hi." Anthony felt as though she caught him in the act of waiting for her, as he soaked her in, drinking in her appearance and scent.

"Hi." Rebecca walked down to where he stood and was stunned how her mind immediately registered everything about him. He smelled heavenly and that woodsy, citrus scent made her mouth water. He was wearing a dark blue chambray shirt and creased-to-perfection khakis. He also wore a rich, highly polished brown leather belt and matching loafers. Even the band on his watch matched his belt and shoes. When she looked up and into his eyes, they were slightly grayer.

"You look terrific." Anthony liked the way her new clothes fit her. There was a lot to be said for quality.

"Thanks! You do too." Rebecca had to admit.

"Thanks." Anthony was warring with his will and brain. He had this uncontrollable urge to capture her face and pull it up to kiss her deeply, but he held his body in check, standing hopelessly still instead.

"I could use a hand with all my old clothes that aren't going to work for me anymore."

"Let me help you with that." Anthony took the boxes into the disposal room where there was an area for unwanted clothes that went directly to local charities.

By the time they cleaned out all of the boxes, Rebecca's parents and brother arrived. The only way that Anthony could describe dinner with her family was *uncomfortable*, perhaps even borderline *painful!* After Anthony apologized to Rebecca's father for not asking for his daughter's hand in marriage, the truth came out. When they described their situation as "not technically a marriage," the proverbial excrement hit the fan.

For Rebecca, most of the meal was bumpy with a side of excruciating to round out her portions, but not for Anthony. Oh no, on the contrary. Rebecca's parents and brother were warm to him. But with Rebecca, man, they let her have it! They were let down with the fact that their *only* daughter was getting married and didn't tell them. They were very shocked that they had to read about it in the newspaper. They were embarrassed when extended family called to ask if their *only* daughter was engaged and why they hadn't been told or invited to the engagement or the wedding. After they found out that their daughter was marrying Anthony under false pretenses, they were grossly uncomfortable with that information—uncomfortable with the fact that their daughter was using Anthony in this scheme, *no, scam, that was the word Mr. McFarlan used!* Anthony simply sat back and watched Rebecca squirm, until she slunk down in her chair. It was priceless!

Once dinner was over, Rebecca looked like she went twelve rounds with *Tyson.* She appeared haggard and shuffled her feet. It was a lot to deal with in one day. Between the movers bringing all of her boxes, the treadmill delivery and the rest of her belongings going into storage, Rebecca was almost out for the count. Add to that the press calling her the "flea market queen" in another paper—yeah today was stacking up, big time, in the "suck" column for her. And as soon as they got home, Anthony could see she was spent.

"I think this has been the longest day of my life." Rebecca admitted to Anthony when they entered the apartment. While she watched Anthony disable the alarm, she wanted to tell him that she thought the first day at the police academy was the worst day of her life, but today was running a very tight second.

"Maybe you should set the alarm . . ." Anthony was nodding his head, smiling.

"Haven't I been through enough for one day? Besides, that is how this entire dreaded day started, remember?"

Anthony smiled. He wanted to scoop her up, kiss her and make love to her. He wanted to tell her that her days with him would only be filled with love and laughter. "No better way to end it if you ask me! Conquer those nemeses!" Anthony made a fist and pumped it.

Rebecca gaped at him. "NO thank you!" Rebecca shuffled off to her side of the apartment, dragging her feet as she went into her bedroom, closing the door behind her.

Chapter Four
Wedding bells . . .

The days that led up to the wedding flew by while Rebecca shopped until she nearly dropped in order to look like a millionaire's future wife. Even though they were only having immediate family, Anthony was getting an earful about the wedding from his mother. Everyone in the family knew he was marrying Rebecca in order to adopt Trevor, but Angelina believed that there was something more to their arrangement and she didn't want her son or future daughter-in-law to miss out on some of the Romano wedding traditions.

"I know son, but what if the relationship turns around?" Angelina held the cell phone to her ear and listened to her son who actually believed that he knew more than she did! *Idiots! Men were positively clueless! Whatever happened to the good old days when you could hit them upside the head with a frying pan and not go to jail?* Angelina smiled, while pretending to listen. She knew there was much more to this relationship, because Anthony was protecting Rebecca and men don't do that unless they are in it for the long haul.

"I highly doubt that." Anthony answered respectfully. "Rebecca has a plan and she intends to stick to it." Anthony felt emotionally and physically drained. Romano weddings had long been established as being steep in tradition and large—extremely large—with preparations normally taking well over a year. Since Anthony and Rebecca were having a much-abbreviated version of a typical Romano wedding, Anthony was taking plenty of heat for it, as he watched Rebecca grow quieter and more withdrawn with their wedding day drawing ever nearer.

For Rebecca, the wedding bells remained silent and so did she. She listened to Anthony describe how the wedding was going to take place on her future brother-in-law's ship called "The Rose." Anthony explained all of the arrangements to her, while she sat quietly on the edge of the couch. She nodded at the appropriate times and when he was finished, she got up, walked to her room and quietly closed her door.

Now that the day was here, Rebecca was somewhat relieved, because she was one step closer to adopting Trevor and that was the only reason she was putting herself through this . . . *right?* She was doing everything she could think of to simply focus on the lost eight-year-old boy who needed a mother and a permanent home.

On Jack's yacht, the guests started to arrive. Besides the bride, the groom and the priest, the balance of the guests were strictly immediate family. Anthony's parents and Rebecca's parents, Anthony's brother Jack, his wife and Rebecca's best friend Francesca, and Rebecca's brother Stephen, who was looking somewhat ornery. Rebecca knew exactly why, because she told her brother that he was not allowed to bring anyone with him to the wedding. The guy never saw one girl for more than three weeks and Rebecca was not taking any chances allowing her brother to bring an unfamiliar, random woman to her wedding that could later go to the press when her brother called it quits. She had to be extremely careful, because the slightest blemish could spoil the adoption proceedings and destroy three years of undercover work.

Rebecca and Anthony's wedding was about six months after Jack and Francesca's wedding. Francesca, who was very pregnant at the time of her own wedding, was now holding her little bundle of joy, who was Rebecca and Anthony's goddaughter, Toni, short for Antoinette. The baby was gorgeous with large, sparkling blue eyes, long black eyelashes and jet black hair. She was the perfect combination of her parents.

"I had to brush my teeth standing sideways otherwise I would spit on my stomach." Francesca was sharing funny stories of her very pregnant final days, which caused everyone to laugh. The jovial conversation continued until Anthony's cousin, Father Michael, cleared his throat signaling everyone's attention. Rebecca wanted the ceremony to be as informal as possible and that is why they opted for the ship instead of the church.

Anthony wore a dark blue suit, crisp white shirt and a dark blue tie. Rebecca wore a light pink satin sheath, cut to the knee. Her hair was pulled up and back away from her face, and the mass of hair that was gathered in the back cascaded in tight curls that sprang as she moved. Anthony handed her a large, blue velvet case moments before the wedding began, which was his wedding gift to her. When she lifted the hinged lid, her mouth opened wide in awe.

"These are incredible," Rebecca breathed, timidly touching the strands of pearls and matching earrings.

Anthony shoved his hands deep into his pockets, lowering his head.

Rebecca placed the case on a small table and put the earrings on first.

The simple act of watching Rebecca put on her jewelry was robbing Anthony of his breath. He watched as she slipped the longest strand over her head. When her fingers trembled, fumbling with the clasp for the shorter strand, Anthony stepped forward, "Let me." Anthony took the necklace holding one end in each hand. He lifted his arms up and over her head carefully setting the clasp, while her scent filled him with potent desire.

Rebecca looked over her shoulder, speaking softly, "Thank you. They're lovely."

Anthony nodded, holding back the words he longed to speak to her. In that intimate moment, he felt such an indefinable compelling pull. It was intensely overpowering.

The wedding and celebration were both melancholy. It passed quickly and by the time the ship set out on its course to their honeymoon destination, it was very late into the evening.

Anthony took a shower, brushed his teeth and put on a pair of long pajama bottoms. While Rebecca used the bathroom, he paced, seeming as though he was waiting for hours. He moved his pacing into the sitting area and turned on the TV in an effort to distract himself, but he couldn't help from peeking into the master stateroom every few seconds to see if she had emerged yet.

Inside the bathroom, Rebecca quickly showered. She had decided on the long "real" silk nightgown with three-quarter length sleeves and a deep scoop neckline. It had a matching robe with a shawl-type collar, but no closures. It was very retro and reminded her of something Lauren Bacall would have worn in an old black-and-white movie. She opened the bathroom door and silently walked over to her luggage. When she turned around, Anthony was standing at the foot of the bed perfectly still. She waited for him to speak, as his eyes traveled over her body.

"Hi." For the last several minutes, which felt like days, Anthony thought she wasn't going to come out of that bathroom. Then she appeared, standing in the stateroom, a heart-stopping incandescent vision, looking positively scared to death.

"Hi." Rebecca stood frozen in place.

They each stared at the other for many minutes unmoving. Anthony thought if he took soft, slow steps that that would ease her fear.

Rebecca watched while Anthony undressed the bed. He removed the decorative pillows and placed them on a bench beneath one of the portholes. He moved about fluidly, while Rebecca studied his quiet steps. She imagined that that's what it must be like to be undressed by this man. Slow and deliberate. He folded down the bedding on each side of the bed on a diagonal and took a step back.

Staring at the bed they were going to share for the first time as husband and wife, Anthony felt his heart getting pummeled similar to the beating a speed bag encounters by the fists of a boxer. "Which side of the bed do you prefer?" He was certain that Rebecca could probably see his heart beating madly, regretting the fact that he hadn't worn a T-shirt.

"I guess the left side, unless you want . . ."

"No," Anthony interrupted her, "you can have the left side."

Anthony watched Rebecca move slowly toward the left side of the bed. He watched as she removed her robe and laid it at the foot of the bed. She sat down and lifted her legs up together and under the covers, pulling them up to her neck.

Anthony switched off the overhead lights and the room immediately became dark, except for the single lamp still lit on the right side of the bed. He snapped off that light, sat down and slowly laid back. Once he was in a reclined position, he remained as still as possible.

"Goodnight." Rebecca whispered curling up on her side as close to the edge of the mattress as possible.

"Goodnight darling." Anthony whispered quietly.

As her eyes adjusted to the darkness, Rebecca felt the ship sway gently. And before she knew what hit her, she silently wept.

When they woke the next morning, Anthony was still in the exact same position he was in when he originally got into bed and Rebecca was at the far side of the mattress, practically sleeping on the seam. It was a wonder she hadn't fallen out of the bed during the night.

"Good morning." Anthony rose exhausted from listening to Rebecca weep most of the night.

"Good morning." Rebecca whispered sitting up. With her back to Anthony, she reached for her robe and slipped it on before she got out of bed. Then she stood up and padded silently into the bathroom.

They took turns using the bathroom, neither wanting to use another bathroom available to them on the ship to avoid the stewards who might mistake that separation for frigidity between the newlyweds.

As they were served breakfast in the main salon, Rebecca watched angry seas strike the portholes with great force. She couldn't believe the storm they were in. "Are we going to dock, or are we going to keep riding this thing out?" Rebecca asked, watching seas that looked mighty dangerous.

"The captain said the worst is over. We should be hitting better weather after lunchtime."

"Really?" Rebecca wasn't convinced. She watched gigantic waves pass by the ship then one of these enormous swells hit the ship. Rebecca braced herself as the surge struck the yacht.

Anthony tried to distract her. "The captain is a retired captain from the United States Navy. He was in the Navy for thirty years and is very familiar with these waters. Plus he knows this ship like the back of his hand. He was hired as a consultant when Jack built The Rose." Anthony stood up to look across the seas with her.

"That's reassuring," Rebecca turned toward him. Without warning, the yacht pitched causing Rebecca to latch onto Anthony.

"We're fine." Anthony held her close enjoying the moment, because he wasn't sure if he would ever get a chance to hold her like this again. Anthony whispered softy to her in his native tongue, "*Rilassare, tu vi salva al sicura.*" He repeated the phrase several times into her soft lavender-scented curls. He gently rubbed her back and when she looked up at him, he lowered his head to place his lips onto hers, slowly, gently.

"Why did you kiss me?" Rebecca backed away.

"I'm sorry. I only meant to comfort you." Anthony sounded sincere.

"Oh." Rebecca held her stomach. "I think I'm going to go lay down."

A few hours later, Anthony woke Rebecca because they had reached their destination. Immediately, Rebecca started to straighten up the bed and remembered that Anthony insisted that they leave the bed disheveled as often as possible to make the stewards believe that they were enjoying another romp.

Anthony immediately started to further mess up the bed, so Rebecca joined in the fun. She tossed a pillow and it accidentally hit Anthony on the side of his head.

Anthony flashed gray eyes at her, *"Che cosa?"*

Rebecca shot him a purely innocent look. Her expression caused Anthony to arch his eyebrow and swat her with a pillow right on top of her head. "It was an accident . . . I swear!" Rebecca tried to amend the situation, but before she knew it Anthony was pounding her with multiple pillows, tickling her and kissing her neck. Rebecca started giggling, tickling and kissing him back.

"Stop . . ." Rebecca used her commanding voice, holding up her hands, breathing hard before stepping away. She was falling in love and trying like hell to stop it.

Anthony was breathing rather heavily too and took a step back to look at the rumpled Rebecca. She was stealing his breath away . . . again. Anthony tried to control his breathing, along with his traitorous heart and body. He wanted her and if he had to be completely alone with her for the next thirteen days, he was going to need plenty of medication or booze. Thankfully, the latter was readily available to him. "Okay." Anthony took a deep breath in and out tossing the pillow he held onto the floor, watching as Rebecca followed suit.

Once the ship was anchored, Anthony instructed the crew to prepare the bungalow while he and Rebecca ate dinner. Anthony didn't want to spend one more night on that ship. The sooner they disembarked and were away from the watchful eyes of the stewards, the better.

Rebecca stared at the island from the railing of the ship. She could not believe that they were staying on an ISLAND! From the ship, Rebecca could see a house come into view. It was an enormous structure, sitting high up on wooden pylons making it appear like a tree house. After Anthony and Rebecca finished their dinner, they were transported to the house in a motorized dinghy. All of their belongings had been brought to the island and unpacked in the master bedroom.

The bungalow was really a mansion on a spectacular, lush tropical island. It boasted three large bedrooms, three and a half large baths, an enormous kitchen and a living room which spanned from the front of the house to the rear.

Once the crew left them alone, Anthony described in great detail how the bungalow was relatively self-sufficient. He described how the rainwater was collected on the roof and held in storage containers that were suspended beneath the floor of the bungalow. The constant wind from the ocean ran turbines that generated electricity for the bungalow. Solar panels supplemented the electricity when the wind wasn't blowing. Most of the waste was turned into compost and whatever wasn't was then compacted and removed from the island. It was remarkable. Rebecca didn't ask who owned the island, but surmised that it had to be privately owned—maybe even by the Romano family. The place was furnished lavishly and was beyond anything Rebecca had ever seen in her life. All of the furnishings were in dark, rich woods. Besides the fact that the furniture was easy on the eye, all the pieces were obviously chosen for relaxing with comfy cushions and plush pillows. It was pure paradise.

"Where are we anyway?" Rebecca asked while studying the bungalow.

"Just past the Virgin Islands," Anthony replied as he took Rebecca's hand and led her into the bungalow. He closed the door then quickly went around to all the windows, pulling the sheers closed for privacy. "The stewards will be here every morning to clean the bungalow and bring food."

"Okay."

"We are still going to have to share a bed."

"That's fine. I mean . . . we already agreed that once we were married we would share a bed . . . if that's okay with you?"

"Yes." But Anthony's mind was screaming . . . *NO!*

In the days that followed, Anthony and Rebecca filled their days with snorkeling, sunning and running. At night, they slept together with the windows in the front and back of the home open to the ocean's breeze, which flowed through the room causing the white, wispy sheers to billow hypnotically, instilling peace. Add to that the sound of the waves, total relaxation.

The ship remained anchored quite a distance from the island, even though there was a dock on the island. And, just as Anthony said they would, the stewards came to the island promptly at eleven every morning. Anthony and Rebecca usually took turns making coffee, then arranged some fruit in a couple of bowls and sat on the deck in the back of the house away from the attentive eyes from the ship. They ate their fruit for breakfast and began their studies of each other in order to prepare for Children's Services. By the time the stewards came, Rebecca and Anthony would go for a run or walk along the beach. Each morning, they messed up the house in a way that would hopefully display to the crew that their nights were filled with wild, reckless passion.

The stewards would arrange their lunch and leave a prepared dinner in the refrigerator, which took only a few minutes to heat and serve. By the time they came back from their run or walk, the bungalow was picture perfect. *Who couldn't get used to living like this?* Rebecca silently assumed the answer was *no one in their right mind!* Rebecca knew that this was what it was like to live like royalty.

By day, Anthony was an unreachable golden god, diving into clear waters, slicing through the water like an exquisite sea creature and by night, he was a clean-cut debonair gentleman who held her chair and smoked pungent cigars. Rebecca sat on the beach under one of the large umbrellas stuck in the sand. Her eyes remained glued upon Anthony when he rose up out of the water, walking the length of beach toward her. Water was dripping from his hard-cut body, flowing over muscles Rebecca couldn't pull her eyes from and at that exact moment, he was beyond handsome. He was striking! And if they had been anywhere else, women would have been throwing themselves at his feet. He was magnificent!

Anthony sat down on a beach towel that was laid out beside her. He took a smaller towel and towel-dried his hair, trying not to lock eyes with Rebecca who seemed to be staring at him all day. Without a word, he stretched out on the beach towel and quite literally passed out.

Rebecca closed her eyes as well and before she knew it, she was sound asleep.

When they woke from their nap on the beach, each was lying on their side looking at the other.

"Hi." Rebecca blinked her big chocolaty, innocent eyes at Anthony.

"Hi." Anthony stared back leaning over to peck her cheek. She was breathtaking in her red bathing suit. She wore a one piece, but Anthony knew she could easily pull off a two piece, but was actually glad that she didn't do that to him. *Every man has his breaking point!* Anthony thought silently.

Sometime later, they headed back to the bungalow. Rebecca used the bathroom first. She stepped into the shower and washed the sand from her hair and the salt from her skin. When she stepped out, she lightly toweled off then smoothed concentrated lavender cream all over her moist skin. She placed a small amount of lavender oil into her palm and rubbed her hands together before running her hands through her hair. Rebecca left her hair wet so the oil would leave her curls glossy and silky. She put on a white lace strapless bra and matching panties and slipped into a white strapless short sundress. She tidied up the bathroom, took her suit with her and opened the bathroom door to find Anthony pacing right outside the door.

"Sorry. I took a little longer." Rebecca apologized.

Anthony could not speak. She was a dream.

When Rebecca turned around, she watched as Anthony openly stared at her. She cocked her head to one side and her expression alone asked the question, *Are you okay?*

"Fine . . . I'm perfectly fine." Anthony pointed to the bathroom. "Are you done?"

"Yes."

Anthony should have used the other bathroom, but he was afraid the stewards would think they weren't showering together and that would set off a chain reaction of rumors. He took his clothing into the bathroom and closed the door catching his reflection in the mirror. He was shirtless and his hair was almost pure white from the sun. He was very tan even though they both used sunscreen and stayed under an umbrella or beneath one of the shaded decks. He showered and shaved quickly. It was their last night together on the island and he wanted to spend as much time with Rebecca as possible. He pulled on a pair of white shorts and a yellow T-shirt that clung to his still-damp skin. He combed his wet hair back and looked at his reflection in the mirror. He resembled his mother's side of the family with their blonde hair and gray-blue eyes, although his were more gray than blue. He didn't care for his features, but that was out of his control. In fact, it seemed that almost everything in his life was spiraling out of his control.

Anthony found Rebecca standing at the table on the far side of the rear deck. A large hurricane lantern acted as the table's centerpiece and was flickering romantically from the ocean's breeze. White Royal Dalton china and cut Waterford crystal complemented the romantic atmosphere. It wasn't the table setting that caught Anthony's eye. It was Rebecca. She was stealing his air again. Her glossy hair had golden highlights from the sun and her skin was perfectly tanned. The white strapless sundress she wore only emphasized her deep tan. Her hand rested on the table bearing the rings he gave her. They had a meaning he hoped to share with her some day, but felt fairly certain that opportunity was never going to come. "Did you do this?" Anthony asked forcibly moving his stare away from her toward the table.

"Yes." Rebecca started to wring her hands.

"That was thoughtful. Thank you." Anthony looked at the white table setting with crystal glassware and delicate china. The white wine was chilling next to the table in a lovely ice-filled sterling silver *repoussé* container with a matching ornate stand.

Rebecca lifted one of the tiny tents and revealed a variety of fish over a bed of yellow rice. "Paella!" Rebecca exclaimed.

"That looks wonderful." Anthony patted his flat tummy. This wouldn't satisfy his hunger, because what he wanted he wasn't allowed to have, he wasn't allowed to taste.

"I'll serve." Rebecca reached for one of the large spoons.

"I'll pour." Anthony needed to keep his hands busy. They ate and drank and spoke amicably to one another. They talked about their childhoods and Anthony was surprised that they had both frequented a local candy shop not far from Rebecca's parents' home and Anthony's aunt's home. "It's a small world," Anthony stated before taking another sip of the cool white wine, which was cruising straight to his head.

With their meal complete and most of the dishes put in the sink, they walked along the beach, hand-in-hand of course, just in case someone was watching from the ship. When they returned to the bungalow, Rebecca went around turning off the lights, as Anthony locked the main doors. She walked over to the windows and pulled the sheers closed. As each one readied for bed, Rebecca felt warm. *Probably too much sun or wine or both* she thought. She was too hot for any nightgown and opted for a short-sleeved lace wrap instead. But when she tried in vain to fall asleep, she couldn't. She decided to get up. Quietly she walked out onto the rear deck. The moon was full and shining brightly, lighting a glittering diamond pathway along the surface of the water. It was dazzling.

Anthony saw the apparition in white move through the bedroom. He wasn't asleep and hadn't slept in eleven days, *but who was counting?* He was wearing only his boxers and after some time, he padded softly to the kitchen door and called out to Rebecca. "Having trouble sleeping?" Anthony questioned softly. When she turned toward him, Anthony's attempt to thwart his eyes from traveling over the beauty donning only a white lace wrap failed. It was exposing and revealed some of her body's secrets.

"No . . . I mean yes." Rebecca responded somewhat startled. She studied the beautiful man she had been living with for weeks. The moon shone on his body revealing a maze of muscles that strapped his upper body, arms and shoulders.

"Did I startle you?" Anthony was apologetic.

"Yes . . . I mean no." Rebecca put her hands to her cheeks. "I'm not making any sense."

Anthony studied her. "Can I do anything?"

"No. I'm okay. I wanted to look at the moon." Rebecca dropped her hands looking at Anthony instead.

Anthony took hold of her lovely shoulders, clad in lace and turned her around more for his own sanity. "It's that way." Releasing her shoulders, he took a step back.

Rebecca giggled. "I know silly." Rebecca turned back to face him feeling a tug, so much like the moon's pull on the water, to move closer to him. She wanted to open her wrap, plead with him to hold her, to make love to her and to never let her go. At that moment, every ounce of her being knew she was in love with him. "I have so much to thank you for . . ." Rebecca started but Anthony stopped her.

"You don't have to thank me." Anthony looked up at the moon in an effort to prevent his eyes from discovering more secrets and to corral his desire to pull her into his embrace.

"Anthony . . ." Rebecca called softly drawing his attention back to her.

"I'm a grown man and made the decisions I made, because I wanted to make them."

"You made those decisions because my best friend is married to your brother." Rebecca knew exactly the reason behind his motive.

"I did it for you. I did it for Trevor. I hate to see children suffer." Anthony confessed, taking a slight step closer. He was trying to show her that he loved her and would do anything for her.

"I don't know how to respond to such generosity?" Rebecca questioned, taking a slight step toward him. "I feel like I have to repay you, but, but . . ." Rebecca moved her hand to encompass their surroundings. "How can I ever repay you for this!? *This* is beyond belief." Rebecca lowered her hand.

"*This* is meaningless." Anthony had '*this*' for years, but without love and someone to share '*this*' with, all of '*this*' was worthless, meaningless. "What you should see is that I am here for you always." Anthony reached out to take her hand. "Whatever decision you make, I will respect it. When you want to move out and take Trevor with you, I will not stop you. If you want to stay, I will not ask you for how long."

Rebecca shook her head and took a step closer. She couldn't fathom this kind of selflessness.

"You're holding all the cards." Anthony paused lowering his gaze to study their linked hands. "At some point you will know what to do. The decision is yours to make, darling." Anthony lowered her hand. He shyly ran his index finger over the curve of her flushed cheek, then quietly turned and left.

Chapter Five
Life's trials . . .

Once they returned from their honeymoon, Anthony and Rebecca fell into a quick and efficient routine. With the adoption hearing right around the corner, they studied each other intently every night. Children's Services could ask them anything and they wanted to be prepared.

"Tomorrow's going be a big day." Anthony thought out loud.

"Yes." Rebecca responded quietly, sipping the hot tea she made herself after dinner.

They were sitting in the family room not really watching the TV that was turned to cable news spewing a political tsunami against the opposing party.

"We have to be in Family Court at nine sharp and the press will most likely be there."

"Who invited them anyway?" Rebecca tried to joke, but knew her quip fell short.

"Rebecca . . ." Anthony wanted her undivided attention.

Rebecca looked up and into the face of the man who was teaching her forbearance.

Anthony turned completely toward her on the couch, "Are you worried?"

"Why would I be worried? We got married under false pretenses, so that we could trick a state agency into granting us an adoption and I've made you my accomplice. Worried? Ha!" Rebecca mocked. Besides that, when she heard who the judge was going to be, she had to call her superior officer to tell him to call the judge so that he didn't blow her cover. *My life is a series of lies,* she thought silently, placing her mug of hot tea on the coffee table before shoving her hands under the afghan.

"I'm going to get ready for bed." Anthony got up and left the family room quietly.

Rebecca watched him leave. She knew she had better get herself together. She needed to go into court tomorrow with a relatively clear conscience.

In the morning, each got ready in their respective rooms and left for court before Sofia arrived. Anthony decided that a Town Car would probably be more discreet, but when they arrived, the press was waiting like a pack of wild dogs circling an injured fawn. Anthony wore a dark blue designer suit and black sunglasses and Rebecca donned a similarly dark blue skirt and jacket with a white and tiny blue polka dotted-blouse that tied at the throat by a famous women's-only designer. Rebecca's huge sunglasses covered nearly a third of her face, yet she still found the flashes from the cameras distracting and disorienting.

When Anthony and Rebecca met up with their attorneys in the hallway, they exchanged pleasantries. "I didn't think it was going to be such a circus," one attorney whispered into Anthony's ear.

"I'm not surprised. Does the press get access to the hearing?" Anthony could feel Rebecca's hand trembling in his and he held onto hers with strength and reassurance.

"I just sent someone from my staff to make certain that they are not allowed access. Adoptions for minor children are usually closed and beyond that, I can't see the judge allowing this madness into his courtroom, especially Judge Delgado." The attorney shot the press a quick glance.

Rebecca overheard a reporter taping her storyline directly behind her. "We are here in Manhattan Family Court with the hottest, newly married couple, Anthony and Rebecca Romano. Even though they have only been married a few weeks, they are adopting a child through the New York foster system. There are many people crying foul, wondering how the Romanos got to the top of the list, while others have waited years to get a chance to adopt. Whoever the child is, he or she has just gotten hold of the *golden ticket!*"

Rebecca was starting to fume. She knew that Anthony and his attorneys were moving vigorously through the usual red tape and that was simply because what Anthony Romano had to offer.

"Do not let them get to you." Anthony warned softly in Rebecca's ear sensing her tensing up, kissing her cheek. "Keep your eyes on the prize. These people have no idea how we are going to radically transform this boy's life."

All the parties were called into the courtroom, with the clerk making an announcement from a written piece of paper. "This hearing will be closed to the public, due to the sensitive age of the minor to which this adoption pertains, under New York State Consolidated Laws, Domestic Relations, Article 7, Title 2, §112-a."

The grumbling and murmuring press filtered out of the courtroom and silence followed once the heavy wooden doors were closed by an officer of the Court.

"All rise," the court's bailiff bellowed. "The Honorable Robert Delgado is presiding."

At one table stood Anthony, Rebecca and four attorneys and at the other table was one state attorney for the New York Family Court.

"Be seated." Judge Delgado barked sternly as he sat down. "I want all the attorneys to approach the bench."

The attorneys quickly scrambled to stand before the judge's bench. Anthony and Rebecca watched as everyone hustled it up from the tables, leaving them behind.

"Do you have a problem with these people adopting this boy, because if you do, there is something severely wrong with the adoption system in this State?" Judge Delgado glared over his half-rimmed glasses at the attorney for the state.

"No."

"Smart." The judge turned his attention to the four legal minds on his right. "Do these people have intentions of staying married?" Judge Delgado asked the attorneys for Anthony and Rebecca.

"Well, Your Honor, forgive me, but I forgot to bring my crystal ball with me this morning."

"Do you want to find your sorry ass behind bars for the balance of the day for contempt counsel?"

"No sir."

"Smart."

"I have no idea Your Honor. Personally, I've been married three times, so I'm the last to say how long their marriage will last," the tallest attorney was doing what he did best and that was to think quickly on his feet.

"In the Prenuptial Agreement, are there any time frames established?'

"No."

"Thank God. I want to speak to Mr. and Mrs. Romano in my chambers, privately," Judge Delgado ordered. He got up and watched as everyone rose. He stepped off the bench and went through a side door.

The attorneys walked back to their respective tables and the tallest attorney told Anthony and Rebecca that the judge wanted to speak to them in private.

"Why?" Rebecca asked, practically petrified he was going to blow her cover in front of Anthony, who would probably blow the roof off the courthouse when he found out.

"I guess he wants to ask you some questions directly and off the record. Just answer him honestly. Lying is not going to work with Judge Delgado. He can spot it a mile away. He has a sixth sense when it comes to that shit."

"Great." Anthony wasn't expecting this move.

"Listen to what he has to say and be honest."

The bailiff walked over to their table and asked them to come with him. They followed the court officer behind the bench and through another door. They came to another large wooden door and watched as the bailiff knocked on the door.

"Yes." Judge Delgado barked through the closed door.

"I have Mr. and Mrs. Romano, Judge."

"Come in," Judge Delgado stated sternly.

Anthony held onto Rebecca's hand and when he walked through the door, the judge rose to his feet. "Mr. Romano. Mrs. Romano."

"Judge." Anthony shook the judge's hand and let go of Rebecca's so that she could do the same.

"Sit down," the judge ordered.

Rebecca and Anthony sat immediately. Rebecca was beginning the wring her hands, so Anthony reached over to take one of her hands up into his, kissing it gently.

The judge witnessed a look between the two and it settled him somewhat.

"Let's get down to brass tacks. Why do you want to adopt a child when you have only been married for two weeks?"

"Judge . . ." Anthony started, but stopped when the judge held up his hand to silence him.

"I'm not done speaking yet."

"Yes sir." Anthony felt like he was back in prep school.

"The press has been looking into all the paperwork filed on your behalf, driving my staff nearly crazy with public document requests. They want to know why you are going to the top of the list. They are reporting that it is the Romano fortune that is speeding up the process when there are families who have been waiting for years to adopt."

Anthony and Rebecca did not move.

"The press is a pain in my ass. Excuse me, young lady." The judge paused to gather his thoughts. "Quite frankly, if I grant the adoption, the story is done, but if I don't, the story lives on."

Again, Anthony and Rebecca did not blink or speak.

"That brings me to my point. I have had it with the Open Public Records Act bullshit turning the courts into a soap opera to give the press something, anything to write about." The judge sighed. "I am going to grant this adoption, but by God, you two had better stay married for . . . five years!" The judge held up his hand, spreading his fingers wide to reiterate the number he deemed appropriate. A long pause ensued and the judge spoke sternly to Anthony and Rebecca. "This would be a good time to speak."

Anthony looked at Rebecca who was pleading with her eyes, so Anthony took the lead. "Ah, Your Honor, I hope that my wife and I reach our golden wedding anniversary," Anthony paused to look into Rebecca's eyes trying to give her some of his calmness and confidence.

In that moment, Rebecca studied Anthony and knew that he had every intention of standing by her side always and championing any cause she wanted to fight.

"But sir, to say that to you would be lying. We want to be honest with you. I love my wife deeply and I am going to do my best, as the head of our household, to keep my marriage and this newly formed family of ours together."

The judge nodded then started to stare down Rebecca. He got a call from her superior officer as well as the commissioner regarding her current undercover work and the judge was wondering if Anthony Romano knew. At the present time, he was guessing *No,* otherwise her supervisor wouldn't have called him.

Anthony pulled his line of vision back onto himself. "Judge . . . our Prenuptial Agreement spells out in detail how Trevor will be provided for, forever. You will never have to worry about this child another day in your life."

"Do you think you're telling me something I don't know?"

"Forgive me sir." Anthony sat back.

"You care to add anything Mrs. Romano?"

"No." Rebecca whispered.

"No?" Judge Delgado shouted.

"No sir." Rebecca's eyes darted toward Anthony and he smiled a reassuring smile, which made her instantly calm. "I agree with Anthony and that is really the best answer I can give you."

"I see." Judge Delgado looked from one to the other. "You can go back to the courtroom. The bailiff will show you the way."

Anthony and Rebecca rose, shook the judge's hand and left quietly. They were escorted back into the courtroom and hadn't even made it to their seats when the bailiff bellowed his "ALL RISE!" behind them, causing Rebecca to jump.

"Be seated," Judge Delgado growled before dropping into his large black chair behind the bench. "I have made a decision to expedite the adoption of the minor child, Trevor Michaels, whose name will remain sealed. I hereby grant this adoption to Anthony Romano and Rebecca Romano because of the incredible opportunities that will be bestowed upon this minor child. I also believe that even though Mr. and Mrs. Romano are newlyweds, there is a profound and genuine love that is shared between them. The deep respect they show each other is, quite frankly, something I would like to see a lot more of in my courtroom. I will order Children's Services to conduct five visits over the next year with the strict instruction that a report must be issued for all five visits. Thereafter, one visit per year until the minor child reaches emancipation. Those reports had better be on my desk within five business days of each visit, with all parties being copied. If I receive one report that causes me any concern, you will be contacted by the attorney for the State and report to this courtroom immediately. Understood?" The judge shot Anthony and Rebecca a glare.

"Yes Your Honor." one of the four attorneys stated as he stood to address the judge.

"I'm not talking to you. I'm talking to your clients." The judge snapped.

Anthony stood to his full height and stated clearly, "Yes Your Honor."

"Good. We're done."

The judge got up quickly and everyone rose just as quickly. Anthony leaned over to Rebecca and placed a tender kiss on her cheek whispering softly into her ear, "Congratulations Mrs. Romano—it's a boy!"

Rebecca beamed and looked at Anthony with love in her eyes. He saw it, but she didn't know that her eyes revealed that to him. Anthony turned to the closest attorney. "When can we pick Trevor up?"

"Right now. He's here. We have to go through the judge's chambers and sign a couple of documents."

"Thank God." Rebecca sighed.

"I want out of here." Anthony whispered to the tallest attorney. Anthony couldn't decide which one he disliked more, hospitals or courtrooms.

The attorneys led the way, as Anthony took Rebecca's hand in his. They all went into another room at the side of the courtroom. Once they signed the paperwork they were led down another corridor. Anthony peered through the glass window of the old wooden door to see the small, defenseless boy sitting at a table with a book in front of him. He was neither reading it nor looking at it. He was only staring off into space. Instantly, Anthony felt a strong, protective and fatherly emotion for this boy, who was now legally his son. It made his heart break to see such a young child so deep in thought, rather than running around tearing up the place.

Trevor didn't notice anyone entering the room, because he was so lost in his own thoughts. He kept wondering what was going to happen to him next. Was he going to another home today? No one said anything to him when he asked. He tried to be a good boy at the last home. He cleaned up after himself and made his bed everyday. But the minute he thought he would be staying there permanently, they moved him to another home. From the corner of his eye, he spotted people walking into the room and quickly registered that one of them was Rebecca!

"Hi." Rebecca walked over to Trevor, who quickly ran over to her, hugging her fiercely.

"Hi!" Trevor exclaimed peering around her to take a look at the tall man standing behind her.

"Trevor, this is my husband, Anthony."

Trevor walked up to the tall, blonde man and studied him. Trevor was very street smart and knew the man had a lot of money. The shiny shoes were a dead giveaway.

Anthony was momentarily shocked that Rebecca introduced him as her husband. "Hello Trevor." Anthony stuck out his hand for Trevor to shake, while he studied the most amazing green eyes he'd ever seen in his life. They were such an unusual shade of green.

"Hello." Trevor put his hand into the man's large hand, never taking his eyes off of Anthony's eyes. Trevor compared his own hand to Anthony's. "You have really big hands."

Anthony smiled, "You will have big hands like mine someday."

"Really?" Trevor couldn't believe that he would ever get that big.

"Absolutely," Anthony assured. "So do you want to get out of this place and stay with us for awhile?"

Trevor looked from Anthony to Rebecca in shock.

Rebecca nodded her head to answer his unspoken question. Rebecca's heart swelled with the fact that Trevor was coming home with them today. She knew that now he would be safe, warm and clean. Some of the things that Trevor had been through gave her many sleepless nights. Now she knew that Trevor would be sleeping in a clean bed, in a stable home with people who loved him and wanted only the best for him.

"Yeah!" Trevor said. "Let me get my stuff."

Anthony and Rebecca watched as Trevor ran over to the table to pick up a small backpack off the floor. Anthony was shocked that that was all Trevor had. "You forgot your book."

"That's not mine," Trevor was sad, because he thought he might like it, but he was too worried about what was going to happen to him today to actually start reading it.

Anthony walked over to the book and made a mental note of the title. "Are you hungry?" Anthony looked at Trevor then Rebecca and watched as they both nodded, which made him smile.

"Wait until you see your room," Rebecca spoke cheerfully. "It is so cool!"

"Really?" Trevor watched Rebecca nod before taking hold of Anthony's hand. Trevor watched Anthony's expression. He wasn't sure what it meant, but soon he would know what each crease and line would mean. He learned at a very young age how to study people's expressions.

Together the three of them left the room to begin their journey as a family.

Chapter Six
One big happy family . . .

Not long after the adoption hearing, Rebecca noticed more men following her to and from work and she was more than a little testy. She tried to bite off Anthony's head one night, very quietly, so that Trevor didn't hear her. It nearly made him hysterical every time he remembered her pacing and ranting in that whispered commanding tone, but Anthony shrugged and told her, "I warned you." Even though someone was watching her every move, Anthony knew that Rebecca appreciated Carlo, her personal bodyguard, because he would wait for her outside work and take her straight home. She didn't have to hail a cab in the rain anymore and when a damn cab wouldn't stop when she tried to hail one, she no longer had to walk home in the rain. And when she did get home and chatted about her day or listened to Trevor's stories about school or Anthony's stories about Romano Enterprises, she seemed to enjoy her time in the apartment, bustling in the kitchen and clucking over her family. But when the clock struck ten, Rebecca was out like a light. That made Anthony smile some more, because there were plenty of nights after she passed out that he would carry her into their room, which gave him another opportunity to hold her, to touch her.

"You could have left me on the couch." Rebecca murmured when he lowered her onto the bed.

"You need a good night's sleep." Anthony whispered, brushing her soft curls from her cheek.

"Thank you." Rebecca would yawn, falling right back to sleep.

The first visit from Children's Services was the furthest from gregarious. A woman showed up one night after dinner, when everyone was doing their own thing. Trevor was finishing up his homework in his bedroom, Anthony was in his office working and Rebecca was catching up on her work files in her room. Christine Cortez, from Children's Services, seemed like a lovely lady; however, when the first report came back, she stated that the family was not operating as a unit, with everyone off in a different direction and that the family admitted to sharing dinner only two times a week. Rebecca cried, Anthony tried to console her and Trevor watched scared stiff. Trevor thought they were going to remove him from his new family.

It was after they read the first report that Anthony and Rebecca decided that they would have to do more things as a family and rearrange their work schedules in order to accomplish their goal.

For Rebecca, that meant that she had to meet with her superior officer and she knew he was going to be less than accommodating.

"We weren't expecting you to marry and adopt a child!" Captain Rice commented in a raised tone.

"What can I say? I did." Rebecca shrugged at her superior officer.

"We've invested a lot of money in this operation."

"Has the operation been compromised?"

"No."

Rebecca stared at her superior, watching him stand up to turn away from her. Whenever she stared down Anthony, he would smile that All-American smile and call her darling making her totally forget her point. Rebecca knew she was making Captain Rice uncomfortable. She also knew she wasn't speaking to her superior officer with the respect his rank commanded. You kind of lose that submissive tone with your superiors when you work undercover for as long as she had. She managed to keep it a secret from her family, her best friend, colleagues at her "so-called" social worker position, her husband and son and everyone else she came in contact with.

Rebecca wanted to nail the biggest human trafficker in the city dubbed Boris. His real name was Mohamed Fahid. Fahid was a child-snatching extraordinaire with a penchant for teenage virgins. Known by all law enforcement officers as one of the city's top ten most wanted scum of all scums. Her effort to catch Mohamed 'Boris' Fahid was not without sacrifice. For three years she worked undercover as a social worker, hiding her real job from everyone and anyone who was close to her. When she became a cop she did so without anyone in her family or friends knowing. She thought they wouldn't approve of her decision and it was easy enough to keep it a secret. But once she got married and adopted a child, it was getting more and more difficult to hide. The worst part was the press dogging the Romanos. The press could blow her cover at any time.

When Rebecca graduated from the academy, top in her class, the sex and human trafficking unit at the precinct where she worked would always direct young girls to her. These girls, lost with nowhere to go, talked about the same man every time—Boris. Rebecca heard the name Boris over and over again. The girls described how he would take care of them. He would buy their clothes and food. He made sure they always had a roof over their heads and a place to sleep. The only hitch was you had to be a virgin and you had to have sex with him first. Three years later, the word was out to Boris that Rebecca, posing as Tina Krane, hated her family, but was such a good Catholic school girl. Boris loved Catholic virgins. To Boris it was what Beluga caviar is to the wealthy. Umm, umm good! *Yeah*, Rebecca thought, *I can almost taste this collar!*

So she made some adjustments, but for now, she was nothing more than the wife of Anthony Romano, the adoptive mother of Trevor Michaels and worked at the mental health clinic. Two nights a week, she transformed herself into Tina, the troubled teen virgin, scouring the city searching for the meaning of life. It was literally like waving raw meat in front of a half-starved lion.

Anthony adjusted his schedule as well. Together they decided that they would have dinner as a family at least five times a week, leaving Mondays and Wednesdays open for late nights at the office. They would start with that and see how Ms. Cortez from Children's Services felt about it in her next report.

While Rebecca went about her routine morning after morning, Anthony, who wasn't really a morning person at all, was starting to absolutely love mornings a whole lot more. Each day, before Rebecca left for work, she would quietly try to wake him. Although Anthony was always wide awake, he pretended to be sound asleep as she tried to wake him up. Anthony wanted her to touch him and touch him she did. Sometimes she would stroke his hair, or run her fingers lightly along his bare chest. Sometimes she would rub her cheek against his before she whispered in his ear,

"Anthony, I'm leaving for work now." No—he wasn't about to start waking up early for any reason, anytime soon. Even their sleeping pattern had changed. At first, when they started sleeping together, she would practically sleep on the seam of the mattress staying as far as humanly possible away from him without actually falling out of the bed. One night Anthony decided to reach out to her. Each time he did that, Anthony guessed that she assumed he was sleeping. Rebecca would carefully take his hand off her shoulder and put it back onto his stomach. But each night, Anthony would reach out for her, hoping, praying for a sign. And whether she was just tired of taking his hand off of her shoulder and placing it back onto his stomach, he wasn't sure, but eventually she turned toward him, snuggling up close to his side. She would rest her cheek against his chest placing her hand over his stomach, as he would wrap his arm around her shoulders holding her close to him all through the night. In the morning, she always woke before the alarm. She would press her lips to his chest before slowly unwinding herself from his embrace. Except for this morning when everything got turned upside down.

"GET UP!" Rebecca was screaming, as she rounded the foot of their bed, with the alarm clock buzzing loudly.

"What?" Anthony shot up out of bed certain the apartment was on fire. "What is it?"

"I OVERSLEPT!!!!" Rebecca shouted, in a panic.

"Is that all darling?" Anthony fell back onto the bed, but she quickly lunged herself on top of him, her short cut nightgown tickling his bare upper body.

"I need help getting everything ready!" Rebecca screamed and shook Anthony's shoulders.

"Darling, you never have to work another day in your life, if you don't want to!" Anthony stated with his eyes closed as Rebecca straddled him.

"Of course I do."

"No . . . you . . . don't!" With one quick movement, Anthony had her pinned beneath him, studying his beautiful wife in her baby doll nightshirt that was cut in a wide, low V that allowed him a pleasurable view of her cleavage. Anthony began to nuzzle her neck, enjoying the sound of her giggling at his playfulness.

He took pleasure in the feel of her body beneath his, all curves and softness, but solid. She liked to work out and it showed on her arms, abs and legs. Without warning, the bedroom door swung open wide. Trevor saw the pile-up and jumped in on top of Anthony laughing.

"Okay . . . seriously . . . I can't breathe." Rebecca managed to squeeze out of her quickly collapsing lungs.

Trevor started laughing harder when Anthony swung him off his back and onto the bed next to Rebecca placing his full weight on both of them. Rebecca and Trevor looked at each other and began to yell.

"Okay you seriously need to go on a diet." Rebecca managed to squeeze past her inability to breathe, stirring the pot.

"Don't make him angry!" Trevor scolded Rebecca.

Anthony was laughing hysterically. In fact, he couldn't remember the last time he laughed so hard. When he rolled off of them and onto his back, he wasn't even remotely prepared for the level of abuse launched in retaliation. Pounding, jumping, pillows smashing on top of him; it was mayhem! It was wonderful . . .

"Enough!" Rebecca shouted in her commanding tone that garnered attention. "I'm late."

Trevor and Anthony watched as she scurried out of the room to her bathroom at the other end of the apartment. They looked at each other and laughed some more. By the time she got out of the shower they were both fast asleep.

"You're killing me today . . . KILLING ME!" Rebecca shouted from the end of the bed.

Both Anthony and Trevor shot up and looked at her with that sleep-dazed look in their eyes.

"In the kitchen," she commanded. "Now!"

As Trevor and Anthony watched her exit the room, Anthony turned to Trevor whispering, "Your mother missed her calling as a drill sergeant."

Trevor blinked at the connection between Rebecca and Mother. Unaware to Anthony, that statement resonated with Trevor, deeply. Anthony got up and Trevor followed behind him with a smile from ear to ear. He loved his adoptive parents. He reached up and took Anthony's hand, padding off to the kitchen together behind Rebecca. Trevor wanted to look exactly like Anthony—tall, straight and muscled.

"Now you are going to have to make Trevor's breakfast and lunch."

"Check." Anthony said as he tried to figure out who this person reminded him of.

"Check." Trevor repeated exactly what Anthony said and how he said it as he looked up at Anthony adoringly.

Rebecca stopped with the commands, because she just noticed that Trevor was holding Anthony's hand. She shook her head and continued. "Make sure all of his books are in his backpack before he leaves for school."

"Books." Anthony looked down at Trevor.

"Books . . . check." Trevor gave his new dad the thumb's up.

"Stop repeating everything I'm saying! It's annoying the daylights out of me!" Rebecca snarled at Anthony.

"Yes darling." Anthony fawned apologetically.

"Yes darling." Trevor mimicked causing Rebecca to laugh.

"Goodbye, I'm terribly late." Rebecca bent over and kissed Trevor on the cheek. "Be great in school today."

"Yes Mom." Trevor promised before he threw his little arms around her neck for a powerful hug. "Don't forget to kiss Dad too." Trevor quietly whispered into her ear, taking hold of Anthony's hand again.

Rebecca froze with realization. *Trevor just called me, Mom and Anthony, Dad. My God, when did that happen?* Her mind was reeling. When Rebecca straightened and looked at Anthony's expression, she knew that he heard what Trevor said.

Anthony stood utterly in shock. Hearing Trevor acknowledge him as "dad" felt as though a cannonball had been strategically shot straight through his heart. He couldn't understand how a deprived and neglected little boy could be so full of love and trust.

"Of course I will." Rebecca announced cheerfully to Trevor in full agreement, while she tried to collect herself. Rebecca took in Anthony's wonderfully disheveled appearance. The man who stood before her was the complete opposite of the man Rebecca saw on a daily basis. Aside from the time they spent on their honeymoon, Anthony was always so neatly arranged. Instead, this morning he wore only his pajama bottoms, his marvelously defined bare chest looked as though he worked out for eight hours a day and his hair was tousled and out of place. He had a soft, sleepy, expression on his incredibly handsome face. Rebecca twined her arms around his neck and whispered, "Be great at work today." She reached up and timidly pressed her lips to his. Anthony's control snapped. Between the boy calling him dad and Rebecca pressing her delectable body against his, he felt powerless to a higher authority that overtook him. With one hand, he laced his fingers through her still-damp hair and pressed his lips to hers. He opened his mouth urging her to do the same. Once Anthony let go of Trevor's hand, he heard Trevor grumble that that was disgusting, vaguely registering him leaving the kitchen.

Anthony reached up with his other hand pressing it against Rebecca's back. Feeling her body making full contact with his, Anthony's passion plummeted into that moment. When she opened for him, he took his time delving into her mouth in a sweet reminder of how love was meant to be made. When he finally gathered the inner strength to loosen his hold of her, Rebecca conversely latched onto him closing the distance between them by tightening her arms around his neck. Anthony relaxed further letting Rebecca take control of the kiss. He wanted her to feel the same desire he felt for her. Today he felt it for the first time. At that moment, Rebecca wanted him just as badly as he wanted her. He knew. Anthony pulled his head back and spoke into the sweet fragrance of her damp hair. "You'll be late for work darling." Anthony lowered his hands slowly to his side.

Rebecca pressed her forehead against his chest exhaling, "I'll see you later."

Anthony waited wondering when she was going to let him go. Finally after several more minutes, Rebecca finally released him, silently leaving the apartment.

Chapter Seven
Finding love along the way . . .

By the time Rebecca got home that night, her head was spinning. For the entire day, all she could think about was Anthony and that passionate kiss that swept her, not only off her feet, but totally off her guard this morning. That kiss revealed feelings she was suppressing, feelings she was hiding from both herself and Anthony. This morning, bottom line, she knew she was in love with him. It didn't matter how hard she tried to fight it. She knew when she left that apartment and rode the elevator down to the lobby that she was fighting a losing battle. She was educated in the way the mind works and trained to control every reflex of her body. Today, she had no control over her mind or her body when it came to how she felt about Anthony.

It was so obvious to her now. *I married my one true love!* Her heart knew it, her mind knew it and her body sure-as-the-stars-above knew it. She belonged to Anthony Romano long before that moment in the kitchen. But did he still want her? She had told him over and over again that there was nothing between them, that the arrangement between them was only temporary until she got Trevor through the first year of inspections with Children's Services.

Rebecca unlocked the door to the apartment and listened to her two favorite men cooking and laughing in the kitchen.

"Hey! Mom's home!" Trevor shouted as he rounded the corner from the kitchen into the foyer.

Gosh that sounds wonderful, Rebecca appreciated. "Hey you! How was school?" Rebecca bent over to press a kiss to Trevor's soft, shiny dark golden head.

"Boring," Trevor shrugged. "Me and Dad are making tacos, because Dad gave Sofee the night off."

Rebecca loved that he called Sofia, *Sofee*, and Sofia loved it too. It was his little pet-name for her and, it was obvious that she loved him. Sofia, in a word, was stunning with her long, jet-black, wavy hair that hung down to her waist with matching jet black eyes. With the exception of the one side of her face that still bore large scars from her attacker, she was gorgeous. One night, Anthony told Rebecca the horrific story. He explained how Sofia was slashed by her attacker. He described how those scars prevented her from finishing high school and finding work, until his father stepped in and gave her a job.

Probably the most surprising thing Rebecca had ever seen in her life was when Trevor first met Sofia. He didn't show any signs of being scared or disgusted by her scars. Instead, Trevor purposely kissed the side of Sofia's face that bore those scars. Almost like a mother kissing a wound. It was so genuine and pure. It immediately gave Rebecca an insight into Trevor's great emotional maturity for his age, despite his rocky start in life.

"Perfect timing darling." Anthony came out of the kitchen with a dish towel slung over his shoulder. "Dad and I . . ." Anthony corrected Trevor, which strangely enough made Trevor smile.

Rebecca looked up to see that Anthony was wearing jeans and a casual off-white button-down shirt, loosely tucked into the waistband of his jeans with a large brown belt. Usually he stayed in his work suit until he went to bed, but tonight he changed into very casual clothes. Tonight he was different. *He knows*, Rebecca thought. *He knows I'm in love with him.*

When Rebecca stood up straight, Anthony pressed a kiss to her cheek taking her jacket from her shoulders. Rebecca looked down at the half table in the hallway and saw that Anthony's cell phone was on the table, turned off. Rebecca reached into her pants pocket, turned off her phone, placing it down next to his. She saw him smile while he hung up her jacket in the closet.

Trevor took Rebecca's hand pulling her into the kitchen to see all their hard work. "Come on. Look! It's a masterpiece!" Trevor announced.

When Anthony shuffled back into the kitchen, Rebecca glanced down and took notice of his feet. "Are you wearing clogs?" Rebecca bent around to get a better look and was totally shocked.

"Yes."

"Yessss . . ." Rebecca dragged the word along like a tune. "Mr. I-prefer-a-suit-when-I'm-at-the-beach is wearing clogs?" Rebecca was curious as to this laidback appearance. Anthony was always so prim and proper, the polished professional, that it truly didn't fit his pattern.

"They were a gift." Anthony stated in that very deep voice that compelled Rebecca to now stare into his gray-blue eyes.

"A gift?" Rebecca asked, even more than a little curious.

"Yes, that's right. They were a gift from a friend." Anthony rattled off the name of a world famous chef in a very nonchalant manner and continued with his preparations for their meal. "He told me that when your feet feel good, you will be inspired to cook."

"Inspired." Trevor repeated the word before snatching another pinch of shredded cheese.

"Really?" Rebecca found it unbelievable that the man knew almost everyone, was incredibly rich, handsome and famous, but he could still roll up his sleeves and make tacos.

"I think it's rather obvious, don't you?" Anthony waved his hand over the tacos with all the fixings chopped to perfection.

"Is it time to eat yet, or do we still have to talk about Dad's clogs?" Trevor asked.

Rebecca and Anthony stared at Trevor. Rebecca could tell that Anthony was experiencing a deep physical reaction every time Trevor called him "dad." It nearly brought him to his knees, she knew.

Now, as they all sat at the huge rectangular island and ate tacos, Anthony looked at his little family in wonder. *My life went from utterly alone to plus two!* He poured homemade sangria from a beautiful glass pitcher for Rebecca and himself and grape juice in the same wineglass for Trevor. He fixed taco after taco for Trevor and taco after taco for Rebecca. "We had a visitor before you came home." Anthony lifted an eyebrow.

"Oh? Who?" Rebecca asked before she bit into her taco.

"Ms. Cortez." Trevor curled his lip.

"Oh no. I missed her second visit! That's going to mean another bad report." Rebecca lowered her taco to her plate and stared at Anthony with fear in her eyes.

"I don't think that will be the case this time—right Trevor?" Anthony turned toward his son.

"Right." Trevor bit into his taco.

"Do I want to know why?" Rebecca asked cautiously.

Anthony nodded.

Trevor put down his taco. "I told Ms. Cortez that she made my mommy cry the last time she was here, because she wrote that really mean report."

"Oh boy . . ." Rebecca groaned.

"It gets better." Anthony interjected.

"I told her that I was glad you weren't home from work yet, because I didn't want her to make you cry again."

"Perfect!" Rebecca sounded more distressed, resting her elbows on the island and dropping her head into her open hands.

"Apparently, Ms. Cortez found that answer to be very interesting, because that is what she said." Anthony looked at Trevor and Trevor nodded to confirm. "We were preparing dinner together and asked her if she would like to stay. We told her you would be home shortly, but she said she would be stopping back again soon."

"Great." Rebecca didn't want to stress Trevor out.

"I'm stuffed." Trevor announced, rubbing his tummy.

"I can't finish this one either." Rebecca looked sadly at the half-eaten taco. "Can I have this wrapped to go?" Rebecca asked Anthony.

"Of course, *señora*." Anthony reached over the counter for her plate. When their hands connected, Anthony felt a shock. He recognized that it was becoming increasingly difficult, as time passed, to breathe her scent everyday, to hold her close every night and still not have her.

"Homework?" Rebecca asked, quickly changing the subject, feeling the intensity grow between her and Anthony.

"Done." Trevor stated confidently.

"Darling, our son is in third grade, right?"

"Right." Rebecca played along.

"He's the youngest in his class . . . right?"

"Yes, that's true too."

"Well, tonight our Son had more homework than I had my first year at college." Anthony teased while he started to clear the dishes.

Without warning, Trevor jumped off his stool, rounded the island and latched onto Anthony's leg in a fierce grip. Anthony looked intently at Rebecca. Putting the items that were in his hands back down onto the island, Anthony reached down and lifted the boy up and into his strong embrace returning his fierce hold. Rebecca joined in, placing her arms around them. Anthony felt tears sting the backs of his eyes. He silently started to barter with God, swearing he would donate more, do more, begging him to make his delicate new family stay together, to love each other and to have peace.

"Dad, you're squeezing the air out of me." Trevor squawked, wiggling, causing everyone to laugh, while Anthony decreased the pressure. When the embrace was complete, everyone helped clean up and Trevor marched off to take a bath.

Anthony and Rebecca could only stare at each other. They were making a family and were absolutely in love, yet they hadn't even touched each other.

Hearing the tub water run, Anthony reached out for Rebecca's hand. He grabbed their wineglasses with the other hand, coupling them together by their stems, leading Rebecca down the hall and into the den. The den was so cozy with deep, dark green walls, glossy honey-colored wood trim and buttery-soft dark brown leather furniture. She helped him put the glasses of wine down on the old door which doubled as a rustic coffee table. Rebecca sat down on the couch and looked up at Anthony who was still standing.

"Don't move." Anthony ordered. "I'll be right back." Anthony held up one hand encouraging her to stay, mentally hoping she wouldn't change her mind.

"I'll be right here." Rebecca assured him, reaching for the afghan she favored that was draped over the arm of the couch.

Anthony whipped around, ran down the hall shouting a few reminders to Trevor then ran back into the kitchen. He grabbed the rest of the sangria and a book of matches. His apartment was on the top floor and that afforded him several fireplaces within the unit. Tonight he wanted to start a fire in the den. He stopped off in their bedroom for a moment before he returned to the den.

Rebecca was sitting in the middle of the couch with the afghan over her lap, her legs crossed. "See! I'm still here!" Rebecca raised her hands then dropped them onto her lap.

"Yes. That's perfect." Anthony exhaled, feeling relieved. "I reminded Trevor to wash, you know, everything."

"Good."

Anthony placed the pitcher of the homemade sangria on the coffee table and went over to the fireplace. He knelt down and slowly started to build a fire.

Rebecca watched, almost mesmerized that he was getting his hands dirty and on bended knee, blowing at the flame to start the kindling. This masculine side of Anthony was completely new to her.

After he quickly rinsed his hands in the bathroom located off the den, he sat down on the edge of the sofa, took his wineglass in one hand and handed Rebecca her glass with the other. He sat back and after several minutes, Rebecca leaned her back against his side. He wrapped his arm around her collarbone and rested his hand on her opposite shoulder, as he desperately tried to slow his racing heart.

"Comfortable darling?" Anthony asked, speaking in a very low, deep tone.

Rebecca was still so unfamiliar with that resonant voice, but was internally wired to receive it and hummed, "Mm hmm."

Well I'm not, he thought silently. *I think I'm having a heart attack!* Their relationship changed in the blink of an eye. *Is this because she loves me or is this because she's in love with the notion of Trevor falling in love with us? I don't care what the answer is*, Anthony silently admitted. *If she wants me, she can have me.* Then Anthony shook his head. *No, I can't let her do that, because when she comes to her senses, she'll hate me. She'll hate me for not stopping her, for not giving her a chance to rethink her decision.*

Trevor came into the den and couldn't believe his luck. He had a new mom and dad. He was living in the most beautiful place he had ever seen in his life and he was so happy. It was really nice that his new parents didn't fight. Trevor was wise beyond his years and when he took in the mood, he was even happier that his new mom and new dad were cuddling with each other. He liked to cuddle too, but something told him he shouldn't wedge his way in between them. *Not tonight!* After a big, long yawn, Trevor announced, "I'm really tired. Could we skip the story tonight?"

"Are you sure?" Rebecca asked, already starting to sit up.

"Don't get up Mom!" Trevor quickly went over to her.

"I guess I must move around a lot, because you're the second person tonight to tell me to sit still!" Rebecca flashed Anthony a grin.

Trevor leaned over and kissed her goodnight.

"Well at least let me tuck you in?" Rebecca loved that he was squeaky clean, in clean pajamas and was about to be tucked into a clean bed. He never had that for the first eight years of his life.

"Mom I'm eight. It isn't cool to get tucked in." Trevor was trying to get her to stay put. He actually loved being tucked in.

"Oh! I had no idea. I'll never let it happen again." Rebecca apologized. She was stunned how mature he was for his age. He acted more like a twelve-year old. *Hard knocks sped up the process,* Rebecca concluded.

"It's okay once in a while." Trevor didn't want to lose that for the world. "Goodnight."

Trevor went over to the side of the couch and kissed Anthony on the cheek. Trevor liked the color of his new dad's eyes. They reminded him of stormy skies, yet he was so calm, so cool. That's the only way Trevor could describe him to his new friends at school. Trevor couldn't believe that his dad was actually a really rich man. He had no idea exactly who the Romano family was until Paul the chauffeur explained how being the son of Anthony Romano meant he was just as important as his new dad. And it certainly didn't hurt to boost him almost instantly to being the most popular kid at school, because he was driven to school everyday in an expensive limousine.

Anthony placed his wineglass on the side table next to the couch and pulled Trevor in, kissing him on the forehead, pressing his lips against the boy's forehead for a moment.

"Goodnight." Trevor said softly.

"Goodnight." Anthony and Rebecca spoke in unison.

A few minutes later, they heard his bedroom door click closed and Anthony was the first to break the silence. "Today was powerful."

"Powerful?" Rebecca asked.

"Emotionally powerful." Anthony clarified. "Maybe that's a better way to describe it." Anthony picked up his wineglass and studied it before taking another sip of the fruity drink.

Rebecca turned around so that she was sitting by Anthony's side with her legs crossed. "Trevor adores you."

"He adores you too, darling." Anthony established.

"Ya think?" Rebecca was so new at this whole mommy-thing.

"He defended you today when Ms. Cortez showed up and he wanted you to tuck him in tonight." Anthony knew. "When he saw us sitting here together, I think he didn't want to interrupt what he saw."

"Ya think?"

"That kid is smart. He ripped through his homework like he was doing an under-classmate's work. And he watches for patterns, just like you."

"I do."

"Of course," Anthony confirmed. "He knows that I am usually working in my office at this time, you are usually at your computer preparing reports for work and he is usually in his room finishing up his homework. He knows that tonight was different. He knows that tonight we were almost a family."

"Almost a family?" Rebecca asked then insisted. "We are a family."

"Are we?" Anthony stared at her.

Rebecca watched the gray in Anthony's eyes grow stormier. She reached up and touched his hair at his temple. It was fine and very soft, which was in complete contrast to his body which appeared the furthest thing from soft. She cautiously ran a fingertip down his chiseled cheek and over his lips, yet he didn't move, only the gray in his eyes intensified while he watched her. "I want to be." Rebecca admitted.

"Before we were married, I told you that I would never touch you. On our wedding day, I made many vows to you. To love you, honor you and cherish you in sickness and in health, but there was one more vow that I made and that was that I would never touch you."

"I remember and I remember our wedding night." Rebecca inwardly recalled how she cried the whole night. She didn't understand why she cried herself to sleep on that special night, but she knew better now. She knew that she loved Anthony. Nevertheless, she fought against her own feelings, robbing herself of love, passion and joy. Robbing them both of their wedding night.

"You shouldn't let what happened with Trevor today change your mind about your true feelings for me." Anthony needed to know now if she might have even the slightest reservation.

"What happened today was amazing! No doubt. Here's this little boy, who was raised by an addict prostitute, showing signs of accepting a new life, a new family, a new mother and a new father." Rebecca pointed to Anthony. "It goes to show you that the resiliency of the human spirit has no bounds. But the truth is that I am tired of pretending that I'm not attracted to you."

Anthony was disappointed with her choice of words, but was he really expecting more.

Rebecca saw an unfamiliar expression dash across Anthony's face, so she tried to rephrase her words. "I'm not very good at vocalizing my feelings. You know that. My profession has trained me to listen more than speak." What Rebecca didn't tell Anthony was that her police training taught her to be silent, because the more people spoke inevitably the more they slipped up. "I'm tired of kissing you and touching you while you are asleep."

"Darling, trust me, I'm not asleep when you kiss me or touch me."

"Oh?" *Wow* Rebecca thought quietly. She was completely unaware that he was awake during all of those early morning tender moments she believed she was stealing. "I'm ready." Rebecca stated clearly nodding her head up and down.

"Ready?" Anthony asked.

Rebecca looked down at her hand holding the glass of wine. "Honestly, I think I was born ready to be a mother. It seems kind of instinctive to me, but being a wife, not so much." Rebecca glimpsed up before pursing her lips. She lowered her gaze then after a long pause she raised her head and spoke very softly. "Do you remember on our honeymoon when I stood on the back deck looking at the moon?"

"Yes." Anthony could feel his palms begin to sweat, because the image of her wearing that sheer lace wrap preoccupied many of his waking thoughts and consumed his dreams ever since that evening.

"I wanted to be your wife that night." Rebecca confessed softly.

"You *were* my wife that night." Anthony made clear in a deep voice.

Rebecca shook her head knowing that she deserved what Anthony was giving her. She lowered her head again and admitted her true thoughts in a whisper, "I wanted you to make love to me that night." Rebecca raised her head slightly, making her desires known. Lowering her head again, she admitted, "I was ready then to be your wife in every way and I now know that I was waging a war against myself. I was fighting a battle I was never going to win."

Anthony waited as she raised her head. He looked into her eyes and could see a change, but asked anyway. "Are you certain?" He wanted to know if she was absolutely sure. He didn't want her regretting anything in the morning.

"Yes," Rebecca admitted shyly again lowering her head.

Say the words, Anthony silently encouraged himself. *Let her know what's in your heart,* "Rebecca . . ."

Rebecca looked up and into his eyes. *Gosh, this is a lot harder than I thought it would be,* Anthony quietly pondered, but he silently encouraged himself to simply say what he felt out loud. "Rebecca, do you remember the night of my brother's accident?"

"Yes, of course." Rebecca lowered her head.

"That night . . . when I bumped into you . . ." Anthony smiled as she lifted her head and looked into his eyes. "In that instant, my heart did a somersault and it seems that no matter how hard I try to control it, I can't stop it from colliding into my ribs every time I look at you." Anthony watched his whispered words soften her expression. He watched her body language change. She didn't keep her head lowered anymore, but raised it up in order to watch him speak every word. "On our honeymoon, that night at the bungalow, I wanted to make you my wife, more than you'll ever know." Anthony watched her expression soften further. "You are beautiful, darling and I long to make you mine." Anthony took her wineglass and put his wineglass next to hers on the coffee table. Sitting on the edge of the couch, Anthony timidly ran his index finger along the curve of her cheek. "I want to tell you exactly how I feel."

Rebecca could only nod. She was captivated by his confessions, transfixed by the deep rich timbre of his voice.

Anthony turned slightly toward her, whispering, "My body thirsts for yours." He watched his words ripple over her as he reached his long fingers through her soft brown curls pulling her slowly toward him for a long, deep kiss.

Anthony's admissions simply engaged every fiber of her being. She fell into his arms, into his kiss, feeling as though she was floating on a cloud. To say that his kiss took her breath away was acutely accurate. His kiss made her . . . forget . . . everything, even how to breathe.

After their deep kiss, Anthony stood up slowly, taking her hand into his, gently pulling her up behind him, the afghan falling to the floor. He led her down the hall and into the room they shared since they returned from their honeymoon. Once inside the bedroom, Anthony closed the door pulling her neatly packaged body in close to his for a long embrace. When Rebecca pulled away and took a step backwards, Anthony felt his heart begin to freefall.

"I need to know something." Rebecca put her hands in her pockets.

"Anything, my darling," Anthony studied her expression, noting the change. He watched in fear as crease lines formed along her usually smooth forehead.

Although they slept in the same bed every night since before Trevor moved in with them, it was as if Rebecca only now regarded their bedroom for the first time. Tonight she truly took in the space that they shared every night and appreciated the centuries-old wood of rich, dark walnut that had been polished to a warm luster. The room was dressed in deep, velvety browns and rich maroon silks, which could be found on the pillow shams, bedding and draperies. She loved the masculinity of the colors, but the texture of the fabrics appealed to her feminine side. She noticed that Anthony had already turned down the sumptuous bedding and lit several candles that sat in a wrought-iron candleholder inset within the small, but handsome, fireplace. Rebecca pointed to the enormous bed that they had been sharing as husband and wife, but not . . . intimately. "How many women have you slept with . . . made love to . . . in this bed?"

Anthony released the held breath he was holding in apprehension to her question. "Not one. Not yet," he inhaled deeply. In an effort to catch his freefalling heart, he focused on the lines of the bed with his fingertips. The four poster king-sized bed was not ornate, yet it had several very detailed carvings of plant life that dated back more than two hundred years. Anthony spoke almost hypnotically, as he delicately stroked the lines of the bed he intended to share with the woman he loved. "This bed is from England and belonged to a king who bedded only one woman in it. That woman was his wife and the only woman he loved," Anthony paused taking in a deep calming breath. "The story is simple. She died during childbirth at a very young age, yet he never took another woman once she perished."

"That's sad."

"No darling. That's true love." Anthony corrected as he winded his way back in her direction. "The rings I gave you are her engagement ring and wedding band."

Rebecca looked down in shock at the rings she wore. She had no idea that they were so steep in history and romantic folklore, but she should have known that Anthony would give her a priceless treasure. "Everyday women come into my office and say, 'my husband doesn't kiss me anymore,' or 'my husband doesn't make love to me anymore.' "What she really wanted to say was, *Everyday I see so much hurt, so much distrust, so much disgust,* but she stuck to as close to the truth as possible.

Anthony stood before her running one hand up and down her arm.

"Why me?" Rebecca asked on a sigh. "I've seen the women you've been with and I'm nothing like them!" Rebecca took a deep indecisive breath envisioning the tall, thin, blonde women who once represented Anthony's publicly preferred choice.

"That's exactly why . . ."

"But I'm making a mess of your life!"

Anthony outwardly laughed, internally acknowledging her doubts. "A mess?" Anthony questioned. Shaking his head he argued, "You have *given* me life, because you are so full of life." Anthony ran his trembling fingertips along the curve of her flawless cheek. "And you're filling my life with meaning and purpose everyday. Can't you see that?"

Rebecca shook her head, not sure of herself. "I see so much abuse and neglect, such vile things everyday. I'm beginning to think that my work is having a negative impact on my ability to trust, to feel, to love." Rebecca carefully measured her words.

"Please quit that damnable job . . ." Anthony pleaded as he took her back into his embrace, getting the feeling that there was something else, as though she had more to tell him.

Rebecca placed her hands on his chest. She wanted to tell him. She wanted to tell him about her undercover work. She wasn't afraid for herself. She was afraid for the young girls that might slip through the cracks—the ones she might miss if Anthony asked her to stop her work. She didn't want to keep any secrets from him anymore, but there were so many lost children who needed someone, anyone . . .

Anthony cupped her cheek, rubbing his thumb along the smooth curve sensing that she wanted to tell him something else. "Tell me darling . . . you can tell me . . . tell me what's on your mind."

"It's nothing . . . I . . ."

Anthony thought she needed reassurance when she stopped speaking. "Our relationship has been backwards from the beginning. I feel almost like a mail-order groom!"

Rebecca giggled, lightly placing her hand on his chest.

"Darling, I pledge that I will always want to kiss you exactly like this." This time he took both his hands and captured her face lifting it up to his. He pressed his lips against hers, waiting for her response and when she willingly yielded, he glided his tongue into her moist welcome opening, feeling her meet his desire. Anthony lifted his face and whispered over her moistened lips, "And darling, the way I make love to you tonight is how I propose to make love to you for the rest of my life." Anthony established a precedence he intended on keeping.

Rebecca's heart was thundering in her chest. She watched his hands run up and down her arms clad in her deep-green silk blouse. Suddenly she noticed him tremble, "You're shaking?" Rebecca took hold of his hand and pressed it to her cheek.

"I'm terrified." Anthony confessed.

"Terrified?" Rebecca searched his expression. She couldn't identify that trait with him, ever.

"Tonight is the single most important night of life." Anthony admitted, running his unsteady finger along the curve of her cheek. "Tonight I have to show the woman I married how much I love her."

"Anthony . . ." Rebecca whispered, stunned with his confession.

"Please, darling," Anthony took a deep breath. "Tonight I am going to make love to you so that you never doubt me. Never doubt my intentions. Never doubt the meaning behind every kiss, every touch. I want you to know that before I touch you, that I love you and, even if you never want me to touch you again, I will always love you, no matter what." Anthony was so nervous he thought his heart was going to implode in his chest as he drew in another large breath.

When she started to speak, Anthony knew she was going to say that she loved him too, but she wasn't ready. He wanted her to tell him on her terms, not because he said the words to her first. So he silenced her with another long kiss. And when he ran his tongue along the edge of her teeth, he felt her sway. Anthony quickly encircled her in a steadying embrace and pulled her deeper into the room towards an ornate bench covered in a deep brown paisley print that ran along the foot of the bed. He turned toward her so that they faced each other. The room, lit only with candlelight, made it warm and cocoon-like. "I'm going to undress you now," Anthony studied her eyes to watch her reaction to his whispered plan.

When Rebecca swallowed audibly, he knew his words were affecting her and that was his goal. Anthony knew with sureness that no other man had undressed her before and he intended to imprint himself on her heart, on her body and on her soul for all time.

Anthony started to unbutton her blouse with stumbling fingertips. He pooled all of his concentration in order to accomplish the simple task that seemed monumental at the moment. When he reached the waistband of her slacks, he tugged at the silky blouse so that he could completely unbutton the garment. Anthony undid her cuffs, one at a time, with great effort.

When he walked behind her, Anthony reached for the collar of her blouse and slowly removed the garment, as Rebecca relaxed her arms behind her. Her bra was a very similar color to her blouse and her back was smooth, begging for his touch, but he didn't, not yet. There would be time for that later. Anthony walked around in front of her and laid the silky blouse over the bench at the foot of the bed. When he stood up, he was stunned when Rebecca reached up and began to unbutton his shirt that was tucked loosely into his jeans.

Rebecca could feel his breath on her fingers as she unbuttoned his shirt. When she reached the point where the fabric was tucked into his jeans, she tugged on the soft, cotton shirt stepping all the way around him until it was free. Carefully she continued her descent unbuttoning buttons that fell over his manhood carefully pulling the cloth away from the bulge, which still remained a mystery. Rebecca didn't need to unbutton his cuffs, as they had been rolled up during his cooking activities. She did, however, take the time to undo the rolled-up fabric before stepping behind him to take off his shirt. Rebecca clearly heard Anthony catch his breath when the backs of her fingers dragged softly along the muscles of his back.

Anthony's control nearly slipped, but he forced himself to stay focused. He waited while she leaned over to place his shirt on the bench, but when she stood up he pulled her against him. Parts of her bare skin touched his and the areas of skin contacting skin burned feverishly. Anthony kissed her with such intensity and passion. His tongue studied the details of her lips, mouth, tongue and teeth. He could hear his breath catch again when she duplicated his movements.

Silently he chastised himself to slow down, but the man inside him was chanting, *take her now*. When their kiss slowed, he rested his lips onto her warm cheek trying desperately to get a grip of his dominating desire. But when she slipped her hands up his chest, he felt his control conversely wane again. Struggling to tamp down his own need, Anthony focused on the next article of clothing. He undid Rebecca's belt and pulled the narrow black leather strip from her waistband. The belt seemed no longer than a foot in length and, although he saw her in her bathing suit on their honeymoon, he was only now starting to truly appreciate the classic hourglass shape before him.

Anthony sat her down on the bench, slowly kneeling before her. He removed her shoes, one at a time and when he stood up and pulled her up to stand before him, he watched her wobble as she latched onto his forearm. He unbuttoned her slacks, lowered the zipper and pulled them down until they pooled at her feet taking in the silky green colored boy shorts she wore beneath that matched her bra. He gently pressed her down onto the bench, pulling her slacks off, one pant leg at a time. He took in the thigh high stockings, something he was unfamiliar with and removed them as well, gliding his large hands over her silky, smooth legs and tiny feet. Slowly he raised her foot to his lips and kissed the very top of one, then repeated his touch to the other. "Such petite feet," Anthony whispered in surprise. "I never knew how delicate."

Rebecca couldn't wait to do the same. She stood up covered only in the deep green satin undergarments bringing Anthony up to his full height and breadth. He reminded her of a mythological golden god. His body was chiseled, with each muscle clearly defined and she couldn't help but skim her fingertips along several of them. When she did, she watched his expression change, which caused her to suddenly stop. She unfastened his belt, but before she could unbutton his jeans, they slowly started to fall from his hips. She saw that he appeared thinner to her now than when they were on their honeymoon. *Maybe it is our marriage arrangement that's taking a toll on him . . .* Rebecca wondered.

She gently pushed at the ripples along his abdomen coaxing him to sit on the bench. She knelt before him and Anthony took pleasure in viewing the deep cleavage before him. He watched as she removed his clogs, smiling her lopsided smile, obviously remembering their earlier conversation.

Rebecca pulled his jeans from each leg, watching his muscles pulse when she brushed her hand along his legs roughened with golden hair. When she removed his socks, she brought his perfectly formed foot to her lips, kissing the top, much the way Anthony did. When she took his other foot in her hand, she pressed it to her cheek for what seemed like an eternity, unmistakably realizing that this simple act taught her—worship.

He showed her that he worshipped her body and she wanted to show him that she felt exactly the same way.

Anthony sat on the bench motionless. It was as if he had forgotten how to be with a woman. Oh, he had been with plenty of women, but not the woman he loved. Not until tonight. He lifted her face up, pulling it toward his and kissed her lips, her eyes, her sweet cheeks and unexpectedly whispered something in his native tongue.

"What language was that?" she gently asked before touching his chest and abdomen with her fingertips, absolutely thrilled by all his muscles.

"Italian." Anthony whispered as he started to nibble her neck, her ear.

"What did you say?" she questioned softly.

"I said that tonight, my darling, I am going to touch you like no other man has." Anthony revealed with confidence his intention, standing to his full height and bringing her up with him.

"Oh." Rebecca swallowed. The next moment Rebecca felt the room tip, because Anthony began to trace the outline of her bra with the tip of his index finger. Rebecca always hated this part. In the past, any man she had been with talked a good game about being a "breast" man, but once revealed, they would gawk at her naked breasts in shock then they would try to avoid them at all costs. Moving quickly, she hurriedly reached for the clasp at her back. She wanted this part to be over with, despising her own body's flaws.

But Anthony stopped her before she released the fabric. He sensed her uneasiness so he had to find a way to reassure her that her body was going to give both of them great pleasure. *It seems as though she doesn't know that?* "*Carissima* Rebecca," Anthony whispered just before he lowered one strap down her shoulder pressing his lips to her flawless skin. Her shoulders were well defined, yet smooth as silk.

"What does that mean?" Rebecca whispered tilting her head to give Anthony access to nibble on her shoulder.

"It means 'my darling'," Anthony softly translated, pressing kisses along her collarbone, watching as she let her head fall back giving him unrestricted access. Carefully he reached for the other strap, lowering it slightly so that he could taste her other shoulder as well.

"I lied to you." Rebecca divulged, her eyes were closed, feeling him kiss the swell of her breasts, which caused her breath to hitch.

"Lied?" Anthony murmured getting lost in the texture and scent of her skin. It was silky and fragrant. Her scent was lavender and he mentally registered the contradiction between how her scent both stimulated and relaxed him.

"Remember when I told you that I didn't like it when you called me 'darling'?"

"Yes." Anthony murmured.

"Honestly . . . I really do love it when you call me that." Rebecca shyly admitted.

Anthony groaned releasing the garment, pulling the material away from her and tossing it onto the bench. Anthony understood immediately how self conscious she was about her body, when he watched her squeeze her eyes shut. So he did what came naturally to him and spoke softly to her in Italian, "*Bellezza.*"

"Okay, every time you say something in Italian, I'm going to need an immediate translation." Rebecca opened her eyes to see that Anthony was *not* gawking at her. Instead she saw something she almost didn't recognize. She witnessed how a man looks when he is cherishing the one he loves . . . *Wow!*

"Just Italian, darling?" Anthony asked softly while running his fingertips along her collarbone careful not to touch her until she watched him. He wanted her to watch him, to recognize his face with his touch and no one else's.

"How many languages do you speak?"

"A few." Anthony skimmed his fingertips along her breast.

"Oh." Rebecca was suddenly finding it hard to speak, to breathe and to stand.

"I said, beautiful." Anthony whispered tenderly. He tentatively touched her breast. Then he held her right breast in his open palm, reveling in the size and weight of it. Listening to her breathing intensify, Anthony outlined one dark circle with his fingertips. "Watch me, *Carissima.* Watch me taste you for the first time." Anthony tenderly instructed, watching her body's reaction to his gentle command. Her buds blossomed to perfection with his words, in anticipation of his touch and Anthony smiled with that knowledge. When he took her into his mouth, he didn't miss her deep intake of breath or her long exhale as she whispered his name on a sigh. He knew in that moment that her previous lovers must have been intimidated by her plentiful bosom, but not him.

Anthony found her curves refreshing. She was a real woman, with real curves that he found appealing and stimulating. Anthony was committing to memory his first taste of her. And when he latched onto her breast, while kneading the other, he felt Rebecca lace her fingers through his hair holding him fast to her. Obviously she was more sensitive here, so he stayed like this until he could hear her breathing coming in shorter and shorter pants. Her breasts were larger than most, yet they fit his oversized hands perfectly. He paused momentarily to slide her green panties down and when he felt her sway backwards, he swept her up into his arms and carried her over to the bed. Placing a knee onto the bed, he carefully and slowly lowered her down. He pulled back the coverlet, watching her scoot over in the bed.

The image that flashed before Anthony's mind was an image of the old photos of the uninhibited pinups he saw down at the family's warehouses as a kid. She was trim yet somewhat muscular and she had lots of curves in all the right places. The thought of her writhing beneath him with pleasure almost caused him to prematurely come. Except there was one more thing he had to do first. He needed to see what her reaction would be toward him and that sobered his thoughts quickly. Many women would tell him that they didn't want him to make love to them when they saw the size of him. His manhood was generous and most of the women he became intimate with were startled by it. When he lowered his boxers, he watched for any sign of fear or disgust, but all he saw was her lovely smile adorn her china-doll face.

Before Anthony had a chance to settle onto the bed, Rebecca was running her hands over his chest, his abdomen and when she touched her tongue to his nipple, he couldn't catch his breath. He was desperately trying to prevent himself from climaxing.

Anthony rolled on top of her pinning her beneath him in order to control her. She was soft in all the right places and it felt wonderful. He wanted to feel this woman beneath him and no one else. He wanted to feel her voluptuous breasts against his bare chest and he used this opportunity to help her gauge him. When he rolled off of her, he kissed her breathless, wanting her to be relaxed, hoping she would find great pleasure with him, not pain. He ran his hand down her thigh and doubled back on the inside touching skin that was softer there than anywhere else. And when he swept his hand toward her center, she submitted willingly, opening only for him. He touched her folds and knew in that moment that she wanted him, as desperately as he wanted her.

"Anthony." Rebecca whispered softly as she began to claw at his arm.

"I'm right here, my darling." Anthony kissed her forehead before slipping his finger into her moist, secret depth, while he stroked her entrance with his thumb in a circular motion. He pressed his thumb to her pearl, which was enough to cause Rebecca to gasp while surging her hips higher.

Rebecca was astounded that he knew her body better than she did. She closed her eyes and tumbled into the trembling sensations, enjoying his touch, while taking pleasure in the thought that he promised to touch her again and again, always like this.

When Anthony inserted another long finger into her center, Rebecca moaned with pleasure. Her nails raked his biceps, chest, neck and back. And when he felt the grip of her orgasm, he watched this beauty fall into complete relaxation.

Rebecca felt marvelously serene. This man, her husband, was touching her as no other man had, as promised. The experience was both soaring and spellbinding. She wanted him to feel the same things she was feeling, so she reached for and gathered him up into her hand relishing in the silky texture and length. She was thrilled with the size of him, as she heard his sudden groan. It was the first time she ever saw or felt a man this endowed. It was astonishing to her that the mild-mannered, soft-spoken, piano-playing Anthony Romano would be so provocatively proportioned. When she thought she couldn't hear him breathing anymore, she opened her eyes and watched him as he lay completely still.

Anthony was immobilized by her touch. He stopped all movement in an effort to rein in his body that begged for release. He didn't want to shorten their first experience, so he implored her, "Darling . . ." Anthony groaned, removing her hold of him. He rolled her onto her back and rose above her. He witnessed her surrender, as she raised her hips to greet him and it astounded him. Anthony thought he was in a dream. How many times had he fantasized this very act, this very moment? For Anthony, there would be no other. She was his life. She was all to him. Now he had to show her exactly what she meant to him.

Anthony entered her slightly then retreated. But when she took hold of him and pulled her body up to complete the circuit, he lost all restraint and plunged into her deeply. The moment of being fully sheathed within the deepest secrets of the woman he loved and desired was captivating. Never before had he entered a woman with such abandon. And when she exhaled his name, he knew he was where he belonged . . . with Rebecca, in Rebecca, loving Rebecca.

When he pitched forward he rested all of his weight on top of her, as she embraced him totally. She reached her arms up and around his neck and brought her legs up high around his back offering her body to him in a living sacrifice.

Longing to prolong their first coupling, Anthony struggled to keep a controlled pace. He sensed that Rebecca wanted something less controlled and that seemed to bring out an irrepressible animal instinct in him. He took her hands from around his neck and pinned her arms above her head. While he drove into her powerfully, without reserve, he devoured her breasts, feeling her arch to encourage his feasting.

At the same time Anthony drove into her, Rebecca felt loved. She found his touch magical and moving. He was kissing her, licking her and suckling her, as she instinctively reached for his next thrust, gasping each time he took her breast into his mouth. The feeling was so unfamiliar to her, but so stimulating. Her body pulsed and in that moment she knew—*the man I married is the only man I will ever love. How did I get so lucky?* "Anthony." Rebecca pleaded struggling for him to release her hands. When he did, she ran her nails down his back and could feel the gooseflesh rise when her nails made their ascent. She kissed his neck and nibbled at his ear, which caused him to rattle off another phrase in Italian.

"I said I love you, my darling." Anthony translated between his labored breaths. But he quickly devoured her mouth not giving her the opportunity to say the same words back to him.

Anthony felt her pushing him to the side and he followed her lead, watching her rise up and over him. He watched her body move up and down in an energized rhythm. Her silky mahogany curls springing about her shoulders, while her breasts bounced wildly. When she covered her breasts with her hands, Anthony struggled to speak. "Please don't hide yourself from me . . . please."

Rebecca obeyed releasing her breasts and Anthony captured them. As he squeezed and kneaded her gently, her head fell back exposing the length of her throat. He was stunned that that vision alone hadn't caused him to ejaculate within her. Instead he rolled her onto her back, before he pounded into her unabashedly. He could feel the rise of his volcanic semen, but wanted her to feel pleasure again and forced his body to remain in control.

Rebecca could feel his manhood swell and, as it did, it caused the wall she had deliberately put up between them to shatter in an explosion of love, contentment and pleasure.

Anthony heard her extended moan, felt a silky pulsing along his entire erection within her, as he drove into her as deeply as he could expelling his life into her over and over again. His body convulsed, overpowered by his need for her. With each thrust, his seed fired into the woman he loved until their releases were full and complete.

Several moments later, Anthony felt Rebecca stir slightly. He spoke softly into her ear. "Stay still, my darling wife. I don't ever want to forget the first time we made love and gave of each other willingly."

That statement from Anthony was Rebecca's undoing and she couldn't help but weep.

"Darling *che?*" Anthony pushed himself up on his forearms and smoothed her mahogany curls away from her rosy cheek with his open palm.

"*Che,*" Rebecca sniffled. "What does that mean?"

Anthony rolled onto his side still very intimately connected to the woman he loved. "It means what? Tell me darling. Was it our lovemaking?" Anthony was terrified that he must have hurt her and tried desperately to comfort her, brushing her curls away from her flushed cheek repeatedly. But before he could finish his tender touches, Rebecca stopped him.

Rebecca took his hand that was stroking her hair and kissed the center of it. "I loved everything about our lovemaking." Rebecca sniffled and in a shaky, shuddering breath admitted, "I never . . . no one ever . . . Anthony . . . the way you touched me tonight . . ." Rebecca sniffled again, struggling to verbalize her feelings into words. She pressed a kiss to the center of his hand again, the one that stroked her so intimately only moments before.

Anthony pulled her in tightly.

But Rebecca stopped him by pressing her lips to his, slightly pushing against his chest. "I'm just . . . you're a remarkable man . . . I will never let another man touch me for as long as I live."

"I'm rather glad to hear you say that, darling." Anthony chuckled, pressing smiling lips to her forehead taking pleasure in the connection of their bodies, feeling and hearing Rebecca's giggle.

Rebecca ran her fingertips lovingly along his jaw line and without warning Anthony unexpectedly lifted her up and onto his throbbing erection, watching her fall right into their unique rhythm.

This time she controlled their peak and when both were spent, she fell forward covering his chest in silken curls and soft curves. Almost breathless, Rebecca sighed. Pressing her cheek against his chest, she finally gathered the courage to whisper those sacred words, "I'm so in love you."

With his manhood still pulsing within her, Anthony reached for Rebecca's face pulling it up so that he could study it, silently questioning her dark mahogany eyes.

"*Che,*" Rebecca asked sweetly.

"Do not *che* me," Anthony threatened softly rolling her off of him and pressing all of his weight on top of her, nibbling her neck.

"Okay, okay, uncle!" Rebecca cried out astonished at how solid he felt.

"Uncle!" Anthony bit into her neck causing her to squirm and laugh.

"Alright," Rebecca captured his face to stop the biting, holding him steady as she studied his mystifying eyes. "I'm in love with you."

"Thank God." Anthony stared at her for many moments caressing her cheek, before kissing her deeply. "Darling, you have no idea how I have longed to hear you and see you say those words to me. I love you." Rolling off her and onto his back he pulled her into his side, holding her satiny shoulders securely in his embrace.

"I think I know when I fell in love with you," she softly whispered.

"When?" Anthony asked kissing the top of her head waiting for her answer.

Pressing her lips into the side of his chest she continued. "Do you remember the night when I was at Francesca's apartment?"

"Yes." Anthony placed his other hand over his eyes, fighting the grin that forged a path from ear to ear. The woman certainly knew how to rattle his cage. But she rattled his cage long before that night and he understood now why.

"Do you remember the next morning when you kissed me and asked me to stay out of the alley, because it gave Carlo the creeps?" Rebecca asked tenderly touching his chest with feathery-light fingertips.

"Yes."

"It was at that moment." Rebecca declared pointedly.

Anthony lowered his gaze and lifted her chin so that he could see her lovely face. How her mahogany hair matched her eyes. "I'm going to need clarification."

"Clarification?" Rebecca questioned softly kissing the finger that lifted her chin.

"Was it my kiss or my words?" Anthony asked.

"Well the kiss wasn't half bad . . ." Rebecca started to explain with the roll of her eyes, which rewarded her with Anthony pinching her tiny waist causing her to yelp.

"Okay, okay, the kiss was wonderful, but your words . . . so calm, somehow commanding, yet not commanding, caring . . . the never-ruffled Anthony Romano. So many things changed for me that night, that morning."

"Never ruffled? Stop! You and my brother ruffle me quite a bit. In fact, I'm certain that if I told my doctor the amount of ruffling the two of you cause, have caused and have yet to cause in my life, he would write a prescription of abstinence from you both. So my words . . ." Anthony questioned her again softly.

"Yes, my love, your words are what won me over." Rebecca revealed. She smiled with the awareness that she could now use these lovely terms of endearment.

Anthony pulled her in close to him. "I still have something from that night." Anthony suddenly remembered sitting up.

Rebecca propped herself up on her elbow, still on her side. She did not hide herself from him, as he asked and he took pleasure in the sight of her. With his left arm, Anthony reached over to his night table pulling open the top drawer. He lifted something from the drawer and brought it around to show her. With both hands, he held the straps to the black, lace bra she had tossed at his head that night, as he listened to Rebecca's giggling.

"Now darling, I'm not a brassiere specialist, but I do not believe that this lacey number is giving you the correct support . . ." Anthony started to joke.

Rebecca snatched the bra from his fingertips and watched him smile. "Give me that! For your information, this is the kind of bra I wear after work. During the day, I wear something sturdier or when I'm working out. Not that that is any of your business!"

"Your body is definitely my business! In fact, it is my priority." Anthony turned on his side to face her, brushing the back of his left hand over her right breast, watching her eyes flutter shut from his touch. "*Bella*," he whispered.

Rebecca found it very difficult to concentrate when he touched her like that and spoke to her in that deep, low voice.

"I fantasized what you would look like in all that lace." Anthony began to softly vocalize his private thoughts.

Rebecca found his deep-sounding baritone voice incredibly stirring, while he tenderly caressed her breast, feeling him pearl her bud between his fingertips.

"I would fantasize how I would take off all that lace and make love to you endlessly." Anthony confessed quietly.

Rebecca's eyes flew open wide. She turned away from him and climbed out of bed in all her glory.

Stunned by her reaction, Anthony jumped up to see what she was doing. He was certain that his secrets, now exposed, scared her away, still so unsure of himself. "Where . . ." Anthony started to ask.

"I'll be right back." Rebecca answered quickly.

Anthony watched as she put on his shirt and darted from their bedroom. He heard the door to her room open then silence. When she came back several minutes later, she closed the door quietly and walked to the foot of the bed. "Thanks for letting me borrow your shirt."

"You're welcome . . ." Anthony could barely finish his reply, because his tongue went dry when she began to slowly unbutton his shirt revealing the infamous bra and matching panties being modeled for his eyes only. He swallowed hard, as she walked around to his side of the bed dropping his shirt along the way.

"Is this what you pictured?" Rebecca asked temptingly.

"Yes . . ." Anthony swallowed hard. "I mean no . . . I mean . . . my God . . . you are beautiful." Anthony had a difficult time answering her coherently. "If you had come to me like this on our wedding night, I don't believe I could have kept my promise." Anthony confessed in his quiet, rich, deep tone.

"I should have come to you *exactly* like this on our wedding night. I made an enormous mistake that night and the nights that followed, but I won't make that mistake again." Rebecca leaned down and tenderly kissed his lips whispering, "Please touch me Anthony . . . I need you to touch me." Rebecca implored.

Anthony had every intention of touching her. It wasn't necessary for her to request that of him. And he made love to her throughout the night and well into the early morning. They both knew they needed to make up for lost time and they did.

In the morning, when Rebecca kissed Anthony the way she always did each morning since she started sleeping in his embrace, he devoured her.

"If we are going to do this every morning, I'm going to have to reset the alarm for an earlier wake-up call." Rebecca wouldn't mind in the least waking earlier for this, as she ran her hand along her husband's jaw roughened with stubble.

"I suggest you reset the alarm, darling." Anthony was smiling, feeling content. He couldn't remember a time in his life when he was happier. "I'll start breakfast for Trevor so that you can get ready for work." Anthony suggested while he swung his long muscular legs over the edge of the bed.

Walking his nude, perfectly chiseled body into the master bathroom, Rebecca watched in gaping awe. "Wow! Even his ass has muscles," she whispered quietly to herself. "I definitely need to kick-up my workouts." Rebecca looked down and patted her flat stomach.

While he was in the bathroom, she had gathered some of her belongings from her bathroom and brought them into the master bedroom, just as Anthony emerged. He was so delighted to see her moving some of her belongings in, that he scooped her up and kissed her loudly on the mouth.

"It's too bad I won't be able to join you." Anthony placed her down carefully on her feet.

"Maybe next time." Rebecca kissed him on the jaw before she bounced into the bathroom.

"I definitely need to workout harder and start taking vitamins." Anthony decided quietly once Rebecca closed the bathroom door. They made love so many times last night that he nearly lost count, but he remembered that after each blending, the resulting feelings were the same—contentment and love.

Padding off toward the kitchen, Anthony spotted Trevor coming down the hall from the other side of the apartment rubbing his eyes, still very groggy. Yeah, the men in this family were definitely not morning people, but mornings seemed a whole lot brighter since last night.

"Good morning Son." Anthony greeted Trevor cheerfully.

Trevor came over to Anthony and hugged him. Anthony had on a T-shirt and his pajama bottoms and Trevor was still in his pajamas. Picking him up and embracing him tightly, Anthony carried Trevor into the kitchen, placing him on one of the stools that was situated around the island. He went to the refrigerator, took out the orange juice and poured Trevor and himself a glass. While he sipped at his orange juice, Anthony studied the contents of the refrigerator aloud.

"Eggs?" Anthony asked.

But Trevor only shook his head taking a sip of his orange juice.

"Pancakes?" Anthony asked, spinning around to see Trevor's reaction.

"Yes Dad. Please!" Trevor sat up straight at the island.

"Come over here and help your old man." Anthony suggested, waving for Trevor to come and help him prepare the batter. Anthony brought in a stepstool that Sofia used from time to time to reach items in the upper cabinets and placed it by the island.

"I'll gather the ingredients and you can stir. First let me start the coffee, so your mother doesn't beat up the coffee machine."

Trevor laughed loudly, because he watched his new mom threaten to murder the machine pretty much all the time.

Anthony went to the pantry and gathered the balance of the dry ingredients for the pancakes. He measured out all of the items and placed only the dry ingredients in the bowl first. Trevor stirred slowly while Anthony added the wet ingredients. Anthony found a flat skillet that was perfect for flapjacks and placed butter and a dash of oil on its hot surface. Anthony held his hand a few inches over the skillet to make certain that it was warm enough, while Trevor watched his new dad's every move.

"I think we are open for business!" Anthony announced.

With the coffee cheerfully percolating and the pancakes stacked high, Anthony and Trevor set the island for two, because Rebecca usually skipped breakfast. When she came into the kitchen with her hair up in a towel wearing a soft white, silk robe, she took in the scene. Anthony was wearing his glasses, holding the business section, while Trevor read an article from the local section. Each was eating and commenting on what the other was reading in the paper.

"Coffee darling?" Anthony asked when she entered the kitchen.

"I'll get it, thank you." Rebecca went over and kissed Trevor on his shiny crown. "Good morning."

"Mornin' Mom. Me and Dad made pancakes."

"Dad and I made pancakes." Anthony corrected his son quietly.

"Dad and I made pancakes." Trevor smiled. "Do you want one?"

Anthony watched her over the rim of his glasses. Although he saw Rebecca have fruit mid-morning, he knew that she never ate breakfast.

"Okay, maybe a small one." Rebecca relented. She tried to avoid breakfast altogether, but perhaps now more than ever. Especially after spending all night with Anthony, who had a body that most women would kill for! Trevor jumped off his stool and brought the stepstool over to the cabinet. He grabbed a dish from the shelf, handed it to Rebecca then placed the stepstool back by the island. Using the tongs, he placed a small pancake onto her plate. Anthony passed the syrup while Trevor passed the butter, but Rebecca decided to avoid the accompaniments altogether.

"Delicious! You and your Dad are such good cooks."

Rebecca ate her pancake, while Anthony ran his hand up and down the middle of her back having difficulty concentrating on any of the typewritten print. Trevor read the caption underneath a picture from the local section out loud and Anthony and Rebecca were stunned that he could read so well. He was a superior reader for his age and his teacher verified that the first day he attended his new school within their district. He stopped at a word occasionally and pointed it out to Rebecca who helped him pronounce it, but all in all, he did great.

"I have to hurry now, but breakfast was delicious." Rebecca placed her dish and coffee cup in the sink and scurried down the hall of the apartment where the other two bedrooms were located. Then she made a quick turn, shrugged her shoulders as she passed the men in the kitchen and headed for her new quarters.

"Mom should move all her stuff into one room." Trevor commented.

"That makes a lot of sense." Anthony turned the page to the newspaper, trying to ignore his growing hard-on.

"Anyway, you don't wake up so easily." Trevor turned the page to the newspaper with some difficulty.

Anthony lowered the paper and looked over the rim of his eyeglasses, remembering how much he despised these glasses, remembering how he hadn't needed them until he started doing all that reading associated with being president of Romano Enterprises. That was his brother's fault and that was a whole other story. "What do you mean I don't wake up so easily?"

Anthony asked, arching an eyebrow before taking a sip of his coffee.

"Mom said that she gets ready in the spare bedroom, because she doesn't want to bother you while you sleep."

"Yes." Anthony nodded.

"Last night I went into your room to tell you that my stomach was hurting. I think it was acid in-ge-ges-tion." Trevor struggled with the pronunciation. "But you and Mom were really asleep. I shook you then I shook Mom, but you guys wouldn't wake up. So I took one of those pink tablets in the bathroom for belly aches and it worked!" Trevor stretched out his little arms shaking the paper just like his new dad.

Anthony was openly shocked and raked a hand through his disheveled hair. He couldn't believe that Trevor hadn't come into their bedroom when they were in the heat of passion. They made love almost all night. Anthony tried to appear nonchalant about the matter, taking another sip of his coffee. However, this time, he couldn't quite manage to get it all down and started to cough, violently.

"You okay Dad?" Trevor peeked over the newspaper.

"Fine . . ." Anthony coughed again. "Fine Son."

Trevor gave Anthony a huge smile. He loved it when he called him *son*.

"I think you better start getting ready for school." Anthony cleared his throat.

"Okay." Trevor jumped down off the stool, taking his plate and glass over to the sink. He padded down the hall and straight into his bedroom.

Anthony tidied up the kitchen even though Sofia would be there at nine. Paul always picked her up after he dropped Anthony off at the office.

"I'm going to get fired." Rebecca declared studying her watch.

"That would be wonderful." Anthony would like nothing better.

Rebecca rolled her eyes. "Tell Trevor goodbye for me."

"Darling, he came into our room last night." Anthony announced while wiping down the island.

"Whaaat?" Rebecca started to shout then whispered. "What do you mean he came into our room last night? When? Oh my God . . . did he see anything?"

"No. He said he tried to wake us because he had acid indigestion!" Anthony started to laugh and held his arms open for her.

Rebecca walked right into his solid embrace and laughed.

"We need to get a lock on that door!"

They kissed only the way lovers do after a passion-filled night and Anthony kept on kissing her into the hallway while they waited for the elevator to come up to the top floor.

Chapter Eight
So in love . . .

"Good morning Mrs. Romano." Carlo was waiting for her downstairs.

Gosh that sounds lovely Rebecca admitted silently. "Good morning Carlo. Can you believe that I'm late again? Two mornings in a row!"

"I think it's a record." Carlo ribbed.

"I'm going to get fired."

"I'm sure that would make Mr. Romano very happy."

"Yeah, he just told me the same thing."

Carlo held the Town Car door open for her as she slid in. She absolutely refused to take the limousine to her job at the city's Mental Health Services, so the Town Car was the compromise.

"I need a little more time in the morning to get ready and to get Trevor ready for school."

Carlo thought that she needed more time with Mr. Romano and that was fine with him. Whenever Carlo drove her, he always left her down the street from the clinic or picked her up down the street from the station when she had to see her superior officer. He knew she was a cop. He also knew that Mr. Romano didn't know that his wife was a cop. And that was one big *fucking* secret to be hiding from him. According to Rebecca, her undercover operations to snag the biggest sex and human trafficker would restart with earnest soon. The only reason why things slowed down was to give the detectives time to see if her highly publicized and photographed marriage to Anthony Romano blew her cover. *It didn't!*

Carlo was so nervous about her restarting her undercover police work that he was actually considering quitting his job, but he couldn't. He agreed to keep Rebecca's secret, because one of his nieces was swallowed up by Boris and Carlo as well as his Puerto Rican brothers wanted Boris dead. He hoped that Mr. Romano never found out about her real job, at least not while he was his employee, because the strong silent types, like Anthony Romano, scared the living *shit* out of him.

128

At first, before Rebecca was engaged to marry Anthony Romano, Carlo recalled how he would follow her around the city. She frequented lots of sleazy bars and even sleazier hotels. Carlo assumed that she needed to supplement her income. *Hey, times were tough for everyone!* But when he saw her in her dress blues down by the precinct, all the pieces clicked.

Carlo knew Rebecca was one tough *bitch*. He saw her push men around in a bar and knew without a doubt that she could take them out without breaking a sweat. She made him swear that he wouldn't tell a soul, because if he did she could get killed. He wondered where she packed her weapon. He knew she had to have at least one on her, if not more and wondered how Anthony Romano hadn't stumbled upon it. Carlo was doing a lot of praying these days. Praying that Rebecca would find the bastard who defiled his niece—the scum who nearly broke her spirit. God only knew how many other young lost girls there were. Once caught, Boris was going to suffer a slow and painful death before he was ever tried in a court of law. Jail takes care of *the real* scumbags. Word on the street, which ultimately reached the prisons, was that Boris was a dead man—that was if the cops didn't kill him first!

Once the elevator doors closed and Rebecca was on her way to work, Anthony came back into the apartment and picked up his cell phone to survey the damage. *Fourteen missed messages!* His eyes widened in shock. "Good Lord! I have got to find a new line of work." Anthony complained. One of the missed calls was from his brother, Jack, so he returned that call first.

"Brother." Anthony greeted his brother warmly.

"Anthony! How are the newlyweds and my new nephew?"

"Good." Anthony replied.

"Good?" Jack asked.

Anthony could tell by the tone of his brother's voice that he was pressing him for more information. Since Anthony was more than a little overjoyed today, he decided to indulge his brother a little. "Great. Everything is really great." Anthony replied quietly.

"I'm so glad to hear that!" Jack replied enthusiastically. "Listen, Francesca and I want to know if you guys want to come up this weekend? The guest suite is done and we could do a little sailing, some fishing. The weather is supposed to be perfect . . ." Jack asked.

"What a wonderful idea! The country air is something I think we could all use. I know Trevor would love it. I'll call Rebecca later. We kind of got off to a late start this morning." Anthony confessed.

"A late start?"

Anthony knew that Jack was pressing him for more details, but this time Anthony ignored him. "Later." Anthony disengaged the call. The other messages he would listen to on his way into the office. He ran to his room and hit the shower.

⤜∞⤛

Just after noon, Rebecca looked down at her cell phone to see that Anthony was calling her. *Perfect timing!* Only a minute ago, she finished her phone conversation with Detective Mitchell. He wasn't supposed to call her during the day, only after hours. She told him as much, but he ignored her, always breaking the rules. He told her that the operation was moving forward and that they were close to setting up a meeting with Boris and Tina, Rebecca's undercover guise. Rebecca knew Boris would take the bait. He couldn't help himself. Boris would never resist a virgin.

Rebecca knew her work was important, but between her husband and her son, she was beginning to wonder if it wasn't time to ask her chief if he could reassign her once Boris was arrested. She was done with this social worker cover anyway. She couldn't stand to listen to these people whine and complain. It was time for an unattached, newly graduated cadet to take over. Besides she was pretty damn sure that Anthony wouldn't approve. "Hi." Rebecca answered her cell phone softly.

"Hello darling. Is this a good time?" Anthony asked.

"Your timing is perfect." Rebecca loved the sound of his voice.

"Wonderful! Francesca and Jack invited us to the farm this weekend. What do you think?"

"Their timing is perfect too."

Anthony laughed. "Yeah it is."

"What a great idea! Trevor will be so excited to spend time with Toni and the animals." Rebecca recalled the first time Trevor met their families. How everyone called him nephew or grandson. How he beamed with each pat on the back or hug, and how his little cousin Toni took to him like a duck to water.

"Terrific. I'll call them and let them know. Do you want to leave Friday afternoon or Saturday morning?"

"Friday please. I can probably leave work early if I skip lunch."

"Excellent. I'll let them know." Anthony figured now was as good a time as any. "Rebecca, I'm going to have Paul pick up Trevor right after school today."

"Why? Is something wrong?" Rebecca questioned quickly.

"No, nothing like that. I just want to spend some time with our son."

"But the after-school program is so good for him. He can play and get some exercise. He can socialize with other children . . ."

Anthony cut her off before she finished her breakdown of the benefits of the after-school program. "I think he should spend some time with his father." There was silence on the other end, so Anthony plowed ahead. "We have a gym and a pool here at Romano Enterprises so exercise is not a problem."

The truth was that Anthony dreaded Tuesdays and Thursdays. The reason was simple. Twice a week Anthony worked out with Scott. Scott was the first fireman at the scene the night of his brother's car accident that killed his brother's first wife. Since that accident, Scott had become a part of the Romano family. When Jack moved up to the farm permanently, he suggested that Anthony and Scott work out together. At first Scott and Anthony eyed each other from a safe distance and clashed, not seeming to have anything in common, but in the gym at RE they bonded. Anthony liked how Scott mixed up the workouts, challenging him, which improved his appearance, but he was hoping that with Trevor's presence, Scott wouldn't be so intense. "I want him to know what I do. You know, teach him the business." Plus it would be fun to show Trevor how to hang out with the guys.

"Well, I guess a couple of days a week would be fine. He can spend time with you and still spend time with children his own age."

"Exactly." Anthony agreed pleasantly.

"Anthony?"

"Yes."

"I can't stop thinking about last night . . . you . . . this morning." Rebecca whispered.

Anthony could visualize her blushing. "I pray you never do." Anthony whispered. "I love you darling."

"I love you too. I'll see you in a little while." Rebecca breathed.

"Okay darling." Anthony spoke deeply. When they disengaged the call, Anthony stared at his cell phone incredulously. In the last twenty-four hours, his life changed spectacularly. Everyday he wanted Rebecca and now it seemed she wanted him equally as much. *Would this change last? Is this only lust?* Anthony silently weighed, looking out at the amazing skyscrapers surrounding the picturesque park. He would have to ponder these questions some other time. As he looked down at his watch, he decided he had better put his nose to the grindstone, because if Trevor was coming to his office twice a week, he would have to get his work done earlier than usual.

Paul, the chauffeur, brought Trevor to Romano Enterprises right after school. "This is where your dad works." Paul hit the button marked thirty-two and held onto Trevor's little hand. The boy was an angel, so polite and well-behaved.

"Oh."

Paul looked down at Trevor, who looked up at him with wide green eyes. "In fact, this entire building is owned by the Romano family."

"Cool!" Trevor eyes widened further. "I guess my dad is really important."

"Your dad makes sure that a lot of people have good jobs, like me."

"Wow!"

As the elevator doors silently slid open, Anthony's personal secretary, Anna, was waiting for them.

"Hello Trevor." Anna bent over to shake Trevor's hand. "I'm your daddy's personal secretary and I'm going to take you to his office."

Trevor looked up at Paul. He had always been told by his first mother never to go with strangers, but Paul gave him the go-ahead nod. Trevor jumped over the crack of the elevator and took Anna's hand. She walked him down a long hallway, while Trevor tried to absorb his surroundings. The walls were covered with paintings and each painting had its own light shining down on it. The carpet was very soft and muffled everyone's footsteps. Trevor saw people in offices on phones and more people at computers typing and more people walking past. "Do all of these people work for my dad?" Trevor asked quietly.

"Yes honey." Anna whispered.

When they came to a heavy wooden door, carved ornately, Trevor knew this had to be the spot where his dad worked. The door alone reminded him of his new dad, strong and solid. Trevor pointed to the door and Anna nodded her head. She knocked quietly and opened the door for Trevor without waiting for a response.

Anthony was on the phone when they walked in. Once he spotted Trevor, Anthony broke off the call instantly, telling the person on the other end that his son just came in. Anthony's father had always greeted him with that kind of attention and, at that moment, Anthony understood that when his father did that, he was showing his son that he was more important than any wholesaler. He wanted Trevor to feel that same sense of importance. He rounded his desk and scooped up Trevor, hugging him fiercely. "How was school?"

"Boring, except when Malcolm threw up all over Carol's backpack this morning," Trevor smiled and giggled.

"Why are you laughing?" Anthony was curious.

"Carol is really mean Dad." Trevor shrugged. "If anyone deserves to have their backpack thrown up on, it's her."

"Mean or not, she is going to need a new backpack." Anthony laughed and so did Trevor.

Trevor dumped his backpack and walked near to the wall of windows. He was fearful at first, until Anthony took his hand into his. Then they both ventured a little closer to look out. "Wow look at that! Is that a park?" Trevor asked, darting his wide green questioning eyes up to Anthony.

"Yes that's *Central Park*."

"Is that a lake?"

"Yes. They have little boats you can take out during the summer months." Anthony was astonished that Trevor was unaware of the park.

"How high are we?"

At first, Anthony was afraid to answer him, fearful that the height might frighten him. "Thirty-two floors up."

"So this is a lot higher than the apartment where we live, right?"

"Yes."

"Your office building is really cool Dad. Paul said you have a lot of people working for you."

"He's right. Romano Enterprises keeps many people working."

"How many?" Trevor asked.

"Well, if I had to guess, I would say about ten thousand."

"Wow! All those people work in this building?"

"No. Romano Enterprises has offices all around the world." Anthony walked him over to a globe that was cradled in an ornate wooden stand near a separate seating area. "We are here," Anthony pointed to New York, "and we have offices here, here . . ." Anthony spun the globe around. ". . . here, here and here."

Trevor looked up at Anthony. "How can you be in all those places at one time?"

"I do some traveling, but mostly by the telephones, video internet and computers. In these offices here in New York, we have our legal department, our translation department and our accounting department."

"What does legal mean?" Trevor asked.

"That is where all the lawyers write long papers." Anthony was trying to answer Trevor simply.

"What do they do in the translation department?"

"That is where we have people who can speak other languages communicating with other countries." Anthony was surprised that Trevor was so interested.

"Accounting?"

"Money." Anthony knew everyone understood that. "They let us know when we are making money or losing money."

"Dad this looks really hard!" Trevor was shocked, because this morning his new dad was flipping pancakes in his pajamas without talking about any of these things. His first mother worried about everything and told him all her troubles.

"Sometimes it is." Anthony laughed ruffling Trevor's hair. "So what do you think about coming to my office on Tuesdays and Thursdays? I thought we could work out together."

"Really?" Trevor shouted then lowered his voice.

"Really." Anthony was so pleased to see that Trevor was excited to spend time with him. "Come on—let me show you the way." Anthony walked over to a closet and took out his gym bag while Trevor retrieved his backpack.

Together they left holding hands walking toward the elevator. Anthony introduced Trevor along the way as his son and Trevor felt something stir deep inside. Something he never felt before—this was the first time that someone was proud to acknowledge him as his son. Someone really wanted to be his father and his father wanted everyone to know.

When they entered the elevator, Trevor watched as Anthony pressed the button to the next floor up. "Dad what would happen if this elevator fell down all these floors?" Trevor asked, waving his hand over all the floor numbers on the panel without touching them.

Anthony suddenly realized that this boy worried, worried a lot. "Well, we'll be together so you have nothing to be anxious about. I will always be there to catch you when you fall. You got that?" Anthony lifted Trevor's chin to study the boy's glowing green eyes that showed an age far greater than his years.

Trevor nodded. When his new dad opened his arms, he jumped up into his strong embrace.

"Now, what do you think about going to my brother's farm this weekend? Me, you and mom," Anthony asked.

Trevor nodded vigorously.

"Good." Anthony laughed. "We'll leave early Friday right after you get out of school. I will pick you up from school first then we will swing by to pick up your mom and drive straight up to the country for the weekend." Anthony relayed the plans to Trevor in detail so that he would not need to worry about anything. Anthony knew that he was going to have to give Trevor lots of details. The fear of the unknown, Anthony guessed, didn't sit well with this kid. Nothing but unknowns for the first eight years of his life ended the day they brought him home, Anthony decided then and there.

When they got to the gym, Scott was already there. He motioned to his watch shouting, "You're late slob!"

Anthony was quite used to this verbal taunting from Scott. At first, Scott's language made his ears hurt, but now it made him smile. Scott called him fat and lazy. He called him a woman. He called him a soft furniture salesman. In fact, some of the adjectives Scott used, together with his vulgar language, were enough to send anyone running to the nearest chapel to pray for his lost soul.

Scott spotted the little boy and stopped the treadmill. "Hey."

"Scott. This is my son, Trevor. Trevor this is Scott. Scott is a very good friend of the family."

Scott stared at Anthony trying to digest the *'very good friend of the family'* intro. Scott knew that Anthony and Rebecca got married and adopted a boy, but he hadn't met him yet. "It's real nice to meet you." Scott leaned down and shook Trevor's hand and liked his grip. "Your daddy is really strong. Do you want to be strong like him?"

Anthony's mouth hung open in shock. *Scott called me a 'soft Girl Scout cookie-selling queen' on Tuesday, with a few fucks tossed in for good measure.*

"Yes. I want to be exactly like my dad when I grow up." Trevor held onto Anthony's hand.

"Good choice. If I was a young man like you, I would want to be just like your dad too." Scott admitted. When Scott straightened up he slapped Anthony on the shoulder.

Anthony looked at Scott with a raised eyebrow, because it was clear that an alien had taken over Scott's body. *Who is this Scott, because this man certainly isn't the Scott I know?*

"So let's see, it's cardio day today. So get changed and we'll get started. MOVE IT ROMANO!"

Anthony rolled his eyes. Scott was fanatical in the gym. The man was like a junkie and exercise was his only fix. Anthony got changed using this time to reset his mind, while Scott set Trevor up on the treadmill.

Trevor watched as Scott and Anthony stretched then stretched some more. Then they did a hundred sit-ups and a hundred push-ups. By that time, his dad and Scott were sweating, but they didn't complain. He heard the men count and grunt, but that was it.

Anthony wasn't about to stop this exercising regime for anything. After the way his wife ran her fingertips over each and every muscle on his abdomen he had so precisely and painfully exercised to define, he hoped she never stopped touching him like that.

"Okay let's get on the treadmill." Scott made sure Anthony had water and a towel then he went over to Trevor and asked if he wanted to stretch like his dad.

"Sure." Trevor hopped off the treadmill and went over to the mats with Scott.

An hour later, Anthony was running at full tilt and Scott was teaching Trevor how to use some of the smaller weights. He was teaching him that if he pushed the weight up over his head, it worked these muscles, touching the different muscle groups. If you do it another way, it worked different muscles. They stood in front of the mirror and Scott did the exercises with him with much heavier weights, pointing out the muscles they were targeting.

When they were done, they all went into the locker room, stripped down and covered themselves with towels before heading into the sauna. Scott explained to Trevor that since his body wasn't as big as his or his dad's, he could only stay in the sauna for a very short time. The dry heat felt intense at first, but Trevor thought it was so cool hanging out with his new dad and his cool friend, doing cool guy stuff. They both had lots of muscles and Trevor wondered when he would look like that. "When do you think my body will look like yours?" Trevor asked Anthony. He lifted Anthony's hand, placing his smaller hand up to compare the two. It was so much larger. Trevor thought he would never get that big.

"What do you think Scott?" Anthony asked before resting his head back against the hot cedar wall, feeling Trevor still holding his hand. Between all the extra-curricular activities that he and his wife partook in all through the night and early into this morning, coupled with this workout, he was thoroughly exhausted.

"How old are you?"

"Eight." Trevor answered firmly with a nod.

Scott tried to hide his shock. He truly believed that the boy had to be older than that. "Eight. Okay. If you workout with your dad and me, by the time you are thirteen, you will be a beast."

"A beast?" Trevor shouted looking at his dad, a little afraid, because he didn't want to look like a beast!

"You will look just like your dad." Scott corrected when he saw the alarmed expression on the boy's face.

"Really?" Trevor asked in surprise.

"Yup," Scott confirmed. "Did you see how hard your dad worked out today?"

"Yup." Trevor imitated Scott.

"Well if you workout like that, you will look like him before you know it!" Scott made it clear that it was going to take hard work. "I used to workout with Jack, your Uncle, before he moved up to the country. I would say that your dad is a lot stronger than your Uncle Jack."

"No way." Anthony quickly refuted that statement, with his eyes still shut and his head leaning against the hot fragrant wood. "Scotty has never seen Uncle Jack angry and I have and he could move this building when he gets like that." Anthony set the record straight.

"Adrenaline can make people move impossible objects, reveal a super-human strength."

"Adrenaline?" Trevor asked.

"Adrenaline is a substance that the body releases to deal with very stressful situations." Scott hoped that answered his question and when Trevor nodded he knew he could continue. "People have been known to lift cars and all kinds of incredible weight, but your dad can bench press more than your Uncle Jack ever could."

"Get out of here!" Anthony's eyes were wide open now, listening intently.

"I would say that your Uncle Jack is very strong, but your dad has more . . . *will* . . . than your uncle."

"Will? What's that?" Trevor asked confused.

"Will—is something that is deep inside of you." Scott pointed to Trevor's chest. "It is your level of determination. You have probably heard people say they don't have the willpower to stop overeating or they don't have the willpower to stop smoking cigarettes." Scott grabbed another towel and wrapped it around his neck. "There is nothing your father can't accomplish."

Anthony found himself, once again, staring at Scott with his mouth hanging open. Scott and Anthony were usually at each other's throats twice a week. Scott called Anthony every feminine adjective in the book. Then when he ran out of English words he would start to curse at him in Gaelic. Scott had been known to push Anthony so far that Anthony would tell Scott to fuck off, which was completely out of character for Anthony, which would in turn cause Scott to laugh, which would cause Anthony to curse even more. So this line of conversation was a complete one hundred and eighty degrees from their usual heated and sometimes hateful exchanges.

Trevor looked at Anthony and asked, "Dad do I have that kind of will?"

"You have more *will* than I will ever have Son." Anthony assured, ruffling Trevor's hair. "I think the heat is starting to get to Scotty's head."

"My head is clear!" Scott defended. Ever since Scott and Anthony started working out, Scott had a new-found respect for Anthony. *The guy's tough as nails, but quiet. He's the poster child for the cliché "speaks softly yet carries a big stick." Yeah, that was Anthony Romano,* Scott thought silently, *and that's what I like most about him.* "The number one thing about working out in a gym is remembering to take a long, soapy shower before you leave. Women hate smelly guys! Right Romano?" Scott wanted back up.

"Absolutely." Anthony agreed. "Come on. How about we get cleaned up and go home?"

"Okay Dad. Thanks Scotty!"

Scott thought the boy was the best—and smart as a whip. "I'll see you on Tuesday right?"

"We'll be here." Trevor gave Scott a high five.

"Tuesday is weight training. Rest up, Romanos, rest up!"

As they made their way through the locker room, Anthony whispered into Trevor's ear, "I hate when he tells me to rest up. That's never good!"

Trevor beamed at his new dad, thrilled that Scotty referred to him as a Romano.

"We have to tell Sofia to make us steak on Monday nights. We are going to need the extra protein."

Trevor nodded and followed along after Anthony.

Chapter Nine
Getting to know you . . .

The apartment door swung open, with Trevor sliding his backpack off and onto the floor. Anthony entered the apartment behind him and quietly set his briefcase down next to Trevor's backpack.

"Hi Sofee!" Trevor stated rather enthusiastically.

"Hello, my Romano men. How was your day?" Sofia asked finishing her dinner preparations.

"Great. Best day ever." Trevor shouted from the foyer, peeling off his coat.

Sofia peeked around the kitchen commenting, "You guys smell really good! Dinner will be ready in five."

Trevor pulled on Anthony's suit jacket sleeve. "Scotty was right."

Anthony nodded while they headed into the kitchen.

"Rebecca beat you home tonight." Sofia nonchalantly announced as she checked on something on the stove.

"Is that so?" Anthony asked without trying to sound too curious.

Sofia was stirring something at the stove in more ways than one. "I think she is running on the treadmill. She said something about not having enough time this morning and pancakes." Sofia smiled over her shoulder.

Anthony arched a dark, golden eyebrow, taking it all in. He wanted to grab a couple of aspirins, because his quads were on fire, but didn't want Trevor to see him needing any relief after his workout. So he 'sucked it up,' which were Scott's famous last words.

Sofia could see that Anthony was calm. She also noticed that Anthony and Trevor came home together. Usually Paul brought Trevor home first then everyone else followed. But today was a day for new things and the apartment held back no secrets.

When Sofia first got to the apartment, she noticed that someone made a big breakfast. So she cleaned up the kitchen in order to start her slow-roasted, garlic chicken with potatoes and green beans. It was everybody's favorite and she made it once a week. After that, she began to clean the apartment. She started in the master bedroom wing first. In this wing, there was Anthony's office, the den, the master bedroom and two full baths. Usually the den was never touched, but this morning Sofia noticed that a fire had been made in the hearth. Two empty wineglasses sat on the coffee table next to an empty pitcher, and the afghan was in a pile on the floor in front of the couch. She straightened up this room first and brought the glasses and pitcher into the kitchen. Then she went into Anthony's office. Usually, he had a glass of water still sitting on a coaster from the night before, but not today and the wastebasket beneath his desk was uncharacteristically empty. It was exactly the way she had left it the day before.

"That's weird." Sofia said out loud. *He's worked every night since I started working for him.* When she went into the master bedroom there were more signs that something was different. Here, melted candles sat in the wrought iron holder that rested inside the base of the fireplace hearth. Those same candles had been in that candle holder unburned since the day she started working for Anthony. "Hmmm."

Sofia started with the bed. She changed the sheets daily in the residence. Although Anthony didn't tell her to do that, she did it anyway. That is when she spotted the bra and panties in between the sheets. "Finally!" Sofia proclaimed out loud.

The rest of the day she caught up on the wash and had Paul take her to the grocery store, because if they planned on making breakfast every morning, they were going to need more supplies. By the time Sofia got back with the groceries and put everything away, Rebecca came home.

Sofia heard the alarm being disarmed and went to the foyer to see who was home early. "Hi!"

"Hi."

"Everything okay?" Sofia was surprised to see Rebecca this early. She was always long gone by the time Rebecca came home.

"It will be once I work out." Rebecca huffed.

"Okay . . ." Sofia could see that Rebecca wanted to talk. But they weren't close enough for that yet. Sofia could see that Rebecca needed a friend, a girlfriend, and so did she. After Sofia was slashed by her attacker, she didn't go back to high school.

She couldn't bring herself to go back. The gossipers in her school were vicious. Her own friends gossiped that she was a tease and that she deserved to get attacked. Eventually, she lost all of what she thought were her best friends.

"I have got to get in my workout. I can't possibly keep eating pancakes and not expect to turn into a blob!" Rebecca puffed.

"No?" Sofia raised her dark eyebrows not sure where Rebecca was going with this line of conversation. So she did what any 'girlfriend' would do and that was to wholeheartedly agree. "Okay."

"Exactly!" Rebecca was happy to see that *someone* understood. "I just have to hit the treadmill a little harder and a little longer." Rebecca nodded.

Sofia nodded in response.

"I can't walk around with this!" Rebecca pointed to her nearly nonexistent waistline. "This has got to go."

"If you say so, Mrs. Romano." Sofia wasn't touching that comment with a ten-foot pole.

"Thanks," Rebecca shouted over her shoulder heading toward her bedroom. "And please call me Rebecca."

"Okay Rebecca."

Not long after that, the men came home. Sofia couldn't help but think that men had a way of filling up all the empty spaces in a home. Plus, she didn't want to miss the opportunity to tell her boss that his new bride was anxious to come home early. "So how was your day, my newest Mr. Romano?" Sofia asked her littlest member of the family.

"The best," Trevor declared jumping up onto the kitchen island stool. "We worked out with Scotty today in the gym at dad's office. It was soooo cool." Trevor started to fill her in.

"That's great!" Sofia patted Trevor on his back. "Well, I picked up some more supplies for breakfast." Sofia started. "I suppose all that working out is going to make the men around here very hungry."

"Speaking of hungry, would you mind if we had steak on Monday nights?" Anthony asked softly.

"Every Monday night?" Sofia wanted to confirm, because a few weeks ago, he told her that it would be better if they ate lighter meals during the week.

"Would it be too much trouble?" Anthony asked while leafing through the mail.

"Of course not. No trouble at all." Sofia was forever indebted to the Romano family. They literally saved her life. When no one believed her that she didn't flirt with the man who attacked her, Mr. Nicholas Romano was the only one who believed her and gave her a job cleaning his home. Even her own father didn't believe her. Once Anthony moved out of his parents', Sofia started to work for him. So if Anthony wanted her to make him steak for breakfast, lunch and dinner and a midnight snack and that made him happy, then by God, she would be only too happy to oblige.

Suddenly the front door burst open and Paul was shouting angrily into the foyer. "Sofia! I've been waiting for twenty minutes already! I'm double parked and I'm gonna get a ticket!"

Sofia jumped at Paul's tone of voice, dropping the fork she was about to place into the dishwasher. Although they dated a few times and she cooked a few meals for him, she hadn't slept with him, nor did she have any intention of sleeping with him. A woman knew. Paul became somewhat annoyed when she told him that earlier today.

Anthony soundlessly walked around the island. "Stay right here." Anthony softly instructed Sofia in a quiet, calm tone. Anthony could see that Paul scared Trevor too. He ruffled Trevor's hair in an attempt to let him know that everything was fine, before he walked out of the kitchen and into the foyer.

Trevor was on his heels in a nanosecond. He watched Anthony nod with his head for Paul to step out into the hallway. Anthony closed the apartment door up to the jamb. Trevor went over to the door to look and listen through the crack. He took note as his dad quietly talked to Paul.

"Paul."

"Yes Mr. Romano."

"Do you think that that is anyway to speak to a lady?" Anthony barely spoke above a whisper, while he placed his hands on his hips under the sides of his suit jacket.

"No Mr. Romano." Paul was leaning toward Anthony, straining to hear him.

"I think you forget the kind of abuse Sofia suffered."

"No Mr. Romano I haven't."

"Yes Paul. The answer is yes you have, otherwise you would not speak to her like that ever!" Anthony spoke softly. "If you or anyone else in my employ thinks for one minute that I'm going to tolerate this kind of unsavory behavior, then they are mistaken. Seriously mistaken." Anthony spoke succinctly and quietly. There was something about Paul that didn't sit right with Anthony, but he could never seem to put his finger on it.

Sofia came up behind Trevor. "What are they saying?"

Trevor whispered into Sofia's ear. "Dad said he doesn't want Paul to yell at you or any woman."

"Dad!" Sofia was shocked. *When did Trevor start calling Anthony, dad?*

Trevor placed his finger over his lips to motion her into silence.

Anthony continued on the other side of the door with Trevor and Sofia listening from inside. "In fact, I will drive Sofia home myself tonight, because it is obvious you need a break from your job." Anthony turned to come back inside causing Trevor and Sofia to crash into each other before scooting back into the kitchen, so as not to be spotted.

"Mr. Romano . . . please . . . I don't need a break from my job. I love my job." Then after a long pause, Paul admitted. "I love Sofia." Paul stated quietly with his head bowed. "But I don't think she feels the same way."

Trevor and Sofia tiptoed back into the foyer to listen. It was here that Trevor learned that when his dad was mad he got very quiet, which was even scarier then if he had screamed and yelled and punched stuff like all the other men his first mom brought home.

"You what?" Anthony challenged in a deep, low voice.

"I love her." Paul answered quickly.

Trevor looked at Sofia, watching her turn red.

"No. No I don't believe that." Anthony could see that Paul was going to speak so he held up his hands to stop him. "Let me make this as clear as I possibly can. I will not tolerate these distasteful manners from you in front of my son, my wife or Sofia. In fact, that goes for anyone in my home or the office or anywhere for that matter, period. Leave Sofia alone. She has been through enough and I forbid you to date her or see her other than to drive her to or from a location. Otherwise, you can find employment elsewhere. Understood?" Anthony continued in that quiet, deep tone. "Sofia is my responsibility and I will not permit you to harass her. She doesn't deserve that."

"Absolutely." Paul agreed.

Trevor and Sofia stared at each other in shock.

When Rebecca came up behind them, she couldn't help but wonder what was going on. "What're you guys doing?"

Trevor and Sofia turned together, pressing their fingers to their lips silencing her. Trevor waved with his hand for Rebecca to join them. All three placed their ears against the door. As the silence grew, they all stared at each other in anticipation of what would be said next. Trevor peeked through the crack of the door to see what his father was doing. Out in the hall, Trevor watched as Anthony stood very still. Trevor could tell that his dad was struggling to stay in control, because his hands were balling into fists then relaxing.

One punch, Anthony thought silently. *One punch right in the mouth and this guy would keep it shut forever.* He couldn't stomach men being abusive to women. Abusive men were very weak individuals in Anthony's opinion. *And who would shout at someone who was attacked the way Sofia had been?* The answer was obvious, *no one . . . no one in their right mind.* So Anthony did what his father always did and took a hard line without tearing someone's head right off at their shoulders.

"Can I please take Sofia home now?" Paul asked.

"No." Anthony turned on his heel then started to enter the apartment.

Trevor, Sofia and Rebecca all bumped into each other desperately trying to make it back into the kitchen undetected.

Anthony closed the apartment door then pulled out his cell phone to make a call. A minute later, he was walking back into the kitchen with a smile from ear to ear. "Hello darling. How was your day?" Anthony kissed his bride on her cheek, which was brightly flushed from her run.

"Great! And you?" Rebecca was still trying to digest what was going on.

"Wonderful." Anthony placed his large hand on Trevor's head mussing his hair. "Sofia, Martin will be taking you home tonight. He'll be up in a couple of minutes."

"Okay Mr. Romano." Sofia was in shock. She was trying to take in how everyone in the family went from polite to loving overnight. And even more shocked at the way Paul had acted and how Anthony handled him. She was stunned that Anthony didn't want her to date Paul and that he was now forbidden to do so. Sofia was starting to believe that she was never going to meet a man who wasn't going to be abusive to her. It wasn't meant to be. Besides, she would rather be alone than to get hurt all over again.

"Sofia, tomorrow we will be going to my brother's for the weekend, so there will be no need to make dinner."

"That will be a nice break for you guys, but I still need to get to the supermarket again tomorrow. I could take the bus?"

"Nonsense. I will have Martin pick you up the usual time and you can discuss with him where you need to go. Martin will be more than happy to accommodate you."

"Okay. I want to write down a few things for the market. Since Trevor is still a growing boy, I think we need more supplies here right?"

"Right." Anthony agreed.

Each one talked about what they would like for breakfast. Rebecca had some lunch ideas. Then Trevor mentioned the steaks again for Monday nights.

"Why Mondays?" Rebecca asked.

"Because me and Dad are doing weight training on Tuesdays with Scotty and Dad says we need protein." Trevor spilled the beans.

"Dad and I." Anthony patiently corrected.

"So you have been working out!" Rebecca poked at Anthony's rib cage. "Wait a minute. You don't mean Scott, the fireman."

"Yup." Trevor answered his mother, swinging his legs back and forth on the stool.

Anthony gave Trevor a look that meant, *what happens at the gym stays at the gym,* but Trevor couldn't help himself. "Dad's a beast." Trevor divulged.

"Is that so?" Rebecca asked, looking in Anthony's direction.

Anthony gave Trevor another look, but Trevor shrugged and that was when the doorbell rang.

"That must be my ride." Sofia went to get her purse and coat from the hall closet and called a goodnight and have a good time this weekend from the foyer.

"Goodnight." Rebecca, Anthony and Trevor chimed together.

Rebecca went around the island and started removing the food from the warmer. "So how was Romano Enterprises?" Rebecca asked Trevor.

"Big! I mean really big Mom!" Trevor said by spreading his arms wide then high up in the air.

"It's a pretty impressive building."

"Dad has a bunch of offices all around the world." Trevor was quick to pass on his knowledge.

"Really?" Rebecca looked at Anthony, who was taking off his suit jacket and rolling up his sleeves. She had no idea the true scope of Romano Enterprises.

"Yup." Trevor watched Anthony as he went over to the sink to wash his hands, so Trevor got up and did the same.

They all sat around the island eating their chicken and talking about their day.

"Homework?" Anthony asked Trevor before biting into another bright green bean.

"I did it already." Trevor answered before popping a green bean into his mouth matching his dad bite for bite.

"I thought homework was for home?" Anthony asked Trevor.

"It is. But when Paul text messaged me . . ." Trevor started.

"Text messaged you!" Anthony replied, shocked.

"Yeah," Trevor shrugged. "He told me that I was going to your office right after school, so I thought I should use my free period to do my homework. We get some free time to do whatever we want each day, so I did my homework." Trevor explained.

"I am still trying to understand the text message part." Anthony asked calmly. "Maybe you can explain that to me again, because I thought no student was allowed to use their cell phone during school hours."

"The teachers kind of let me do it anyway." Trevor admitted.

Anthony didn't like the sound of that one bit, arching a golden eyebrow. He was definitely going to have to discuss that with his son later. On second thought, Rebecca was hawking him with wide eyes apparently waiting for him to discuss that with Trevor right now. Anthony paused gathering his words. "Well, I would like you to remember something." Anthony started by placing his hand on Trevor's shoulder, reassuringly. "When someone with authority allows you to do something that is against the rules, it doesn't make it right."

Trevor stared at his dad unafraid at his correction, only trying to understand. "So you mean I should follow the rules all the time."

"Yes!"

"Okay Dad, I will. I thought they were being nice to me, because I was new in school."

"Maybe they were, but it still doesn't make it right. *Capisce*?" Anthony asked.

"What does 'ka-peesh' mean?" Trevor asked.

"It means, do you understand?" Anthony smiled and rubbed the boy's shiny head of hair.

"I *ka-peesh*." Trevor tried to pronounce the Italian word.

"Not bad." Anthony patted his son's back. "I think you are learning faster than your mother." Anthony quipped.

"Hey! I really had a hard time in English class. English is my first and second language." Rebecca shot back.

They all laughed and ate dinner together then everyone helped to clean up, even though Sofia told them time and time again that she would take care of it in the morning. While Trevor cleared, Anthony rinsed the dishes and placed them into the dishwasher. Rebecca put the leftovers into containers and into the refrigerator.

When Trevor went to his room to get changed into his pajamas, Anthony walked over to Rebecca, took the things from her hands and captured her face, lifting it up to kiss her deeply.

Rebecca blinked, looking into his eyes.

"Now that is a proper hello." Anthony stated quietly.

"I would say so . . ." Rebecca sighed.

"I missed you darling." Anthony confessed, skimming his thumbs over her soft cheeks. "I cannot wait to go away this weekend."

"Me too." Rebecca returned. "It's going to be great to get away this weekend and see everybody."

"How about we promise no cell phones this weekend? Do you think you can do that?" Anthony continued to run his thumbs over her smooth cheeks studying the color in her eyes. But when Anthony watched her hesitate, he pulled back. "Forget it. It really isn't that important. Besides, what if a patient needs you?" Anthony dropped his hands to his sides and started to walk away from her, but Rebecca quickly grabbed his arm, turning him back to face her.

Rebecca wasn't going to let another opportunity slip through her fingers like she did on her wedding night. "No. It is. It's very important that we turn off the world and be together as a family, as husband and wife."

"Are you sure?"

"Yes. I'm sure. I'm not even going to take the damn thing with me, I promise." Rebecca crossed her heart.

Anthony lifted her up and placed her on the island. He pressed his body between her legs and kissed the top of her head. He yearned for her. "Rebecca." Anthony whispered before he pressed his lips against hers, pulling her hips toward him. He felt her wrap her legs around him, as his desire swelled. "I want you so badly." Anthony whispered into her ear.

Rebecca's body trembled, turned on by that deep, rich voice. Rebecca ran her fingers through his hair. "I'm going to take a shower, because I want to smell as enticing as you do right now," she whispered. "And, tonight when our son sleeps, I plan on touching you." Rebecca wanted him to know that she wanted him as much as he wanted her. "A lot!" Rebecca added.

"I'm not sure if I can wait." Anthony admitted before he devoured her neck. He pulled himself away and lowered her off the island to the floor, as if she were the most precious, fragile object on the face of the earth.

"It'll be well worth the wait. Trust me." Rebecca went up on tippy-toes and kissed his defined jaw before she turned away, running down the hall into the master bedroom suite to take a shower.

Anthony stood alone in the kitchen looking down at his manhood which throbbed in his suit pants. Raking a hand through his hair he said, "This is going to be a major problem if my wife gets me this hard with only a few kisses." Anthony went to the cabinet for a glass, filled it with ice-cold water then downed it. He refilled it and went down the hall to the master bedroom suite. He could hear the shower running and was very tempted to join his wife. Instead he changed into his jeans and a T-shirt, keeping his feet bare. After, he went into his office to call his father. He wanted his father to find another position at Romano Enterprises for the very outspoken, disrespectful chauffeur. Ever since he took over as president, he let his father address these very sensitive employee situations. There was less gossip that way. Besides, his father would give Paul speech after speech about how to treat women which would fry Paul's brains in no time. His father's lectures were lobotomy-resulting, except without the anesthesia and scalpel.

Anthony smiled broadly when his father agreed to take Paul away from RE for awhile. *Oh yeah, Paul was in for the lesson of a lifetime,* Anthony sat back in his chair grinning. *"Grazie."* Anthony thanked his father before he ended the call. Then he began to rifle through some of the mountains of paperwork on his desk. When an entire spot was cleared off, he was shocked that he managed to do that in minutes. He realized at that moment that he was so preoccupied with thoughts of Rebecca, then Trevor, that he simply couldn't concentrate, which prevented him from accomplishing anything.

"Dad where are you?" Trevor was calling him from down the hall.

"I am in the office, Son." Anthony called back.

"Wow, you did a lot of homework tonight." Trevor looked surprised.

It was the first time Anthony could see the top of his desk in months. "You know what?" Anthony asked.

"What?" Trevor asked.

"I think I'm done for tonight, so how about a story?"

"Okay. I'll go get a book." Trevor darted out of the room, down the hall and into his room. He grabbed the first book on his shelf and ran back in a flash.

"That was quick."

"Where do you want to read the book?" Trevor asked.

"How about the den? That way I can show you how to build a fire. Then we can read for a while."

"Cool." Trevor shouted.

There they built a fire together and Anthony listened while Trevor read the story to him, as the fire snapped and crackled in the hearth. When the story was over, Trevor had a question. "Dad?" Trevor looked up into Anthony's gray eyes. "Yes Son." Anthony loved that he called him *Dad.* "When we got home Sofee called me Mr. Romano and Scotty called me Romano too. But my last name is Michaels, right?" Anthony nodded. "I guess they think your name is the same as mine, but the adoption isn't complete."

"But I want my last name to be Romano."

"I see." Anthony nodded. "There is a legal process and it's going to take some time."

Trevor scowled.

"Okay . . . I'll speak to the attorneys and see what we can do to speed it up. Is that a better answer?"

"Yes. Thanks Dad." Trevor jumped onto Anthony's lap and hugged him around the neck. "I want you to teach me to play the piano and speak the way you speak."

"All in one night?" Anthony asked laughing.

"How long will it take?"

"For you, maybe a few weeks since you are so smart." Anthony knew.

Trevor smiled.

"Come on, let's go tickle the ivories."

"Ivories?" Trevor asked.

"The piano keys." Anthony held onto Trevor and walked him into the living room. Anthony sat down on the piano bench, with Trevor on his lap, spreading his hands on the keys. "Place your hands over mine."

"Like this?"

"That's right." Anthony watched Trevor place his hands over his and Anthony began to play chords. "These are chords."

"Cool."

"And when you get very good at that, then you can play music like this." Anthony began to play something classical, watching Trevor look back into his eyes then at his hands.

"Wow that is soooo cool!"

Rebecca heard the music and walked into the living room to see Anthony playing the piano with Trevor on his lap.

"Hi guys."

Trevor jumped down off Anthony's lap. "Did you hear that Mom?"

"Yes. That was beautiful." Rebecca reached down and picked Trevor up before taking a seat next to Anthony who began to play again. Rebecca rested her head on his shoulder enjoying the music that filled the room with soothing sounds.

"Dad is going to teach me how to play the piano and speak Italian."

"Oh no . . . not you too . . . then I won't understand what anyone is saying around here." Rebecca watched Trevor and Anthony heartily laugh a thick-as-thieves laugh. She was glad to see them bonding. It was so important. "Bed." Rebecca glanced at the grandfather clock.

Trevor nodded.

"Would it be okay if I tucked you in tonight?" Rebecca asked cautiously.

"Okay." Trevor responded.

Anthony was smiling, thinking, *this boy, now my son, is such a joy and gives everyone else joy.*

"Goodnight Dad." Trevor reached over to give his dad a kiss.

"Goodnight Son." Anthony captured Trevor's precious face and kissed each cheek. "That's how we do it in Sicily."

"Why?" Trevor asked.

Anthony arched an eyebrow. "That's a good question. Maybe it is because one kiss is never enough. You will have to ask *Nonno* the next time you see him."

"*Nonno?*" Trevor asked repeating the word perfectly.

"Grandpa." Anthony translated.

"Okay." Trevor reached up with his small hands, took hold of Anthony's chiseled face and kissed each cheek.

Anthony laid his hands over Trevor's and whispered, "I love you, Son."

"I love you too Dad." Trevor wanted to say it to him this morning, but didn't.

Anthony got up lifting Trevor up with him before he handed him to Rebecca. "I will tend to the fire while you say goodnight to our son." Anthony leaned down pressing a kiss to Rebecca's still damp, fragrant, soft curls.

Trevor took hold, hugging Rebecca close. She was stunned that Anthony told Trevor that he loved him. *Did he? Of course he did,* she thought silently. *Anthony loves me too,* Rebecca affirmed privately. She was only now discovering that Anthony was a very loving man.

Rebecca walked down the hall to Trevor's room, lowering him until his feet touched the bed. Rebecca closed the door and asked, "Okay what was going on with Sofia and Paul?" Rebecca wanted Trevor to dish the dirt.

Trevor plopped down onto the bed and started to spill the beans. "Mom, Dad does not like yelling."

"Really?" Rebecca sat down on the bed and began to tuck Trevor in.

"Really." Trevor opened his green eyes wide to drive home the point. "He gets very mad. But when he gets mad, he gets very quiet. That's when you know he is SUPER mad!"

Trevor emphasized the word, as Rebecca studied the most incredible green eyes she had ever seen before in her life. "What happened?"

"Paul came into the apartment yelling at Sofee that he was waiting then Dad walked out of the kitchen and jerked his head like this," Trevor imitated Anthony's move, "and Paul got out of the apartment. That's when Dad told him he was not allowed to yell in his home. He was not allowed to yell at Sofee or any girl. What does forbidden mean?"

"Not allowed to." Rebecca defined the word.

"He told Paul he was forbidden to see Sofee. Then I thought he was going to punch him Mom."

"Really?" Rebecca found that hard to believe, but anything was possible. Some people had a knack for pushing other people's buttons.

"Yup."

"What happened next?" Rebecca was impressed that Trevor understood so much of what was going on around him, but that was due to his upbringing.

"Nothing!" Trevor sounded surprised. "Dad stood real still, but his hands went like this." Trevor showed her how Anthony rolled his hands into fists then released them.

"Wow. Your dad does not like disrespect." Rebecca concluded.

"Disrespect?" Trevor asked.

"That means that we should all be polite to each other. Be nice to each other."

"Yeah he really doesn't like disrespect." Trevor repeated the word.

That didn't surprise Rebecca. "So how was the gym?" Rebecca was wondering about her husband's workouts.

"Cool. Scotty said Dad is stronger than Uncle Jack."

"No way." Rebecca waved her hand in the air discounting that statement. *When did Trevor start referring to Anthony's brother as Uncle Jack?* Her mind was trying to keep up with all of these little gradations.

"That's what Dad said! But Scotty said it was true. I think Dad is a giant . . . a gentle giant!"

"I think you would be a very good psychologist when you grow up." Rebecca pressed a kiss to Trevor's forehead.

"You do?"

"Yes I do. But I think you could be anything you want to be, because you are so smart." Rebecca made sure she covered all the bases.

Trevor smiled, because his dad told him tonight that he thought he was smart too. "I think I want to be exactly like Dad when I grow up."

"Good choice." Rebecca waited a minute, almost needing to gather the courage to say something she felt from the very first moment she met Trevor, but wasn't sure if it was the right time. "I love you Trevor."

"I love you Mom." Trevor jumped up and hugged her one last time then popped right under the covers.

Rebecca tucked him in, got up and closed his bedroom door behind her. She made her way down the hallway, stopping in the dining room to check out the wine selection in the wine refrigerator. She studied the different bottles wondering what Anthony might like to have. She noticed an open bottle of Port and decided that that might work. She found the little port glasses. At least she thought they were the little port glasses. Who knew? Because there were, without exaggeration, twelve different sizes of glasses in the crystal cabinet. She filled the two glasses about one-third up and went down the hall to the den. There she found Anthony sitting in front of the fire staring into the flames.

"Hi." Rebecca didn't know why, but suddenly she felt shy. She turned around and closed the door to the den with her blue lace clad foot peeking out from beneath her sweat pant leg.

"Trevor all tucked in?"

"Yup." Rebecca answered. "Port?" Rebecca asked holding out a glass.

"Perfect choice." Anthony took the glass from her extended hand and held out his other to help her sit beside him.

"Is this the right glass?" Rebecca joined Anthony on the carpet in front of the fire.

"Yes." Anthony smiled. "A toast?"

"Okay." Rebecca agreed, but Anthony nodded for her to do the honors, as she watched him breathe in the rich bouquet. "Oh, you want *me* to say a toast. Let me think. To my husband, the person our son wants to be like when he grows up." Rebecca raised her glass and tapped it against Anthony's.

"What do you mean?" Anthony probed.

"Trevor told me he wants to be just like his dad when he grows up." Rebecca revealed.

"Wow." Anthony looked surprised. "I guess the pressure is on. *Salute*—that means cheers."

Rebecca smiled as he remembered her request for immediate translations, as she watched him take a sip of the rich wine.

"Trevor asked me if he could change his last name to Romano."

"Wow." Rebecca took a sip of her Port.

Anthony nodded and chuckled. "I don't believe that would be possible until the adoption is complete."

"Oh. Did you tell him that?"

"I told him I would look into it, but I explained it to him."

"How did he take that?"

"Not great, but I told him that there is a process and that it might take some time."

"Okay. Do we have any idea when Children's Services is coming by again or is there going to be another surprise attack?"

"I don't think we are ever going to be warned. But if she comes by this weekend, she is going to be out of luck." Anthony smiled.

Rebecca smiled and sipped her wine.

Anthony lowered his head bringing his lips close to hers. "I missed you today."

"I missed you too." Rebecca felt her lips tingle with anticipation.

"I want to touch you." Anthony breathed.

"What are you waiting for?" Rebecca whispered back wondering what was taking him so long.

Anthony touched a damp curl. "You."

"Me?"

"I guess I'm still . . . unsure." Now Anthony struggled to gather his words.

"Well I'm not. In fact, at lunch today, I did a little shopping . . . went to *The Pink Pussycat . . .*" Rebecca heard Anthony's quick intake of breath. By his reaction, she knew that he had knowledge of the boutique. Rebecca stood up calmly, placing her glass of Port on the coffee table. "Came home early so that I could wash it and have it ready for tonight." Rebecca unzipped her warm-up jacket revealing a midnight blue lace top with very thin satin straps. The lingerie was cut in a very deep V. She purposely wore the longest strand of pearls he gave her as a wedding gift.

When Anthony heard where she did a 'little shopping,' he nearly swallowed his tonsils. His eyes grew wide, as they hungrily devoured her body. The first thing he noticed was the pearls he gave her as a wedding gift and that surprised and pleased him. He let his eyes devour her and could see the outline of her breasts through the lace and could not believe how sexy she looked or that she went out of her way today to get this for tonight. When she started to slip out of her sweatpants, he grew hard. The deep blue lace continued like a dress cut way too short with matching bikini style panties. There was also a garter belt with tiny satin straps that ran down the front and back of each leg. The straps were attached to dark blue hose in the same lacey, delicate pattern. Her feet remained shoeless, but covered in dark blue lace.

"Wow." Anthony tossed back the rest of his drink, set his glass on the coffee table and stood up.

"I don't think I've ever heard you say *Wow* until tonight." Rebecca retrieved her glass and took a sip while watching Anthony study her figure. "Wait!" Rebecca held up her free hand. "Let me show you the back." She slowly turned around to reveal a long, very low, teasing semi-circle which tastefully revealed the beginning of her bottom.

Anthony took a step toward her trying not to look like an inexperienced, gawking teenage boy. Carefully, he ran a fingertip along one of the satiny straps on her shoulder. Her shoulders were stunning, quite muscular and defined.

Rebecca continued to turn holding the strand of pearls in one hand. Although it was made of lace, the garment was silky-soft. The panties were very high-cut on her hips and revealed parts of her firm derrière. "It was pretty tricky to get into it, but getting it off should be no problem for a big, strong boy like you." Rebecca teased.

"Since I can't feel my fingers or arms at the moment, I think that might be a very big problem." Anthony shamelessly admitted.

Rebecca laughed.

Anthony leaned down, kissing her smiling mouth.

Rebecca leaned over quickly to put down her glass. When she straightened, he kissed her deliberately and swiftly. Each kiss became a little longer and a little more demanding until his hands were wrapped around her, caressing her bare back, while tongues dueled to see which one could give the other the greatest pleasure first. "Anthony." Rebecca whispered as he started to devour her neck.

"*Che* darling?" Anthony asked.

This time Rebecca understood him and told him exactly what she wanted. "Shirt off." Rebecca pulled on his T-shirt in an effort to remove it. She wanted to feel his chest and he granted her that wish. She ran her hands along his clearly defined stomach muscles and had to ask, "Did you do this for me?"

"Yes." Anthony struggled to speak, his need mounting.

"Why?" Rebecca was curious, pressing a tender kiss to his impeccably chiseled chest.

Anthony was shocked how quickly his body responded to her slightest touch. He swallowed unable to get the words out at first, but tried again. "I wanted you to find me attractive in any way." Anthony grasped her head and brought her lips back up to his. He plundered her lips and dipped into her mouth for another sweet taste.

"I find you attractive in so many ways." Rebecca breathed over his moistened lips.

"Good. That's very good." Anthony was caressing her shoulder.

"I believe a lot of women would find you attractive. You look . . . like a . . . mythological god."

Anthony smiled. "There is only one woman I want to attract and if I knew that you found my words more attractive than my body, then I wouldn't have been killing myself working out at the gym with Scott."

Rebecca studied his body with her eyes and her fingertips. "Thank you."

Anthony smiled, running his fingertips along the lovely curve of her cheek.

"You're beautiful." Rebecca told him exactly what she thought of him.

"No darling, you're the real beauty. Now I think I should apologize in advance if I happen to tear this enticing ensemble."

Rebecca's mind was whirling. *Did he say tear it?* She was getting hotter by the minute and the image of her husband ripping off her lingerie was not cooling her temperature. "I don't mind. Think what Cassandra will say when I tell her that the outfit was so hot that my husband ripped it right off my body."

"Who's Cassandra?"

"The salesgirl . . ." Rebecca whispered, touching his chest.

The next minute, Anthony tore her outfit right down the front, exposing her breasts. He tossed the soft afghan onto the carpet and pulled her down to the floor in front of the fire. "I thought about you all day."

"You did?" Rebecca was pleasantly surprised, but when Anthony began caressing her breast she was finding it difficult to speak, let alone think.

"Yes. I was afraid that you might have regretted last night and would never want me to touch you again." Anthony watched her forehead crease.

"Oh no." Rebecca shook her head, running her fingertips over his jaw that appeared to be cut from stone.

"No second thoughts." Anthony whispered cupping her cheek.

"No second thoughts. I love you Anthony. I have never told any boy or any man that ever in my life. I was a bit of a skeptic about love. I didn't believe that love existed until you showed me it did." Rebecca immediately stopped speaking, because he suddenly ran the back of his hand over her breast. She collected herself and said, "I hope you always want to touch me like this."

"I will." Anthony promised.

"I want you to show me whenever you want me . . ." Rebecca stopped to think about what she was saying. "I think that was too many 'wants' in one sentence." Rebecca mumbled touching her fingers to his chest.

"Darling, I *want* you." Anthony watched her swallow and followed the column of her throat with his long fingers down to the center between her breasts. "I've wanted you since the first day I bumped into you and I haven't stopped wanting you since." Again he swept the back of his hand across her breast watching Rebecca close her eyes. When he replaced his hand with his lips, her hand dropped to his shoulder holding onto him, as her breathing changed. Anthony nudged the strand of pearls to the side with his lips, watching as she melded into the afghan on the floor. He watched the flames dance off her skin and hair—a vision that would forever be etched into his mind.

Rebecca started to feel akin to molten lava, but tonight she wanted to give Anthony all the pleasure. So before she fell under his spell she took hold of his face and brought his mouth up to hers. "Kiss me. Please . . ." Rebecca pleaded.

Anthony went up on his knees, captured her face and kissed her until she was breathless.

Rebecca absolutely adored how he kissed her. *He's not a wet kisser . . . no,* Rebecca thought silently, *but a really good kisser. Probably the best-I've-ever-had-in-my-life kisser. No! Correction! THE best I ever had, period.* He just didn't kiss her lips and twin his tongue with hers. Oh no. Instead he would faintly run his tongue along her teeth and over her lips outlining them. That was . . . *WOW!* He kissed her lips by pressing his lips to hers at first then he added a little more pressure, kissing with more force without being forceful, and controlling the speed and intensity of the kiss without being controlling. *Holy crap! He's such a great kisser!*

Rebecca gathered her thoughts while he kissed her again. She undid his belt, which was directly in front of her, with trembling fingers. She came up on her knees as they continued to kiss, sliding his pants down. Rebecca gently pushed on his shoulders and Anthony sat down on the afghan while Rebecca, in her now-tattered outfit, slid his pants down his legs. She tossed them to the side and asked warmly. "Can you do something for me?"

"Anything darling." Anthony was going to fulfill any and all of her wishes, as he ran his fingertips along her cheek.

"Lay back and place your hands under your head."

Anthony did as he was told, placing his large hands beneath his head.

When he did that, Rebecca couldn't help but study the intricate and perfectly defined muscles on each arm. "Now keep them there until I tell you to move them." Rebecca whispered.

"Alright darling." Anthony chuckled.

"Promise?" Rebecca questioned softly.

Anthony nodded feeling his desire intensify.

Rebecca knelt down and placed her hands on the waistband of his knit boxers. Anthony raised his hips slightly, in order to assist her in the removal of his garment. She pulled down his boxers, softly touching his manhood before tossing the garment to the side. Anthony's maleness was a surprise to her last night and an even greater surprise tonight, while Rebecca quite literally examined him in awe. Rebecca sat back down and placed her legs together folding them to one side. "Wow!"

Anthony laughed. "Can I touch you now darling?" he asked. Her breasts were partially exposed in her torn lace outfit and it was driving him a little crazy not being able to touch her body.

"No. No. I haven't even started yet." Rebecca went back up onto her knees and leaned over him. "I hope you don't mind . . ."

"Mind what?" he whispered.

"If I kiss you . . ."

Anthony shook his head.

Rebecca kissed him deeply and lingeringly, but when she pulled away he still reached out for her mouth. She ran her fingernail down his neck then kissed it. She ran her hands along each arm and kissed his bicep. She kissed the spot where his shoulder met his chest. She deposited feather-light kisses everywhere she touched. When she kissed his underarm, Anthony chuckled again in that sexy, rich, deep tone that she was unexpectedly so attuned to. When she ran her fingers along his chest, Anthony's muscles leapt with the connection of her touch. Rebecca touched and kissed her way down and when she heard a faint moan, she knew he was enjoying her touch.

"*Rebecca.*" Anthony whispered.

"Thank you." Rebecca said.

"*Che?*" Anthony asked in a deep whispered voice that came only when his desire increased.

"For this amazing body . . ." Rebecca spelled out, noticing the intensity of the gray in his eyes. With an open hand, she started at his bicep and ran it down the length of his body in the faintest of touches. When she completed that journey, she continued by touching the thick, light-colored mat above his manhood. She smiled. "I hope you don't mind if I kiss you like this."

And when she took him into her mouth, Anthony began speaking rapidly in his native tongue, as he raised his hips to place more of himself into her warm, wet mouth.

"Translation . . ." Rebecca giggled, pausing for a moment.

"I haven't finished speaking . . . yet!" Anthony could barely get the words out. He started speaking rapidly in Italian all over again, when Rebecca retook him into her mouth. "I said I have to touch you." Anthony gasped during the translation trying desperately to catch his breath.

Rebecca stopped to listen before drawing him in, watching as he pressed his head against his hands fighting to keep his promise, exposing each muscle in his neck, arms and shoulders.

"I . . . want you." Anthony squeezed his eyes shut. When he felt his desire rise, he knew that Rebecca had no intention of stopping, as he felt his semen climb. "*Rebecca . . .*" he warned, but she didn't stop and when he came right into her mouth, feeling her lick him clean, he exhaled, "*Rebecca . . .*"

Unexpectedly, he didn't feel her anymore. He immediately opened his eyes to see that she was standing up trying to wriggle out of her torn lingerie. "I could give you a hand or two with that."

"Not yet." Rebecca tore more of the lace in order to free herself of the outfit as it slipped to the carpet silently.

Anthony instantly grew hard again as he watched her unclip the garter belt in order to remove her panties. When she tossed them to the side and quickly reattached the garter belt to the hose, he knew she was trying to torture him. Clad only in her dark blue lace hose fastened to her garter belt and the long strand of pearls, which he was so thankful he gave her as a wedding gift, he watched in wonderment as she positioned herself over him. Two days ago, the only part of her skin she showed him, willingly, was from her neck up and from her wrists to her fingertips. Now she was fitting herself to him, which caused Anthony to start speaking in Italian all over again, while he raised his hips up to enter her more fully.

"*Mia moglie bella . . .*" Anthony spoke again in his native tongue while gasping for air. "My beautiful wife . . . I said . . . I will never . . . ever make this promise again."

"I'll just have to use the handcuffs next time."

Anthony's eyes and mouth flew open in shock at the same time.

"Oh yeah, they sell those too!" Besides having her very own as part of her regular uniform, but she kept that to herself.

"*Santa Madre . . .*" Anthony exhaled.

Rebecca was reaching for what only Anthony could give her, riding him harder, forcing him deeper. The feeling of him deep within her caused her to forget all her worries, all her fears and to simply take pleasure in this sexual union with the man she loved.

Anthony stopped all movement, feeling her pulsing warm silk enveloping him, struggling to control himself in order to prolong their lovemaking. "Rebecca." He watched her lower herself, as she placed her forehead to his chest.

"Anthony I can't wait anymore . . . please touch me . . ." she pleaded.

Anthony's hands were on her hot flesh in a flash. He was more than a little aggressive and although he tried repeatedly to regain some kind of control, he couldn't seem to stop himself. He rolled her over and impaled her, continuing where she left off. Feeling her embrace him, they mated in front of the fire. And no matter how hard he tried, he couldn't seem to stop himself from manhandling her, driving deeper and deeper with each thrust. He pushed the strand of pearls aside with a growl, grabbing at her breasts, squeezing one mound then the other with more force than he ever used on any other woman in his life, all while she sweetly called his name. The gentler she spoke to him, the crazier he became. When he lowered himself on top of her and bit into the side of her neck, she delicately ran her nails down his back, which snapped the very last vestige of his control.

"My husband." Rebecca sighed, cupping his jaw, watching him rise up above her, his eyes the color of thunderheads, revealing an inner intense storm. Rebecca held on while the velocity of his storm escalated. "I never thanked you properly for these beautiful pearls." Rebecca softly whispered, holding the pearls in one hand. "Thank you."

Anthony barely heard her over the roar of thunder in his head. He couldn't stop himself. He squeezed, pulled and bit, as rumble after rumble roused the passion within him. He tried to stop his rapid descent into his own desires, but he was losing the fight. He scooped her head up with one hand, while he braced himself with the other, in order to bring her mouth up to his hungry devouring mouth, all while impaling her center as deeply and as powerfully as he could.

Rebecca strapped her arms and legs around him and reached for his next thrust, welcoming the power of his stormy passion and the longevity of his intensity. She felt celebrated and adored and never wanted that feeling to end.

Anthony tried in vain to regain some semblance of sanity, but it was as though touching her wasn't enough, being within her wasn't enough. He couldn't seem to stop the gale of need that persisted to build inside of him. Then he faintly heard her whispering to him, while she tenderly stroked his jaw.

"I love you Anthony."

Anthony struggled to wait for her to reach her next pinnacle before he reached his own, but Rebecca's gentle declaration together with her temperate touch caused Anthony to give up the fight, surrendering unequivocally to the forces within him. Anthony lowered her head and himself while projecting his life into her. It seemed his body had waited for her body his whole life. His body acted in a manner that was wholly unfamiliar to him, while he released his life into his wife's silky depths. When he heard her low moan coupled with a pulsating sensation, he felt complete. After many minutes, Anthony rolled to his side with his bride still very intimately joined to him.

Rebecca found that connection so fulfilling. Remaining sexually linked, even though their lovemaking was spent, simply astounded her.

Anthony pressed his lips to her forehead, desperately trying to catch his breath. "Please stay away from that intimate apparel shop." Anthony whispered between short quick pants. He could feel her laughter at his very center, embracing her fiercely. "I was . . . a . . . little . . ." he couldn't even bring himself to say the word. He was completely stunned by his own body's reaction to her and his inability to control it whenever she was within arm's length of him.

"Rough . . ." Rebecca finished his sentence for him. She was still trying to catch her breath as well, while she pressed her lips against his pulsating neck.

"I'm sorry. I don't know what came over me." Anthony glided his open palm over her cheek pushing her curls away from the spot he wanted to kiss. "I'm so in love with you Rebecca." Anthony was still trying to catch his breath, before pressing his lips to her warm, rosy cheek.

"I kind of figured that." Rebecca started to trace the outlines of his muscles on his chest, as she exhaled.

"I'm serious about that boutique." Anthony took another deep breath in and out. He couldn't believe that he was still trying to catch his breath even though he had been seriously working out for almost a year.

"Umm . . . it's a little too late for that." Rebecca admitted, biting her lower lip.

Anthony dropped his chin to look into her mahogany eyes.

Rebecca studied his eyes, watching them vary from gray to blue to all gray. "Well . . . I didn't just buy one thing when I was there!" Rebecca admitted with a shrug, tenderly touching the most handsome face she had ever seen in her life, still not believing how she had fought so hard against her own feelings.

"What do you mean?" Anthony was actually scared. *Maybe scared to death is more accurate . . .*

"I bought several outfits. I thought I could take them with me this weekend." Rebecca bit her lower lip again.

"God help me." Anthony pressed his lips to her forehead, listening to his wife's soft laugh.

They fell asleep in front of the fire and a few hours later they walked, completely naked, down the hall into their bedroom. They turned down the bed, snuggled together face to face and slept fitfully.

In the morning, they woke early and showered together. Anthony noticed some bruising on his wife and winced. "Does that hurt?" Anthony caressed her breast tenderly kissing some of the purpling spots.

"No." Rebecca soaped his chest. "I just bruise easily."

"I will be more careful from now on." Anthony was horrified.

"Please don't stop touching me like you did last night. It was wild and wonderful and I slept like a rock." Rebecca ran her soapy hands over his muscular shoulders and arms.

Anthony chuckled in a deep tone, "You were snoring a little."

"What!" Rebecca swatted him with the sponge. "I do not snore!" Rebecca pinched his flat stomach, smiling.

Anthony smiled and kissed her smiling lips.

"I don't think I want to go to work anymore." Rebecca admitted quietly. "I think I would rather stay home and make love to you all day."

"Hmm . . . that could very easily be arranged." Anthony tenderly captured her face lifting it as he lowered his lips to kiss her delicately.

Chapter Ten
Weekend in the country . . .

Anthony hustled through his day and left the office at one. He planned on driving them all up to his brother's farm himself. In fact, he traded in his Mercedes coupe for a Mercedes SUV figuring that he would need something with more room since he went from a bachelor to a married man with a son, overnight. Since his last car had only two seats, he needed something they could all fit into comfortably. Besides, Anthony did not want his family to be chauffeured around, especially on those are-we-there-yet trips.

When he entered the apartment, although Anthony gave Sofia the day off, he could tell that she came anyway. The coffee cups from this morning that were left in the sink were no longer there. And as he made his way into the master bedroom, he found the bed made and the place vacuumed. Anthony hung up his suit, put his shirt in the laundry bin and dressed in a pair of jeans and a long-sleeved T-shirt. He slipped on more casual shoes and pulled a jacket from the closet. He packed a few things in a leather duffle bag and put it by Rebecca's that she had packed this morning. His fingers were itching to see the lingerie she secretly packed into her overnight bag, but he quashed the urge. Next to Rebecca's bag was Trevor's bag as well. He took all three bags into the foyer then went into his home office to check his email one last time before he left. There on the middle of his desk was Rebecca's phone with a little note.

"Let's turn off the world!"

Anthony smiled, so pleased that she had remembered their pact. With his new vehicle equipped with satellite technology, he had no problem leaving his cell phone behind. Besides, one bodyguard, if not more, would be discreetly following them anyway. He placed his phone next to hers then quickly went into the hall. He swung the overnight bags over his shoulder and left the apartment. Once he loaded the bags into the SUV, he hopped in behind the steering wheel and pulled out of the underground parking garage. He made his way to Trevor's school first. Parking as close as he could to the school, Anthony walked to where some other adults gathered. A few women waved to him, so he assumed they were parents and waved back.

When the front doors split open wide, kids of all shapes, sizes, ages and colors came pouring out. Anthony spotted Trevor and started walking toward him. Trevor ran the distance between them and launched himself into Anthony's open arms. "Hey Son." Anthony lifted him up and kissed him on each cheek. "How was school?"

"Bor-ring!"

"I'm fairly certain that that comment would not please your teacher."

"It is! Anyway, it's way too nice outside to be locked up in school." Trevor grumbled.

"Locked up?" Anthony laughed. Trevor sounded exactly like every other young boy on a cloudless blue-skied afternoon like today. "I remember those days, but . . ."

"I know, I know." Trevor stopped his new dad from giving him the, *you have to study and do well in school* speech.

Anthony placed him back down on the sidewalk and Trevor waved goodbye to his friends. Anthony nodded to the mothers, who waved back, while they walked back to the car. He hit the button on the clicker and placed Trevor's backpack in the trunk with the other bags.

"Homework?" Anthony asked, looking down at his son.

"Nah Dad. It's Friday. There's never any homework on Friday." Trevor kicked a rock.

Anthony couldn't believe that Trevor actually sounded disappointed that he had no homework. "No." Anthony corrected. He wanted Trevor to speak properly.

"No." Trevor repeated looking up at his dad, grinning.

"Come on, we better hurry. Your mom is probably waiting." Anthony looked down at his son.

"Okay."

They both got into the vehicle and buckled their seatbelts before Anthony pulled out heading toward the mental health clinic. It was about ten blocks down from the school and they were lucky to find a spot only a block from Rebecca's work. The parking was definitely an unfamiliar challenge to Anthony, who hardly drove himself anywhere. Anthony handed Trevor some change and he hopped out to feed the meter. Together they walked hand-in-hand down the block to her office. Once they rounded the bend, Anthony had to do a double-take. Rebecca was standing outside her office building talking to some guy. Trevor let go of Anthony's hand and started to run toward Rebecca while shouting for her.

Anthony couldn't prevent the deep doubt that gnawed at him. According to the bodyguards, he knew that Rebecca was promiscuous and he wasn't sure if this leopard could or would ever change her spots. He knew that she loved him, but could she remain monogamous?

Rebecca waved to Trevor then caught a glimpse of Anthony not far behind and from what she could tell, he did not look too pleased to see her talking to another man. Rebecca had been standing outside waiting for Anthony and Trevor when Detective Mitchell suddenly showed up and started talking shop. He said he tried to reach her on her cell phone and she apologized and told him she accidentally left it home. She told him that she didn't feel comfortable talking to him in broad daylight because the initial set-up for Tina, her undercover identity, to meet Boris, the sex trafficker, was already in place. She was concerned that he might blow her cover, but Mitchell ignored protocol. That's the way most know-it-alls liked to roll.

Anthony watched Rebecca kiss Trevor on the cheek, so he wasted no time eating up the balance of the distance to place a resounding kiss on Rebecca's lips. "Hello darling."

"Hi." Rebecca started the introductions. "Anthony, Trevor, this is Detective Mitchell. Detective this is my husband, Anthony Romano and our son, Trevor."

"Hi Trevor." Mitchell stuck out his hand to shake Trevor's.

"Hi." Trevor stretched out his hand to shake the detective's hand. Trevor watched the detective, who looked nervous, as the detective looked at his dad.

"Romano." Mitchell nodded.

"Mitchell." Anthony did the same. The mere sight of Detective Mitchell, who had been a thorn in the side of the Romano family for years, was enough to ruin Anthony's weekend. But Anthony wasn't about to let anything ruin his weekend with his wife and son, not even Detective Mitchell!

"Looks like you guys have plans?"

Anthony said nothing and Trevor quickly grabbed onto his dad's hand. Trevor knew that when his dad got quiet, really quiet and very still, that usually meant that he was angry, very angry. Anthony dropped his face and gave Trevor a lopsided smile.

Rebecca looked at her watch. "Wow! Look at the time! We really do need to go." Rebecca smiled at Anthony, taking his hand.

"Good to meet ya, Trevor." Detective Mitchell stated nodding at Anthony, before he started to walk away from the group.

Once they reached the car, Rebecca pulled Anthony to a stop, kissing him passionately on the lips, causing Anthony to smile broadly. "I can't wait to get out of the city." Rebecca declared.

Anthony smiled.

Trevor jumped into the backseat and Anthony made it clear. "Buckle up!"

"Check."

"You're next young lady." Anthony opened up the car door and watched Rebecca slip into the passenger seat. She was wearing a long, khaki riding skirt with a black turtleneck and long, shiny black leather boots that reached her mid-thigh, disappearing under her skirt. Anthony watched her get dressed this morning and knew exactly what she wore beneath that outfit. And when she paraded around in those satiny black undergarments in those long, shiny black boots, he nearly devoured her, stunned by his own carnal desires.

Once Rebecca was settled into the passenger seat, Anthony dropped his head in and gave her a deep kiss.

"Thank you." Rebecca was so happy to be going away for the weekend. She didn't realize it until that moment that she needed some time away.

"Buckle up, love."

"Check." Rebecca teasingly whispered.

Anthony arched a golden eyebrow which caused her to giggle. He closed the door and rounded the vehicle looking down at the beginnings of the throbbing need in his jeans. Apparently, that organ had a mind of its own whenever he was in the slightest vicinity of his wife. He hopped into the driver's side and pressed the button to start the car's engine. Smiling at everyone he asked, "All ready?"

"Yup." Trevor called from the backseat.

"And not a minute too soon," Rebecca chimed in placing her head against the headrest looking at her husband contentedly. "Okay." Anthony started to pull out of the spot and stopped when Trevor shouted from the backseat, "Seatbelt!" Anthony quickly belted up then pulled out of the spot making his way towards the highway.

They all spoke about their day and Anthony reached over to take Rebecca's hand in his during the ride. He was going to remind her constantly that he was near, always. That she belonged to him and no one else. The ride went relatively quickly between chatting and listening to Trevor talk about the silly things his classmates did in school. When they got to the farm it was a little past four in the afternoon and there were police and fire vehicles all over the property.

"What in the world . . ." Rebecca stared at the sight.

Jack was coming out of the animal hospital and from one look at his body language, Anthony could see that Jack was ranting and raving about something. His hands were flailing as Frankie calmly walked back into the animal hospital. Anthony pulled up, away from all the emergency vehicles. That is when he noticed that Trevor looked afraid. Trevor had already unfastened his seatbelt and was leaning over into the front seat. "It's fine Son." Anthony attempted to alleviate Trevor's uneasiness. He wasn't sure if the sight of police was disturbing him or if it was Jack swinging his arms around like a chaotic lawn ornament.

Trevor was very grateful that Anthony was his adopted dad. Anthony was so calm. *Uncle Jack looked downright mean,* Trevor thought silently.

They all waited in the car while the police cars and the fire department's red shiny trucks left the farm, one by one.

Anthony stepped out of the car and saw the dog come charging up from the water. Although Bruno had calmed down dramatically since his goddaughter, Antoinette, was born, he was still a handful.

Trevor jumped out of the backseat and called for him. "Bruno! Come on boy!" Trevor called, urging the dog on faster. Bruno obliged, by hunkering down and ripping up more dirt and grass the instant he recognized the small child's voice.

Anthony went around to Rebecca's door to help her from the vehicle, which she absolutely loved. When Anthony and Rebecca first brought Trevor up to the farm, Anthony picked up Trevor so that the dog wouldn't plow into him, but the dog had stopped on a dime a few inches from him then and did the exact same thing today.

"Hey boy." Trevor stepped over to the dog petting his massive head gently. He just loved how soft he was. Trevor reached around and hugged Bruno around the neck. When Trevor released him, Bruno rewarded him with a big, long lick right on the cheek, which was full of dirt and grass causing Trevor to giggle. "Dad, can we *please* get a dog like Bruno?" Trevor begged, with his little arm wrapped around the dog's neck. Little Nick, his Great Uncle John's chunky bulldog, was still running, trying to catch up.

"We're not allowed to have pets in the apartment." Anthony shrugged. "We might have to move here, if you want to have pets."

"Really! Can we?" Trevor shouted.

Anthony walked around to the rear of the vehicle to take out the luggage, while Jack made his way over. He shook his brother's hand, rubbed Trevor's head and kissed Rebecca on the cheek.

"What happened?" Rebecca asked.

"Don't even get me started. My wife insists on letting this python . . ."

"Wow . . . like in snake?!" Trevor interrupted.

"Yes—like in snake." Jack spoke softly to his new nephew, tousling his hair even though he was furious as hell.

"Cool." Trevor whispered.

"I have to admit that thing totally creeps me out." Rebecca shuddered openly.

"I know! Me too." Jack agreed. "Well the damn thing wrapped itself around Francesca so quickly that Nelson and I couldn't free her. So Maggie called the police, because everyone who works at the fire department has a fear of snakes, but they come anyway to see if they can try to overcome this phobia with exposure! I mean, give me a break!" Jack threw his hands up in the air. "Uncle John won't go near the thing and there is only one officer on the whole police force who can handle that slimy thing without taking his weapon out of his holster, an Officer Cleary. I should give that man combat pay every time he comes here and unravels my wife!" Jack shook his head. "Call me crazy, but I don't like that thing twisting itself around my wife in half a second!"

Anthony, Rebecca and Trevor said nothing, while they watched Jack have his fit.

"What—" Jack was openly shocked with their silence. "Tell me you don't agree with me!"

"I remember that snake from when she first opened the hospital and from what Francesca told me, the snake is not trying to harm her." Anthony tried to reason with Jack, but he could see it was useless.

"Listen to me Anthony. It's a snake. It bites like a snake and eats like a snake!" Jack stated his case in an open and shut manner. "Would you want some twenty-foot long snake wrapped around your son?"

"No." Anthony stated immediately and very clearly, smiling at Trevor, who smiled back.

"Precisely . . . now how about your wife?" Jack asked.

"Perhaps on those mornings when she is barking out all kinds of orders to me and Trevor . . ." Anthony winked at Trevor and in that instant Rebecca swatted Anthony with her oversized handbag in his stomach. "Umph . . ." Anthony reached for his stomach.

"Seriously . . . !" Rebecca walked away from the men, because they were starting to grate on her last nerve.

Trevor was laughing when he spotted his cousin, Antoinette, who everyone called "Toni" for short. And when she spotted Trevor, she squealed in a high pitched scream, which prompted Bruno's very high-pitched playful bark accompanied by Little Nick, the stubby-legged bulldog.

"Son, stay away from that snake!" Anthony cautioned his son.

Trevor looked back toward his dad with a smile from ear to ear.

"I mean it!" Anthony warned. He didn't want his son anywhere near that thing and he certainly wouldn't wait for the police to free his son. He would have no problem taking care of that thing—and for good.

"I swear—my wife and these animals. It's like a zoo here!" Jack ranted.

"Brother, you're kidding right? You knew she was a vet before you married her."

"I know. But I thought that after Toni was born she would slow down, but that's not happening." Jack swung his arm over his brother's shoulders and could feel how solid he was. "Still working out with Scott?"

"Please don't remind me." Anthony shook his head.

"I know. The man is a little over-the-top about his workouts."

"Over-the-top doesn't even begin to describe it." Anthony lifted the bags out of the trunk.

"Come on let me show you the new guest quarters."

Rebecca went into the animal hospital and said hello to Maggie, the receptionist and Robin, who recently graduated from veterinarian school and was working at Frankie's hospital full time now.

They were all chatting amicably when Frankie came out of the examination area. She spotted her best friend and ran to her. "Hi. I had to get cleaned up. Snakes carry a lot of salmonella."

"Ewww! You might want to leave out that little detail when your husband is around, because that's disgusting!" Rebecca didn't care what disease her friend might be harboring, because she didn't hesitate to give her an enormous hug.

"I've missed you!"

"I've missed you too!"

"Robin is going to finish up the rest of the appointments for me so we can visit."

Rebecca smiled at her friend, realizing at that moment how much she truly missed her. Texting, e-mailing . . . it wasn't the same as spending time with her best friend.

"We are going to have dinner on The Rose tonight and leave the yacht dockside because we want Trevor to get used to the feeling of the boat on the water."

"That sounds great."

"Let me show you the new guest quarters. It's perfect."

Frankie and Rebecca said their goodbyes to everyone and headed out into the clear, blue day. The colors were spectacular this time of year and Rebecca looked around in wonder. "Everything looks and smells so fresh here."

"I know. I always say this is my favorite time of year. Then summer comes and we swim and sail and I think, no, that is my favorite time of year. Then the fall comes and the colors are absolutely breathtaking. Then it snows and everything is covered in this pure white gleaming powder and I think, no, that's my favorite time of year. I guess I love all the seasons and look forward to each one."

"You're right. I forgot how pretty it is here, then I come back up and it reminds me all over again. I wish we could move out here." Rebecca's thoughts came out unconsciously.

"Why don't you?"

"The commute?" Rebecca shrugged. "Work?"

Rebecca and Frankie turned the corner and saw the new three-car garage structure with the new guest quarters above the garages. It was built to make it appear as though it had been constructed at the same time the house was built, which was well over one hundred years ago.

At the other end of the property, Uncle John and Nelson put Trevor and Toni on one of the horses and were walking them around the ring. Trevor held onto Toni as she leaned against him, giggling and smiling.

Rebecca waved to them and they all waved back. Uncle John made sure the kids were entertained and having fun. Rebecca could see how much John loved those kids. *If it wasn't for my father-in-law, John would have missed out and never would've known his great nephew and great niece.* He had removed himself so far from his family, but Nicholas Romano dragged him back in, practically kicking and screaming all the way, but it was worth it. All the pain, the ridicule and strife finally led him to a place of forgiveness, peace and love, Rebecca silently considered Uncle John's journey.

Frankie took Rebecca into the guest quarters and when she opened the apartment door, they found Jack and Anthony standing in the living room deep in a quiet conversation.

"Hi!" Frankie called to her brother-in-law.

"Hello Francesca. You look well." Anthony went over and kissed his sister-in-law. "I'm glad to see you aren't all tied up anymore."

Frankie rolled her eyes. "Jacqino thinks that I should only be doctoring puppies and kittens."

"What's wrong with that?" Jack countered, raising his hands up then dropping them quickly to his side.

But Anthony ignored their conversation and walked over to where Rebecca stood. He took her hand in his and looked into her eyes, while his brother and sister-in-law discussed her patients.

When Frankie and Jack realized that Anthony and Rebecca weren't listening to them at all, it was clear that they wanted to be alone, so they quietly left the apartment. "Something has changed between them . . ." Frankie considered.

"Love has a funny way of straightening everything out." Jack spoke tenderly to his wife's beautiful upturned face, remembering their own struggles.

"I know." Frankie sighed before Jack kissed her tenderly. Love managed to straighten out their lives, but Frankie was still surprised, because Rebecca had told her that their arrangement was only temporary or at least until the adoption process was complete. However, after seeing how they looked at each other now, it seemed to Frankie that their arrangement has changed.

⎯⎯⎯⎯⎯⎯⎯

That night, dinner on The Rose gave everyone a chance to catch up. They ate and joked and everyone couldn't help but notice how Rebecca and Anthony were constantly holding hands or looking into each other's eyes longingly.

After dinner, Jack decided to show Trevor around the ship. He wanted a little alone time with his new nephew. He explained that he built the ship and went into great detail about the time it took and the obstacles.

"Wow!" Trevor couldn't believe that his uncle built ships. That was so cool. Everything about the Romano men, Trevor was discovering, was way cool.

"Your mom and dad took The Rose on their honeymoon."

"What's a honeymoon?"

Jack thought about this for a bit then decided to go for the truth. "It is when a bride and groom take a trip right after their wedding so that they can get to know each other a little better." *Good answer,* Jack inwardly praised himself, completely shocked by how inquisitive this eight-year-old age bracket was. "It's a Romano tradition."

"What is?" Trevor wasn't following his uncle. Trevor had to stretch his neck all the way back to look at his uncle, who was even taller than his dad.

"Taking our new brides out to sea for the honeymoon," Jack answered, tapping Trevor on his forehead.

"Why?"

"Ask me that question in about ten years." Jack was onto this kid now, watching his nephew's green eyes squint.

Trevor studied his uncle and thought . . . *ten years! That's such a long time.* "Why do I have to wait that long for an answer? What if I forget to ask you that question in ten years?"

This kid is a whip, Jack thought. "Oh you won't. Trust me." Jack slapped Trevor on the shoulder, deciding to change the subject. "Have you been working out?"

Trevor nodded, smiling broadly at his new uncle.

◌◌◌

The next morning, Rebecca, Anthony and Trevor walked over to the farmhouse to have breakfast with the family. "Good morning." Anthony went over to Retta, the family's cook and housekeeper, kissing her on the cheek, before snatching a strip of bacon.

"Good morning to you too. Sleep well?" Retta asked.

"Like a baby." Anthony replied.

Francesca, Toni and Jack came into the kitchen and Toni squealed when she spotted Trevor.

Rebecca picked up the baby kissing her soft cheek. "Good morning Little One." She dubbed Toni, watching the baby smile.

Anthony stared at Rebecca in wonder, simply amazed how she seemed to go all soft around children.

Everyone enjoyed a hardy breakfast, except for Rebecca who sipped her steaming mug of coffee.

"So, is everyone up for sailing?" Jack asked rubbing his hands together quickly.

Toni squealed to her father.

"Good girl!" Jack patted his daughter's chubby, little arm.

Toni creased her forehead, her blue eyes filling like crystal pools of water, as she looked at Trevor.

"Yes, Trevor too." Frankie made sure her daughter understood. "But first we all have to get cleaned up."

Toni started wailing.

"Toni, you have to take a bath and so does Trevor." Frankie quietly reasoned with the toddler, who was suddenly beyond consoling.

"I will take a quick shower and be right back, Little One, okay . . ." Trevor promised her, squeezing her little hand, using the nickname his mother used only moments before.

"See!" Frankie said to her darling daughter. Frankie was actually getting a little panicky. Trevor was leaving in a day and she had a sinking suspicion that her daughter was not going to take that very well. She was so glad to see that Trevor looked happy, that her best friend and brother-in-law looked so in love and that her daughter had a cousin of her own, but she was sensing that the fallout was going to be bad when they left. Really bad!

Later that morning, armed with several picnic baskets prepared by Retta, the group started out on their short sailing journey. Toni absolutely loved it and was beaming from ear to ear. Jack and Frankie had been taking her out on the water since before she was born.

When they started out, everything seemed fine. Jack kept the sailboat at a slow, even pace. Then, about a half an hour into the trip, Anthony looked over at Trevor and immediately knew that something was wrong. Trevor looked at Anthony and Anthony spotted it. It was a look of sheer terror upon the young boy's face, something he had never seen before. Anthony could tell that Trevor was completely immobilized by fear. The look in Trevor's eyes caused Anthony to react instantly, but slowly. Anthony calmly walked over to his son, smiling serenely. He sat down beside Trevor before he pulled him up and into his strong embrace, taking his goddaughter into his arms as well.

Anthony whispered to Trevor in Italian, *"Bambino panico?"*

Trevor wrapped his little arm tightly around his father's neck keeping his other little arm secured around Toni. The baby just giggled and drooled on them. "I'm scared." Trevor admitted into his dad's ear quietly.

"I'm right here Son." Anthony whispered before pressing a kiss to his son's forehead then duplicating the kiss onto his goddaughter. "Tell me what frightens you." Anthony wanted to know. He wanted to crush all of his son's fears. He wanted to show him that nothing would ever harm him.

"I'm afraid that the boat will crash or flip over and we will drown." Trevor raised wide glistening bright green eyes to Anthony.

"I can see how that might be upsetting to you. But since you are wearing a lifejacket and Toni is wearing a lifejacket, you will both float on top of the water." Anthony replied softly, rubbing his back.

"But you aren't!" Trevor whispered fiercely. "And neither is Mom or Uncle Jack or Aunt Frankie."

Anthony's thoughts halted, assimilating the fact that Trevor just referred to his brother as Uncle Jack and his sister-in-law as Aunt Frankie. "I see." Anthony calmly continued to hold his son tight. "But Uncle Jack and I are very strong swimmers and we have been sailing our whole lives so . . ."

Trevor cut him to the quick, "What if something hits your head and you can't swim?"

"Good point." Anthony got up and placed Trevor on the bench. "Stay right here and hold onto Toni." Anthony smiled, placing Toni onto Trevor's lap. Trevor held onto Toni, as she leaned back into his arms. Anthony went over to a bench in the middle of the sailboat and opened the lid. He reached in and pulled out four more lifejackets. He put one on and clipped up the front. Anthony tossed a jacket to Jack and Jack did the same. Anthony walked past Trevor smiling, then handed one to Frankie and Rebecca, kissing his wife's sun-warmed cheek. He walked back over to his son and took hold. "Better?"

"Yes." Trevor quickly replied before he grabbed onto Anthony.

This time Trevor's grip wasn't so desperate. Anthony held onto his son and goddaughter sensing a stirring in the deepest part of his soul—it was a commitment to protect.

Rebecca came over and sat down with them. Trevor jumped over and onto her lap. When Toni cried, Trevor picked her up and placed her on his lap. "They're breaking my legs and I love it." Rebecca whispered to Anthony, leaning against the man she loved.

Anthony wrapped his arm around his wife's shoulders holding her tightly while stroking his son's leg with his free hand.

Frankie walked back over to Jack who was still stationed at the helm and put her arms around his waist. "They look so happy." Frankie whispered up to her very tall husband, before she turned to watch Anthony kiss her best friend's cheek.

"Yes. I'm glad Anthony remained patient while Rebecca found his love."

Frankie nodded, suddenly feeling very emotional, because she was so happy for her best friend.

In no time at all, Trevor relaxed and stood on a box in front of Jack to take the helm. Jack could see how excited he was, as Trevor looked up at him with gleaming green eyes.

Trevor looked out and saw a fortress high up on a mountain. "What's that?" Trevor pointed in surprise.

"West Point," Jack answered his new nephew. "Right there is Triumphant Point."

Trevor looked back and Jack knew that his nephew had questions. So Jack described the United States Military Academy. Jack was amazed how quickly Trevor absorbed information. *The kid is like a sponge!* To Jack's surprise, Trevor was already referring to the sailboat in sailor's terms after only hearing them once.

By the time they returned to the farm, Frankie could see that Toni was about to pass out and needed a nap. Retta took Toni inside for one with no argument.

Frankie thought while her daughter was napping she would check on her patient. Trevor asked if he could go with her. When Frankie and Trevor entered the animal hospital, the waiting room was empty and clean. The receptionist's area was very tidy with files in a rack by the computer. Everything was labeled and Trevor read off some of the labels. "Pat-i-ents."

"Patients." Frankie corrected his pronunciation.

"Billing and Re . . ." Trevor wasn't sure how to pronounce the last word.

Frankie looked and said, "Receivables."

"Oh."

"That means people who've paid for their visit."

Trevor nodded his head understanding the need to get money. His real mother told him when he had to leave the apartment so that she could make some money. He knew that people needed it all the time.

Frankie took him in the back where the hospital area was located. At the moment, she only had one animal in the hospital. Robin, her assistant, left a note when she last medicated the boxer that was staying in the hospital.

Trevor started to look around. He knelt down and looked at the dog in the crate. He looked so much like Bruno, but had more black than brown and floppy ears instead of pointy ones. "Who is this Aunt Frankie?" Trevor pointed.

"This is Buddy." Frankie had a gift that enabled her to see into the future. It was an amazing sense to have and Frankie was aware of this gift since she was a very young girl. The dream she had last night showed a young man with her daughter. He was strong and tall and wore a perfectly pressed uniform. The details were what gave her little glimpses into the future, because the young man could have been anyone, except for one distinguishing characteristic, green eyes. They were Trevor's incredible, sparkling green eyes. Like most dreams, Frankie would keep those sweet details a secret and let everyone see for themselves what the future held.

Trevor tried to reach through the bars to pet the dog.

"Here honey, this is a better way to pet him." Frankie opened up the crate and Trevor reached in to pet the large dog. "Buddy's going to like that, even though he is asleep because of the medication we gave him. He will still know you're here."

"Is he sick?" Trevor looked at his aunt.

"Yes. When we got him he wasn't doing so well, but he's getting better slowly. Buddy is a boxer just like Bruno, but someone abandoned him and when the police found him, they brought him to my animal hospital."

"Why?"

"Well they know that I have a boxer and they know I could care for him." Frankie cupped the back of her nephew's head studying his deep-green eyes that seemed far too old for his age.

"He doesn't have a family?" Trevor knew how that felt.

"Well, we are his family now."

"Like me?" Trevor asked.

"Exactly honey." Frankie reassured.

Trevor continued to pet the dog. He felt a connection to this dog and couldn't resist touching the fur right between the dog's eyes that was shiny black and very soft. Trevor never saw a dog lie so still. "How long is he going to sleep for?"

"He's on some strong medicines right now and that makes him sleep a lot. He will probably sleep on and off for the next few days."

"Aunt Frankie, would it be okay if I stay here while Toni takes her nap?" Trevor asked.

"Sure. I have some paperwork to do, so that would be fine." Frankie got up and went over to her desk.

As Frankie worked, Trevor petted and spoke softly to Buddy. "It's okay, boy. Aunt Frankie is going to make you all better." Trevor watched as the dog struggled to open his eyes. Trevor smiled and reached over kissing the dog right on the top of his head. Buddy closed his eyes and lowered his ears, as Trevor continued to stroke and console the sick animal. A few moments later, Trevor was asleep, half in the crate with Buddy and half on the floor, with his hand resting on Buddy's head.

Later on that evening, they all ate outside on the terrace that overlooked the river and during the meal Frankie could see that Anthony and Rebecca needed some time alone. She insisted that the kids sleep in the farmhouse tonight and Toni started to wail.

"What?" Frankie asked her daughter softly.

"Twevor?" Toni asked on a wail, mispronouncing his name.

"Yes, Trevor is staying in the farmhouse tonight too. Is that okay Trevor?"

"Sure." Trevor took hold of Toni's little hands and helped her to walk along the path, with the dogs trotting along behind them.

"Oh boy. Toni is going to be a basket case when you leave. She is SO attached to Trevor." Frankie spoke quietly to Rebecca, watching Trevor help Toni walk to the gazebo.

"I know." Rebecca seemed worried too. "Maybe we should mark the calendar when we are coming back for a visit. That might help her handle the separation better."

"I hope you're right!" Frankie wasn't too sure.

Later on after dinner, Anthony and Rebecca walked back to the guest cottage alone. Once inside, Anthony instantly took Rebecca into his arms and started to kiss her deeply. "Darling," he groaned, watching her lean back to look into his eyes. Anthony studied her face before he carefully swept her up, off her feet, carrying her into the bedroom.

"Alone at last." Rebecca whispered.

"What if Trevor becomes frightened and needs one of us during the middle of the night?" Anthony lowered her feet to the floor carefully.

"We'll keep our clothes close." Rebecca suggested as she toed off her sneakers.

"Good thinking." Anthony did the same before he leaned down to kiss her lips. He swept his tongue along the seam of her lips urging her to open for him. Slowly he met her tongue with gentleness, tenderness. Anthony circled his tongue around hers and felt Rebecca sway. *She likes to get kissed,* Anthony secretly knew. So he continued the kiss by turning his head to the right, then to the left, never breaking the seal of lips to lips. When she moaned, he knew he had her right where he wanted her. Slowly, Anthony removed her sweater, dropping it to the floor. "Wow." Anthony was shocked to see that she was wearing a teddy beneath the sweater that continued into the waistband of her jeans.

Rebecca giggled.

"Santa Madre." Anthony swept the back of his hand across his forehead that instantly broke out in a sweat.

Rebecca giggled. She reached for his pullover lifting it up and over his head, dropping it onto the floor near hers. "Wow." Rebecca copied Anthony. "If you walked around without a shirt in the city, women would be begging you to marry them."

"Like you did?" Anthony teased.

Rebecca giggled. "Guilty as charged."

"Really . . ." Anthony was caught off-guard by her response.

"Uh huh . . ." Rebecca ran her fingers lightly over each pectoral muscle. *Simply irresistible,* she thought.

Anthony unbuttoned her jeans, pulling them down to her ankles before helping her step out of them. He stood back to study the teddy. "Does this come with an instruction manual?" Anthony ran a fingertip along the bow at her waist.

Rebecca laughed. "I don't believe so . . ." Rebecca unbuttoned Anthony's jeans, watching them fall to the floor.

"Hmmm . . ." Anthony peeled off his boxers and kicked both his jeans and boxers to the side before he led her over to the bed. He sat her down on the edge studying the lingerie.

Rebecca watched as Anthony's eyes devoured her, sending the thrill of anticipated pleasure along her skin.

Anthony gently nudged her to lay back. He spread her legs and noticed two snaps. He undid the snaps and in one movement, slid his long finger into her warm silky depths. He heard her gasp and watched her eyes close, as her head arched back when he stroked her essence with his thumb. Each circular movement was coupled with deeper and more forceful strokes until her breathing changed to pants.

"Anthony." Rebecca moaned, struggling to open her eyes.

Anthony continued to stroke her and when she began to moan louder, he replaced his finger with his tongue listening to her softly call his name. He felt her pearl swell with pleasure as he took it into his mouth.

"Anthony . . . Anthony," she murmured.

He knew she was on the verge of coming and it was at that moment that he rose above her. Standing at the edge of the bed, he pulled her toward him, impaling her with his length.

"Oh God." Rebecca groaned as the first orgasm gripped her, causing her legs to quiver.

"Again." Anthony growled, holding back his need to expel his semen into her warm silky depths.

"Anthony . . ." Rebecca held out her arms, encouraging him to hold her.

Anthony lowered himself feeling her wrap her trembling legs high around his back as he pushed into her. Not powerful thrusts but deep, slow thrusts. He kissed her and when she arched her neck, he knew she was close. He felt her run her fingers through his hair, then her sighs grew into a loud whimper. Anthony felt her climax contract along the length of his membrane until he could no longer wait. He came fast and feverishly, as he pumped powerfully into her, feeling his sperm hurtling deep into her smooth depths.

"Wow." Rebecca breathed. "No one's ever done that to me before."

Anthony rolled to his side. He studied her lovely face, skimming light fingertips along her flushed porcelain cheek before he whispered, *"Cara mia."*

"I was wondering when you were going to start speaking to me in another language." Rebecca instantly closed her mouth, because he had started to remove the rest of her teddy. When she watched Anthony take her nipple into his mouth, she sighed. "Oh that feels so good . . ."

Chapter Eleven

Their need for each other grows . . .

Nearly a month later, while at Romano Enterprises, Anthony was charging through his work determined to get out of RE by six, the latest. He was leaving for France late that night and wanted to spend as much time with his wife and son before he left. He needed to meet a wholesaler who was giving the new buyer for RE a hard time. This wholesaler did not take kindly to working with women in general, let alone a woman from America. Anthony was on the phone with this nitwit in a last ditch effort to resolve their differences, when a soft knock on his office door interrupted his thoughts. He was pleasantly surprised to see Rebecca peek her head in. Anthony smiled broadly, stood up from behind his desk, motioning for her to come in. He watched as she walked in soundlessly closing the door behind her, secretively securing the lock on the handle.

Rebecca turned back to Anthony returning the smile. He was speaking in a foreign tongue which, funny enough, Rebecca currently found to be very stimulating. She was impressed with how many languages Anthony was fluent in and it spoke volumes about his intellect.

Anthony wondered why Rebecca was wearing a raincoat, when the sun was shining so brightly today that he was forced to lower the blinds in his office. Besides the raincoat, he noticed that she wore a pair of very black, unusually high spiked heels with red soles. Anthony watched her make her way past the seating arrangement of the large, overstuffed high-back chairs that circled a low, round glass table. Ever since the press had hammered her about her clothing, Rebecca was extremely careful about what she wore and Anthony just assumed it must be a new fashion trend. He watched as she ran her red fingernail along the top of one chair, then the other circling her way back toward his desk.

Anthony was listening to the wholesaler's complaints about the new buyer and that the prices she wanted to pay for the furniture were ridiculously low. He whined that Anthony would make a hundred times that when he sold it in America. It was the same story, but a different country and a different wholesaler.

Anthony placed his hand over the receiver whispering to her, "Take off your coat. I'll only be another minute."

Rebecca mouthed the word 'okay.' She knew that tonight they would probably have very little time before he left on his business trip. So she figured she would make the most of her lunch break. Slowly, she started to untie the belt to her raincoat, letting the sash fall to her sides still looped through the belt-loops. Pausing, Rebecca raised her head, because she wanted to see her husband's reaction.

Anthony watched as she started to unbutton the top button, then the next and the next and the next. Anthony was speaking to the distributor when Rebecca opened her coat slowly to reveal that she wore only a black lace strapless bra and matching bikini panties with those black high heels. She dropped the coat to the floor and in that same instant Anthony dropped the phone, sending it crashing to his desk.

"I'm so hungry . . ." Rebecca breathed, placing one hand on her tiny waist and the other over the lowest part of her abdomen. "And there is only one thing that is going to satisfy me." Rebecca turned around to reveal that the lace panty was actually a g-string that revealed her highly defined derrière.

Anthony could hear the distributor from the discarded phone shouting. Anthony felt for the phone blindly, never taking his eyes off his wife. After several failed attempts, he finally managed to hang it up. Backing away from his desk, he began to speak in his native tongue.

At first, Rebecca couldn't make out the language, because he was speaking so rapidly. Ignoring his reaction, Rebecca wound her way back around the seating arrangement toward Anthony's desk. Sliding between him and the desk, she pushed him further away from his desk. She jerked on his tie then pushed her tongue into his mouth. She wanted to have sex. She didn't want to make love. She didn't want Anthony to be sweet or tender. She didn't want him to whisper in her ear. She wanted to be pawed and pulled and plowed. She wanted to feel good *and he had better be damn quick about it!*

It became vibrantly clear to Anthony what she wanted. He pulled her hair back to get her tongue out of his mouth, which caused her to smile. Then he plundered her mouth with the force she was looking for and heard her moan. She pulled at his clothes and when his tie was removed and his shirt unbuttoned Anthony ripped the lace bra apart by grabbing the fabric with both hands at the center between her deep V. Her breasts tumbled out and he ravished her. He bit the soft flesh then heard her sigh. He tugged and squeezed to her audible groans. When she reached for the hook and eye on his trousers, he batted her hands away. He was in control now. He released his shaft, pulled the lacey fabric bottom to the side and drove into her without any regard for foreplay or delicacy. He took her right there on his desk, holding her fast to him while he forcefully impaled her.

At that precise moment, Rebecca realized that this was it. Anthony was the only man for her. *He's 'the one!'* He was her life and no other man would ever come close. When she exhaled in ecstasy, he pushed into her deepest depths barely pausing for her release to be completed. *What a lover! What a man! What a husband! One who fills my every need, my every wish,* Rebecca silently acknowledged.

Anthony's release was powerful and with it drew the knowledge that he would never love another. It was Rebecca for him, always and for all time.

When each was thoroughly spent and reality crept back into their minds, Anthony lifted her up from the desk brushing back the curls that were stuck to her forehead. "I hope that satisfied you, darling?" Anthony asked softly, once again finding himself completely out of breath.

"I think that should hold me over until dinner!" Rebecca quipped, listening to Anthony chuckle in that deep tone, while he tenderly touched her breasts.

Anthony was already noticing the reddened spots where she was probably going to bruise over, giving each spot a feather light touch followed by a tender kiss. He stepped away from the desk to pick up her raincoat. He watched as she paraded her nearly nude body on those dangerously high, high heels toward him. He helped her slip her arms into the sleeves leaving the coat open, obviously still wanting him to touch her, which, of course, he was only too happy to provide.

Rebecca listened as he spoke many unfamiliar words in Italian to her. She turned her head to the side waiting for the translation, while he tenderly touched her.

"I said, 'My vixen, my very hot wife, my very sexy vivacious wife.'" Anthony was still caressing her breast. "Please feel free to stop by for lunch anytime." Anthony smiled making the translation complete.

"I'll do that." Rebecca giggled while she caressed his chest before buttoning his dress shirt.

Anthony looked around and saw the contents of his desktop on the floor and he couldn't stop the smile that formed upon his face. "Darling, how did you get here?"

"I took the subway," Rebecca answered in a soft, careless tone, as Anthony took another taste of her. His head shot up and when he opened his mouth wide ready to launch a fit, she stopped him. "Relax, relax. Carlo took me," Rebecca reassured rolling her eyes. "The man is the human version of a barnacle."

"Carlo." Anthony sighed, quietly thanking God for sending the perfect bodyguard for his extremely overactive wife. "The man is a saint!" Anthony decided. "Remind me to give him a raise."

"Why? That will only encourage his present bad behavior." Rebecca lifted on tiptoes to place a kiss on her husband's handsome jaw. *God, that jaw is the sexiest part of him,* she thought. *No, all of him is sexy, some parts more than others.*

"Is he waiting for you?" Anthony tenderly skimmed his thumb along her rosy cheek.

"Pleeeaaassseee, look for yourself." Rebecca rolled her eyes dramatically.

Chapter Twelve
Sailing through uncharted territory . . .

Anthony sat in his suite in Paris at a lovely French writing desk on the second day of his business trip, totally unable to control his wandering mind. All he thought about was his wife, *his wife*. Wow, the phrase still seemed so unfamiliar to him. Although their days were filled with work and Trevor, their nights were filled with indescribable passion and tenderness. It was nothing short of amazing, bordering on the unbelievable.

Sipping his rich dark coffee, Anthony stood up and looked out onto the quiet street below. Paris moved at a snail's pace compared to New York and it seemed that no matter where he was or what he was doing, his thoughts constantly drifted back to Rebecca and their small son, Trevor. He wished he could have brought them with him. *Maybe when school lets out,* Anthony considered silently. For the first time in his life, he felt complete, whole and enriched beyond measure. But something deep down in his gut told him that Rebecca was still holding something back. *I just can't put my finger on it.* Anthony pressed his lips together tightly. *We are so close to having it all, but something or someone is blocking our path!* He prayed that he would discover whatever the hell it was before it interfered with their marriage.

Later that morning, Anthony was finishing up with the distributor who was clearly going to be a problem with the new buyer for Romano Enterprises, as he discreetly checked his watch. Instead of thinking of a way to maneuver this distributor into working with the new buyer, he was mentally calculating how many hours until he would be home. With the six hour difference between New York and Paris, he should be back in New York by eight, maybe nine at the latest. Flying by private jet knocked a good hour off the normal commercial flight check-in and baggage retrieval aggravations.

Several hours later, with absolutely no progress made, Anthony was on his way home. He tried to call Rebecca on her cell phone, but it wasn't going through. He tried the apartment and Sofia picked up.

"Hello?" Sofia asked into the phone.

"Sofia it's Anthony."

"Hi! How is Paris?"

"Boring." Anthony used Trevor's favorite word he associated with school.

Sofia laughed. "Oh boy . . . you sound exactly like Trevor."

Anthony chuckled. "I couldn't get a cell call through to Rebecca."

"We're having a terrible storm here. Raining and thundering. Maybe that's why. Trevor is watching it from the living room."

"Is Rebecca home?" Anthony was missing his family and wanted to get home as soon as possible. Jetting all over God's green earth for this one-of-a-kind piece of furniture or that crystal-ware had definitely lost its appeal.

"No. Not yet. Let me get Trevor. Hold on." Sofia called for Trevor with her hand over the receiver. Trevor came running into the kitchen and Sofia explained who was on the phone. "It's your dad!" Sofia exclaimed.

"Dad!" Trevor shouted, because his dad was in Paris which was really, really far away.

"Hello Son. How are you?" Anthony spoke softly.

"Good." Trevor lowered his voice, because he could hear Anthony just fine.

"How was school?"

"Boring," Trevor grumbled.

Anthony chuckled, certain that Trevor was bored with school, because he was so much brighter than his grade level. He was considering having him tested, but that could wait until he had a better time to discuss that with Rebecca. "I will be home in a few hours, hopefully not too late."

"Really, that's great, because me and Mom have been missing you . . . Mom and I," Trevor corrected himself.

"I miss you too." Anthony was thrilled to hear that they were missing him. "Where is your Mom?"

"She's still working."

"Oh okay. When is she coming home?"

"I don't know. I'll put Sofee back on. We are getting a really bad storm Dad, so be careful."

"Okay I will." Anthony smiled simply amazed that an eight-year-old was telling him to be careful.

"Love you Dad."

"Love you too Son."

"Hello." Sofia took the phone back.

"When is Rebecca coming home?"

"I'm not sure. She said she was working very late, so I brought an overnight bag with me."

"Oh I see. Well, I should be arriving at the airport in about three hours, but you can stay so you won't have to go out in the storm. Let Rebecca know when she can expect me, alright?"

"Okay. We'll see you later."

Anthony disengaged the call then began to worry. *Why wasn't Rebecca home yet? Why couldn't he reach her on her cell?* He started to pace the cabin until the weather started jostling the jet around, forcing him to take his seat. He sent her a few text messages, but she didn't respond. Two hours later, his cell phone started to ring. He thought it might be Rebecca, but saw the call was from Jack.

"Anthony." Jack spoke carefully.

"Hey. I'm on my way home from Paris. What's up?"

There was a long pause.

"Rebecca," Jack spoke in a whispered tone, his phone crackling from the lightning.

Anthony jumped up from his seat, feeling a jolt from head to toe as though the plane had been struck by lightening. His mind whirled with scenarios. Anthony felt a shiver run down his spine, his heart beating wildly in his chest.

There was no easy way to say it. Jack silently prayed for the strength his brother was going to need to get through this. "She's been shot," Jack whispered.

"My God." Anthony expelled the words on an exhale before falling into his seat.

"I don't have all the details. We are at the hospital now. I have a car coming to get you because I have Paul and Martin picking up Rebecca's parents and Mom and Dad."

"How serious is it?" Anthony asked, but deep down he already knew the answer, because Jack was sending for their parents.

"Very . . ." Jack didn't hesitate and didn't want to lie to his brother. The doctors already told him it was highly unlikely she was going to survive.

"I can't believe this." Anthony was in shock.

"I know. We are praying for her, brother. Francesca and I are here."

"Okay." Anthony calculated the time. "Maybe another forty-five minutes tops."

"We'll be here."

When they hung up, Anthony began to pace the aircraft like a half-crazed, caged animal. *Doesn't know the details? How did this happen? I can't believe this. Is it that serious? Yes!* Anthony's mind was replaying the conversation over and over again, making him slowly go out of his mind.

In the hospital, it seemed like every cop in the city was standing in the halls and in the waiting areas. It was swarming with men and women in blue, because that's what they did when one of their own got shot. Some were in plainclothes and others in their street uniforms. Two officers, who were in more decorative uniforms, approached Jack.

Jack took a deep breath. "I told him that his wife was shot, but I didn't tell him anything else."

Chief Franks and Captain Rice nodded. A sharp blade of lightning, followed by a loud rumble of thunder lit and shook the hospital.

"I told him that I would send a car to get him. I have to make a phone call." Jack was clearly shaken and Francesca was crying softly by his side.

"I'll pick him up. I'll leave now," Captain Rice insisted.

"Thank you." Jack turned away from them and tried to console his grief-stricken wife. Jack couldn't believe that Rebecca was a cop and that she had been working undercover for the past three years. Even his wife, who was Rebecca's best friend, had no clue! Obviously she was very good at undercover work, because nobody knew anything and no one saw this coming.

"She told me a long time ago that everyone has secrets." Frankie began to sob again.

"Shhh, sweetheart, she's in the hands of the best doctors in the world." Jack held her tightly trying to absorb her pain.

Jack's parents arrived at about the same time Rebecca's parents and brother did and they couldn't believe how many police officers were at the hospital.

"Was an officer shot tonight besides Rebecca?" Rebecca's mother questioned before taking another shuddering breath.

Jack gathered everyone together in one of the waiting rooms and made them all take a seat. He told them all that Rebecca was an undercover cop and that was precisely when Rebecca's mother, Victoria McFarlan fainted. While the nurses helped to revive her, the other women cried. Mr. McFarlan was trying to comfort Francesca, while Stephen, Rebecca's brother, was doing his best to comfort Jack's mother.

Nicholas took Jack to the side and in a low voice so that no one would hear him he said, "I can't believe this."

"I know. I can't believe it either."

"Anthony doesn't know that she is a policeman, I mean, policewoman?"

"No. According to the chief he had no idea." Jack pointed to the man wearing the only white shirt among the multitude of officers. "She was undercover."

"My God, this is terrible. And the boy?" Nicholas asked, feeling his stomach rolling uncontrollably.

"Trevor is at home with Sofia. I didn't want to tell her such terrible news over the phone, so Captain Rice went to speak to her in person before he went to the airport to pick-up Anthony."

"What are the doctors saying?" Nicholas was rubbing his hand along his forehead that was pounding fiercely.

"Nothing good." Jack filled him in.

"Anthony . . . he is going to be inconsolable." Nicholas didn't even have the words to express the grief Anthony would experience if he lost Rebecca.

"I know."

"And they have just found each other. I mean truly found each other."

"I know." Jack lowered his head, shaking it from side to side, finding this whole situation so hard to believe.

Chief Franks walked up to Jack and the senior Romano. He knew all the wealthy campaign donors well. "Captain Rice has informed me that he has arrived at the airport and your brother's jet just landed."

"Thank you." Nicholas was relieved that his son could be here with his dying wife, shivering visibly when he heard the low, menacing rumble of thunder.

"Sir . . . do you want me to tell him, or do you want to tell him?" Chief Franks would have preferred the latter, but at this point, he was prepared to do his job.

"Maybe we should find a room and we can all tell him. Then he can speak with the doctors." Jack suggested.

"That might be best."

Once at the hospital Anthony ran behind Captain Rice who, after introducing himself on the tarmac in the pouring rain, remained eerily silent for the entire drive to the hospital. Anthony kept peppering him with questions like, 'why is a Captain from the NYPD picking me up,' but Rice clamped his mouth shut.

Anthony ran right up to his father and Jack. "Where is she?"

"She's still in the operating room. Come this way, we have a room so that we can talk." Jack saw how pale his brother looked.

Anthony nodded. "Why are there so many cops here?" Anthony whispered, positively floored by the number of police vehicles outside and the number of uniformed officers inside.

They filed into a small room off the main hallway and once the door was closed Chief Franks began. "I am very sorry that your wife was shot tonight Mr. Romano."

"Thank you." Anthony didn't know why this high ranking police official was here. There must have been some type of police involvement in this entire situation.

"Rebecca has been an undercover officer with the Thirty-fourth Precinct . . ."

"WHAT?" Anthony bellowed cutting him off. "UNDERCOVER! What the hell are you talking about?"

"Anthony, let him finish . . ." Jack placed a hand onto his brother's shoulder to try to calm him.

"This is true?" Anthony spun around, yanking his brother's hand from off his shoulder.

"Yes."

"Oh my God!" Anthony raked a hand through his wet hair.

"Officer Romano has been working an undercover assignment for nearly three years."

"Officer Romano . . . three years . . ." Anthony whispered.

"Yes sir. She has been trying to apprehend the single most-wanted sex trafficker in the world. He is a radical from the Middle East with a penchant for American teenage virgins."

"Oh my God." Nicholas fell into a vacant seat. Hearing the words 'Officer Romano' and 'sex trafficker' sent his mind reeling.

"Tonight, everything that could go wrong did go wrong . . ." Chief Franks continued, speaking without emotion. "Officer Romano, who always set herself up as a lost teenage girl, was shot in the line of duty." A low rumble of thunder announced that the storm wasn't even close to being over.

Anthony couldn't process this information. "This can't be happening."

"Officer Romano's injuries are life threatening because, as an undercover officer, she could not wear her bulletproof vest or carry her service weapon. Unfortunately, she was completely vulnerable."

"Service weapon . . ." Anthony muttered.

"It takes a special kind of person to do this kind of work."

Anthony stood stone still. He kept thinking how Rebecca watched everything she ate, how she was constantly running, constantly staying as fit as she could. "She works at the mental health clinic. I don't understand."

"She has degrees in psychology and criminal justice, sir and we arranged for her to get a job at the mental health clinic in order to get her on the inside. A supervisor at the clinic was sending lost teenagers in our target's direction. Especially virgins."

Anthony walked over to the corner of the room feeling the urge to vomit.

Jack looked at the chief signaling him to stop, but Franks ignored him and continued.

"Your wife, Mr. Romano, saved more of our lost young girls than any other officer on the payroll of this great city. She has never been honored or celebrated for her tireless work."

Anthony turned back toward the room full of occupants, but he only saw his father who was cradling his head in his hands, as pale as a ghost.

"We believe the supervisor at the mental health clinic figured it out." Chief Franks paused gathering his thoughts. "This supervisor personally set up the meetings between the teenagers and this . . . scumbag. Officer Romano would go to some of the sleaziest places in the city to talk the girls out of it. That is when we would relocate the girl from the area. Some never wanted to go home and in some cases, we would relocate entire families because this man wanted his virgins and would stop at nothing to get them." The chief paused again to take a deep breath. "Officer Romano was early, she was always early and she was setting up when Boris, our perpetrator, walked right into the hotel room. He had the keycard that opened the lock. Once he was inside, she was trapped. When the officers arrived about ten minutes later, they heard loud noises coming from inside the room. The door was bolted from the inside, but several detectives broke down the door and stormed in. Officer Romano was badly beaten."

"Jesus . . ." Jack whispered as he leaned against the wall, no longer able to stand on his wobbly knees.

"Boris was beaten worse. Officer Romano is one tough cop and she was not going down, not without a bullet. He was waving around his semi-automatic and started shooting randomly when the other officers broke in. He knew he was going to die and like most radicals, they don't care to leave this earth without taking a few innocent souls with them. We had strict orders from the Justice Department in Washington that we could shoot-to-kill."

Nicholas took a deep strangled breath.

"His first shot hit Officer Romano right here." Chief Franks pointed to his heart.

Tears streamed down Anthony's face and Jack and Nicholas ran to comfort him. "I can't lose her . . . I can't." Anthony fell into his father's open embrace.

"Shhh my son." Nicholas tried to absorb his son's hurt. His daughter-in-law was such a brave, strong woman who worked to save others. Why, even the boy she adopted was just another lost soul who needed a mother and a father and she gave of herself willingly. At that moment, Nicholas felt such love for her.

"She wanted to help others. She is so noble." Nicholas spoke softly, which only made Anthony cry harder.

Anthony was already beyond in love with her and when he thought he couldn't love her anymore, he now found another reason to love her. *She carried my name into battle. She fought for children everyday. My God, she is such a gift to humanity.*

Chief Franks continued in that same unemotional tone while tears streamed down his face. "Boris is dead and the supervisor from the clinic who coordinated the rapes and human trafficking is dead as well." Chief Franks swiped viciously at his tears. There was still one more part that Chief Franks decided to leave to the doctors. He had said enough. "I know that the doctors want to talk to you." Chief Franks embraced Anthony with incredible strength then both the chief and Captain Rice left soundlessly.

Nicholas and Jack took hold of Anthony, enveloping him with their strength and comfort. "I called Cousin Michael. He should be here any minute." Jack spoke softly.

Anthony knew that they called their cousin, Father Michael, to give Rebecca her Last Rites.

What followed was more terrifying news! Doctors who were not performing the surgery came in next and introduced themselves, but Anthony couldn't remember their names. He couldn't squash the fear that kept rising up to tear him down. The doctors were there strictly to explain the situation. With an anatomical picture, along with a model of a heart, they started to explain the position of the bullet. Anthony's mind literally shut down. All he could think about was that the woman he loved, the woman he could only love, was dying at this very moment and there was nothing he could do about it. *Nothing!*

"Many of the officers are giving blood, because at this rate we may have to transfuse your wife many times before the night is over."

Doctors never mince their words. Jack shook visibly recalling when his first wife died.

"There is another complication."

Instantly, Anthony snapped out of the trance he was in. "Complication?" Anthony muttered, thinking that there was no hope for the woman he loved.

"The pregnancy," one of the doctors explained.

"Pregnancy?" Anthony asked softly. "I didn't . . . she didn't tell me."

"A month tops. She may not have known yet, herself."

Anthony fell to his knees, *"My God."* After several minutes Anthony felt someone lift him to his feet, it was his father. Anthony clutched his father like a drowning man holding on for dear life. He was exhausted, as though he had been treading water for days. Forcing his mind to work he asked, "Where was Carlo?"

"She lost him then a cop pulled him over for a minor traffic infraction. It was all part of the operation. Rebecca had to lose him, or he could have blown everything they had worked on for years. He never caught up with her after that, but kept combing the city looking for her. By the time he stumbled onto the commotion on Bleecker Street, it was already too late."

Anthony was absolutely sick to his stomach unable to comprehend how his wife kept all of this to herself, kept all of this from him. *This was the missing piece!* He prayed he would find the missing piece to the puzzle, the thing that was blocking their complete harmony and love and now that he found it, he didn't want it. Anthony walked over to the corner placing his hands high up on each wall, hanging his head in sheer exhaustion.

☙

Captain Thomas Rice quietly knocked on the door.

Sofia answered it after peeking through the peephole and disabling the alarm. The tall officer came into the foyer quickly removing his hat. She knew Captain Rice a long time. The first time she met him was immediately after she was assaulted.

"Ma'am. I thought I would come by and give you an update and check on you. Do you or Officer Romano's son need anything?"

"No." Sofia answered quietly, her voice audibly shaky. "Please come in."

Captain Rice followed Sofia. "I have stationed a man right outside the apartment door." Captain Rice stated concisely.

"Thank you." Sofia walked straight into the kitchen. That was the only place she found comfort. So many things were running through her mind . . . like the time a madman slashed her face in an effort to rape and kill her. Her attacker would have been successful, if not for the help from a Good Samaritan. She openly shuddered, thunder rumbling in the distance.

Captain Rice noticed her shivering, but busied his hands by rolling the rim of his hat between his fingers, not sure what to do or say next. As long as he lived, Thomas would never forget Sofia or that night. He was new to the police force, still technically a rookie. As his mind traveled back in time, he remembered he was working the dreaded graveyard shift. The call came over his radio of an assault and when he arrived on scene, there she was . . . *Sofia.* She lay motionless on the ground with a dead man on top of her. Half her clothes were ripped off of her body and blood gushed from her face and scalp. The knife that the perpetrator used on her was sticking out of the neck of her attacker, his blood pooling on the ground. Thomas pulled his mind back to the present watching as she moved around the kitchen silently putting the makings of a meal together.

"Ma'am, I didn't come here to eat."

"Please call me by my name." Sofia stopped to look at him. "We've known each other for almost twenty years Thomas."

"Yes Sofia, we have."

The thunder rumbled and the lightning clapped again, making her jump.

"Sofia. I came to tell you that it doesn't look good . . . ya know . . . for Officer Romano . . . Rebecca and the baby." Thomas ran an open hand over his shaved head. *Christ, this was one hell of a night! Every time he had the worst night of his career, Sofia was involved . . . what the fuck?*

"The baby?" Sofia's strangled voice cracked.

"Yes."

Sofia's hands froze above the food she was preparing. She lowered her head, unable to hold it together a minute longer and began to cry.

Thomas walked up behind her and carefully turned her around pulling her into his steady embrace, softly consoling her, resting his head on top of her smooth, black hair.

Many minutes later, Sofia lifted her head to look into glittering blue eyes. "Trevor is so smart. He will know that something is very wrong when I am here in the morning and his parents aren't. I don't know what to do."

"Let me make a few phone calls and find out what the family wants to do. Come here." Thomas walked her over to the island and helped her onto a stool. He swept away a tear that was traveling down the side of her face where the angry scars from her attack remained. He turned out of the kitchen and into the foyer, keeping his voice low on the phone.

⨭⨭

Father Michael, Anthony's cousin, hurried into the hospital and led a long healing prayer for Rebecca. When he spoke, all the officers went down on bended knee praying for their sister. Tears poured down Anthony's face unchecked and his grief resonated through his family, Rebecca's family and the throng of police.

⨭⨭

Once the chief addressed the family his next job was to start handing everyone who was involved in this operation their asses, literally one by one.

"Our sister officer is dying because of YOU!" The chief shouted in Detective Matthew Mitchell's face. "You FUCKED UP!"

Mitchell didn't move.

"I was told that you showed up at her undercover job."

"I wasn't able to contact her on her cell phone, sir."

"Ya know what?" When Mitchell didn't answer, the chief continued. "I think you showing up at her undercover post tipped off her fucking supervisor, that son of a bitch!" The chief had been a cop for more than thirty years and coincidences didn't happen—fuck ups happened! And sure enough, most criminals had an uncanny ability to spot fuck ups . . . *fucking creeps!*

Mitchell knew his career was over. He already sent his letter of resignation to his immediate supervisor.

"Anthony Romano is one of this city's finest and most generous citizens especially to the NYPD and what do you do, you go get his wife KILLED!"

Mitchell stayed perfectly still.

"I can't understand how little fuckers like you keep getting through the academy." The chief poked at his detective's chest. "Just because your daddy's daddy was a great cop, doesn't make you one. Get out of my FUCKING SIGHT!"

Mitchell darted from the room, ashamed.

⤸⤷

Anthony checked his watch and paced the long hallway lined with officers. Some of the officer's faces looked the same and some looked new. Anthony realized that some had recently gotten off duty, while others had to leave to go on duty. He paced back and forth before these walls of blue listening to their prayers and compliments about how brave his wife was. They were there to fortify him and at that moment, he knew that he would have crumbled if they hadn't been there. Someone handed him a picture of Rebecca in her graduation uniform. Anthony couldn't stop the tears that flowed down his face, while the young officer explained how Rebecca helped him with the running portion of the training.

"We had to carry a wounded officer for one hundred yards, sir, in twenty seconds or we failed out of the academy. The record was seventeen seconds and Officer Romano carried me in fifteen seconds, even though I weighed forty-five pounds more than her. She broke a lot of records at the academy and even got the 'hot shot' ribbon in our class. She had the highest score during firearms qualifications, sir."

Anthony was so proud of her, nodding his head unable to speak past the huge lump in his throat. When he handed the photo back to the officer, the officer pressed it back into Anthony's hand. Anthony embraced him, thanking him soundlessly.

It was now exactly eight hours since the doctors' last spoke to them. His parents and Rebecca's parents were asleep in the lounge. Stephen, Rebecca's brother, was speaking to the chief and Jack was sitting in the lounge with Francesca sleeping at his side, watching him pace.

Finally, the door opened. The waiting was over. One doctor came out in clean scrubs and motioned for Anthony to join him.

Once the door closed, the doctor began, *"Christ,* that was one hell of a fight, but your wife is in phenomenal physical condition." Protocol was out the window at the moment, as the storm continued to rage outside the hospital walls. "That is the only reason why she survived the surgery. Anyone else and they would've been DOA."

Anthony nodded, trying to hear the doctor's words over his pounding heart.

"Okay. So the good news is that we have her stabilized. The bullet grazed the heart, but did not puncture it."

Anthony tried to still his shaky knees, staring at the doctor unblinking, almost unable to comprehend that the love of his life was still alive.

"We are giving her another unit of blood. That should be her last for now. She is breathing on her own, miraculously, but the baby . . ." the doctor trailed off.

Anthony leaned a hand against the block wall. During the long wait, Anthony had plenty of time to think, mentally calculating that they must have conceived the baby when they went to the country for the weekend.

"One month, maybe five weeks, tops . . . we picked up the pregnancy in her blood work. Her hCG hormone level was elevated and we confirmed it with an ultrasound. It's too soon to tell . . . she suffered so much trauma." the doctor explained. "The high doses of pain meds could cause her to spontaneously abort the pregnancy."

"I understand." Anthony took a deep breath.

"She's young and there will be other pregnancies. If we discover that the pregnancy is impeding her recovery, we will abort it immediately. We're not taking any chances."

Anthony swallowed nodding again, because the process of speaking was not an option at the moment. He didn't want to lose his wife. "Can I see her?"

"They are moving her to intensive care now, one floor down, room five-o-five. Give them fifteen minutes." The doctor turned to leave, but added as a last thought, "I don't know if anyone told you, but she was severely beaten, her right hand is broken in three spots," the doctor pointed to three areas on his hand. "Her face is swollen and will appear unrecognizable to you. The next twelve hours are critical."

Anthony nodded, still unable to speak due to the lump in his throat.

"She isn't out of the woods yet, but she's damn close."

Anthony nodded. He wanted to hug the doctor—it wasn't proper etiquette, but he did it anyway. "Thank you," he whispered.

Anthony walked back out into the hallway and told everyone that she survived the surgery, but that she had a long way to go. The officers couldn't help themselves and cheered with relief. Many officers and his family embraced him.

Anthony took the elevator down alone to the intensive care unit. Once he reached the door, a nurse met him and took him to a room to put on a sterile gown, cap, face mask and booties over his shoes. They also made him scrub his hands with antibacterial soap, before he put on the rubber gloves. They obviously weren't taking any chances.

Once he entered the hospital room, his stomach rolled threateningly. Rebecca lay unmoving in the bed connected to machines and IVs. Her face was swollen, exactly as the doctor said, beyond recognition and it was a complete shock to see his beautiful Rebecca this way. For the first hour, he sat by her bed waiting for any response, stroking her left hand softly. Her right hand, which was in a cast, lay over her abdomen unconsciously protecting their baby. For the second hour, he started to pray and by the third hour he was incredibly frustrated and just plain pissed off. He started to curse in Italian then in French topped off with a little Greek, when suddenly he heard a faint noise coming from the bed. Anthony rushed over to Rebecca's bedside whispering, "Darling I'm here, I'm here."

"English," Rebecca struggled to get the word out. "For the love of God, speak English," she groaned.

Anthony laughed and cried at the same time. He embraced her without disturbing the tubes that ran into her arm and back to machines, his tears spilling onto her face.

"Do I still have my teeth?" Rebecca mumbled.

"I think so." Anthony exhaled, smiling tenderly, tentatively touching her bruised, swollen lips.

"*Son of a bitch* punched me in my mouth," Rebecca took a deep breath. "I really hate those cheap shots." Rebecca paused, because her brain felt fuzzy. "Naturally, I hit him back right in the mouth." Rebecca breathed in and out again with some difficulty. "I think that's when I broke my hand," Rebecca slightly lifted her right hand. "I laughed at him when he spit some of his teeth out at me. That really set him off," Rebecca sighed.

Anthony shivered dreading the day when he would probably have to hear the entire story. "A cop?" Anthony questioned softly.

"Yeah . . . about that . . ." Rebecca broke off for a moment struggling to stay awake. "Can you tell my parents? You're so good with those kinds of things." Rebecca closed her swollen eyes succumbing to the medication.

Anthony smiled, remembering the time she had asked him to do that very thing before. "I love you darling." Anthony placed a protective hand over her lower abdomen next to hers praying for her and their child.

Epilogue
Time to make a move . . .

Rebecca came home nearly a month later, after spending almost two weeks in the hospital followed by two weeks at the hospital's rehabilitation facility. Of course, Anthony was by her side every day.

On the day she was released from the rehabilitation facility, they were led by a full police escort. Rebecca was wheeled into the apartment with officers all around her, Captain Rice leading the way along with Anthony. Trevor was sitting on her lap carefully holding her broken hand, which was still in a cast. Trevor leaned over to whisper into Rebecca's ear, "I changed my mind."

"About?" Rebecca asked keeping her tone quiet.

"I want to be just like you when I grow up."

"Don't tell your father!" Rebecca whispered eyeing him cautiously. "I'm not sure if your dad can handle that right now. But we can start practicing on your target shooting." Rebecca secretly planned.

Trevor's green eyes gleamed with excitement.

Anthony was praying a whole lot more these days, so thankful that his wife was still alive as well as their baby. They didn't tell Trevor yet, because the baby was only two months along and there could still be consequences. The doctors were quick to disclose all of the potential gory, graphic details.

Captain Rice was equally as equipped as the doctors in the "gory details" department. He made it very clear to Anthony that there was still a very real danger since Rebecca was the one who set up the biggest sex trafficker in the world. "It all comes down to money and she cost these traffickers millions."

Captain Rice recommended retired military personnel for protection and Anthony didn't hesitate to take his advice. Some of the highest-trained men and women from the United States military would be protecting Rebecca and Trevor around the clock and that gave Anthony some peace of mind, but he still wanted his family out of the city. Captain Rice made it clear that there would be a new head sex trafficker to take the place of the dead one. "They're a dime a dozen."

Anthony shivered with the thought, thinking of his niece, praying for so many young lost girls.

That night, after Trevor was happily tucked into bed, Anthony and Rebecca sat in the study on the couch sipping their hot tea. Anthony thought this was the perfect time to discuss his plans, with his arm circled around his wife's shoulders, pulling her in close to him. He missed her on so many levels. Before they left the facility today, her doctor secretly confided that Rebecca asked him if she could get back to normal relations with her husband and he told her, *absolutely*. But Anthony would follow her lead. Both the doctors and her superior officers told him that Rebecca could have a period of post trauma, that nightmares and general signs of depression were common. *Geez*, Anthony thought, *I've been experiencing those very things myself.*

"Maybe it is time to think about buying a home?" Anthony kissed the top of his wife's fragrant hair.

Rebecca leaned back, curled up by her husband's side looking up into quiet gray-blue eyes that projected peacefulness. It was something she had searched for her whole life and was one of the lucky ones, because she found it.

"Where?" Rebecca asked.

"Jack said there is a place that adjoins his land that is for sale." Anthony ran his fingertips up and down Rebecca's arm that was draped over his chest. "Trevor could have a yard to play in and be close to his cousin. And you would be close to your best friend. I know how much you miss Francesca."

"I do miss her and Trevor would love it there." Rebecca rested her head back onto his strong shoulder, wondering if he was going to touch her tonight.

"And I could see my brother more," Anthony was thinking out loud.

"That would be nice. But the commute—how are you planning to get to work?"

"There are actually several ways I can get to work. I can go by boat, helicopter or the conventional way, car."

Rebecca nodded. The first two would be quicker. "What about schools, Children's Services and Trevor's friends?" Rebecca was thinking about Trevor and how a change like that could impact his current progress.

"The area is actually a golden ribbon school district, but Trevor will probably have a period of adjustment meeting new children his age. Ms. Cortez from Children's Services is going to have a long ride to pop in on us."

"Sofia?" Rebecca was thinking about the scars on her face and how she was never, ever going to find employment.

Anthony smiled, loving the woman who was curled up by his side even more. She actually gave a damn about others, unlike so many people today who had their own agenda and no one and nothing else seemed to matter. "I have scheduled Sofia for an appointment with a team of plastic surgeons in California and if we have to drag her there kicking and screaming, so be it. I already asked my father to get on it."

"No one ever says *no* to your father."

Anthony smiled. "Besides, I have an idea for Sofia. Come on, let me show you." Anthony placed their mugs of hot tea on the coffee table and pulled his wife up behind him. Slowly they walked to his office and Anthony had Rebecca sit behind his desk. He leaned over and pulled up the recent e-mail from his brother. Clicking the mouse, he brought up the first picture.

"Is that a barn?" Rebecca asked, looking closer.

"Yes. It was converted two years ago into a house, but it isn't complete. The owners ran out of money. I thought this would be a great place to raise our family . . . what do you think?"

"I think that's awesome." Rebecca watched as Anthony clicked through the photos of some other buildings and the shoreline.

"This is riverfront like Francesca and Jack's property."

"Oh wow, that's pretty."

"So?"

"Yes."

"Just like that . . ." Anthony was stunned.

"Yup, just like that." Rebecca would follow her husband everywhere and anywhere he wanted to lead her. Besides, her father-in-law already laid down the law while she was at the rehabilitation facility. In that moment, Rebecca recalled her tall, powerful father-in-law. Whenever he entered her room, the nursing staff seemed to dive for cover. His mere stature and presence evoked authority and instilled fear. He paced along the foot of her bed, telling her that he could not rest knowing that his son's wife was in harm's way at any given moment. Then he said something to her in Italian and said he expected more grandchildren, muttering another phrase in Italian. He told her that he was proud of her. But he also told her that she was forbidden to do any further undercover work. He promised that he would personally follow her around if need be and not to underestimate him. And when he told her that he loved her, in that split-second, she was through with undercover work. He had her eating out of his hand like a baby bird.

"Alright, now check this out." Anthony pulled up the next screen to reveal a photo of a restaurant.

"Oh that's pretty too. Is that an inn?"

"It's a bed and breakfast, The Black Bear Inn."

"I like the name." Rebecca smiled over her shoulder at her husband.

"I like the name too, but the place is badly rundown. Jack is convinced it is worth saving, but I have my doubts. I think it needs a wrecking ball!"

Rebecca laughed and studied the pictures as Anthony clicked through them.

"It was originally a home that was converted into a bed and breakfast and restaurant, but it hasn't been open for business in years." Anthony clicked on more of the pictures which showed how the restaurant sat on lakefront.

"How far is this from where we will be living?" Rebecca asked, clicking back through the pictures.

"About ten miles." Anthony guessed, resting his hands tenderly on her shoulders.

"Sofia could turn that place into a goldmine."

"My thoughts exactly." Anthony lifted up his wife and settled her down onto his lap. "So what do you think?" Anthony twirled a curl that fell over her shoulder around his index finger.

"I think that you and your brother have already conspired."

Anthony was openly shocked. "I have to start working on my poker face. It would be very bad for business if people could read me that easily."

Rebecca giggled.

"Jack has already begun some preliminary negotiation talks. The properties need a ton of work, but Jack would turn them around in no time." Anthony didn't tell her that when he spoke to his brother, he told him that he would pay whatever the sellers wanted to get his family and Sofia out of the city as quickly as possible.

"No doubt. I mean just look at what he did with Francesca's farmhouse. I'm sure he can turn these diamonds in the rough into flawless gems."

"Can you leave your work behind?" Anthony was almost afraid to ask, afraid that if she couldn't, he would have to accept that. They didn't speak about her police work at all and Anthony was unsure if she was willing to give it up and leave it all behind.

"I have a new assignment," Rebecca paused to place her hand still in a cast low on her abdomen protectively. "But I reserve the right to keep my options open." When the doctor told her in the hospital that she was a month pregnant, she cried. Instantly, she remembered that when they went away for the weekend, she forgot her birth control pills. She didn't think that skipping a day or two could leave her open to getting pregnant, but it did. Then when the doctor explained to her that she might lose the baby, she felt such guilt, because her actions could possibly destroy what she and Anthony created.

Anthony didn't particularly care for the "keep my options open" comment and would wage that war another night, but not tonight. "Let's seal the deal with a kiss."

"Is that how you conclude all of your transactions at Romano Enterprises?"

"Yes." Anthony reached his fingers into his wife's fragrant hair pulling her face close, pressing his lips to hers. Slowly he rose up out of the chair, lifting his wife up with him and carried her into their bedroom. Anthony placed Rebecca carefully down next to the bed.

"My heart is pounding." Rebecca confessed softly, as she placed her hand over her heart.

"Mine too." Anthony admitted as he took her hand from over her heart and placed it over his.

Rebecca stood very still. "What a fool I was! I'm so sorry." Rebecca whispered on the verge of tears.

"Che?" Anthony asked, ducking low. Anthony studied Rebecca's eyes, at eye level, stroking the face of the woman who turned his life upside down and inside out, all while making him the happiest man on the face of the earth.

"I might have robbed us of our first child." Rebecca whimpered covering their unborn child protectively. Tears started to pool in her eyes threatening to spill over.

"The baby is safe. Nothing can hurt her now." Anthony reassured her, placing his hand over hers.

"I have made your life a living hell."

"No you haven't." Anthony smiled kissing her forehead. "Every moment with you is like one thousand moments. And every moment of my life spent without you, doesn't even exist for me." Anthony wanted her to know what she meant to him, watching his words of love shimmer over her. He recognized that look upon her face. And he knew that when he spoke the words before any touch, his touch would have everlasting meaning.

"My husband." Rebecca whispered, tears racing along the curve of her cheek, because his words were dispelling the dark shadows of guilt.

"My wife." Anthony whispered kissing her tears away. "Tonight I am going to make love to you because I've missed you so much. I need you, I want you and I love you." Anthony watched her tears travel down her lovely cheeks. He swept her tears away with his thumbs, sliding his hands to capture her face before pulling her up for a deep kiss.

Rebecca had a thought. "Wait. I'll be right back." Rebecca pulled away from him, ran into the closet, gathered some items from a drawer then darted into the bathroom, smiling wickedly at Anthony on the way.

Anthony watched while she ran into the bathroom and closed the door. Inside the bathroom, Rebecca unfolded the lace wrap she wore on their honeymoon. Struggling with her hand still in a cast, she undressed as quickly as she could. Her fingers touched her scar over her left breast. *My God, what a risk I took!* Refocusing her attention, she pulled on the lace wrap then tied it closed as best she could. She plumped her hair and dabbed a little lip gloss on her lips.

In the bedroom, Anthony waited a few minutes then decided to busy himself. He removed some of the decorative pillows from the bed and turned down the comforter. When he slipped off his shoes and socks, he heard the bathroom door open. He turned and instantly froze. Rebecca was wearing the unmistakable white lace wrap that she wore on their honeymoon. He walked forward to study the beauty in white lace before him. The bridal wrap was lace with satin trim and hit Rebecca at the middle of her highly defined thighs.

She was cut and he didn't understand her obsession with eating right and exercising, until it was revealed to him that she was a police officer. Anthony reached out to touch the fabric. He traced his index finger along the satin trim watching her take a deep breath.

"The night I wore this, I wanted you to touch me . . . to make love to me . . ." Rebecca stopped speaking, because Anthony suddenly guided his fingertip over the outline of her orb covered in white lace.

"I wanted you so badly that night." Anthony lowered his head to lick at the bud pressing up against the lace.

Rebecca almost stopped breathing. She closed her eyes, savoring the sensation. She was getting that funny feeling that the world was starting to tilt again.

Anthony felt her sway and whispered, "Stay with me darling."

Rebecca opened her eyes watching Anthony move his head to treat the neglected right bud the same.

"*Delizioso.* Delicious." Anthony stood up making the translation. He pressed his lips to hers and teased her mouth open. He kissed her gently, tenderly twining his tongue with hers.

Rebecca pulled at his shirt until it was off. She ran her fingertips along every muscle following the pattern each one made. She skimmed her hands along his abdomen.

Anthony pulled the sash on the wrap. He opened both sides of the lace wrap, sliding it over her shoulders and down her arms until it drifted to her feet. He saw the scar over her heart and shivered. He touched her scar tentatively before lowering his head to kiss the spot, inhaling a shuddering breath. For him, this scar would be a constant reminder of how close he came to losing her.

When he lifted his head, Rebecca undid Anthony's belt and slacks, watching as they pooled at his ankles.

Anthony stepped out of his slacks, kicking them aside before he advanced on her. Using just his fingertips, he ran them along the muscles on her abdomen.

Rebecca intended to keep pace and followed suit. She lowered his boxer-briefs until they were at his ankles, running her fingers over his countless muscles, watching as they leapt to attention. Slowly she took his maleness into her hands, as she watched Anthony's gray eyes grow dark, closing slowly. He wanted to be touched, she knew. And when she knelt before him and placed him into her mouth, she heard him moan her name.

"Rebecca." Anthony groaned sliding his fingers into her hair. *"Rebecca."* Anthony felt loved. No one ever touched him like this except for her and the sensation was pleasure with an edge of danger, as his pulsating penis grazed along her teeth.

"Delizioso." Rebecca whispered before she drew him in again.

Anthony chuckled at her repeating the Italian word he used to describe her, but once she retook him back into her mouth, his laughter stopped. Anthony wanted to make this first night home with her special. After a few more seconds, he lifted her face from his body and helped her stand before him. He reached down taking hold of her bottom, lifting her until her legs were wrapped around his waist and carried her until her back was balanced against the wall. With one hand, he found her center and entered her in one powerfully thrust. Anthony drove into her, watching her eyes close. *"Bella."* Anthony called to her, blinded with passion while driving into her over and over again.

Rebecca cupped his face with her left hand, hooking her other hand in its cast around his neck, struggling to hold onto him. "Anthony." Rebecca called out his name before her head leaned back against the wall. She could feel her release building and after several more thrusts, they both climaxed.

Anthony groaned on his release, burying his head into Rebecca's neck, while Rebecca rested her head on top of his.

Rebecca could still feel him pulsing within her, feeling his labored breath along her neck, while her own climax continued. When she lifted her head up, she noticed how his shoulder muscles bulged dramatically from him supporting her and couldn't resist running her hand over the taut muscle group. When he lifted his head up, Rebecca was fascinated to witness the face of a man who was completely in love. But the best part was that she was the recipient of his love.

Anthony lowered her feet to the floor carefully. He watched his rapid breath move her hair to and fro. He cradled her face, kissing her sweetly. "My darling," Anthony whispered, desperately trying to capture his breath. "I am so in love with you," he whispered between his labored breaths, chuckling slightly.

"I love you Anthony." Rebecca touched Anthony's chiseled face, feeling blessed, so very blessed. "Thank you for being so patient with me."

"My pleasure darling and very well worth the wait." Anthony chuckled again.

Rebecca giggled. "Do you forgive me for my secrets?"

"Do you really need to ask?" Anthony swept her up into his arms and carried her to the bed. He lowered her to the bed slowly, watching Rebecca scoot over to give him room to join her, but he didn't join her. Instead he devoured her visually. He studied her legs which were trim and muscular from her running. "Thank you for this body." Anthony trailed his fingers along her muscular legs.

Rebecca laughed and smiled remembering that she had said the very same thing to him.

Anthony ran his fingertips over more of her. He ran his fingers along the muscles on her chest, the muscles on her arms and the muscles on her abdomen. His eyes studied her hips, lightly skimming his fingertips where he envisioned their baby might be, their miracle that still survived. He watched her lay back against the pillows, placing one arm behind her head while the other in the cast rested along the curve of her waist. Anthony studied her breasts which were pronounced and rising and falling with each breath she took. He watched her centers rise in anticipation of his next touch and noticed the effects of the baby here. "The baby is changing you here." Anthony ran a fingertip along the darkened circle on her breast.

Rebecca closed her eyes, enjoying her husband's touch.

"Anymore secrets darling?" Anthony softly questioned continuing his feathery-light caresses.

"No." Rebecca murmured closing her eyes.

"Are you certain?" Anthony touched the darkened circle around her other bud watching his wife shake her head. "I hope you weren't planning on sleeping my love, because tonight, while our son sleeps, I am going to make love to you again and again and again . . ." Anthony declared when he slowly lowered himself down onto the bed, slipping into her silkiness.

"That sounds perfect." Rebecca sighed, "Absolutely perfect."

The End

Here is a Sneak Peek At
The Wedding Vow
Book 3 in the Romano Family Trilogy

Chapter One
Exit, stage right . . .

Captain Thomas Rice sat quietly in his dress blues on stage at the awards celebration. There were other superior officers on either side of him, including Lieutenant Ryan who could never look Thomas in the eye again. *Maybe that has to do with the fact that that jackass stole my fiancée from me who just happens to be sitting in the front row to my left, wearing all red from neck to toe. God help me . . .*

With his speech neatly tucked inside his jacket, he decided to concentrate on anything else, but his depressing love life. There were hundreds of men and women from the New York City Police Department who were also dressed in their stiffly starched dress blues. Chief Franks stood next to the commissioner who was at the microphone calling out another name for another award.

Thomas took notice that two rows in from the front sat the Romano family. Thomas saw Officer Rebecca Romano sitting with her husband Anthony Romano and their son, Trevor, who sat in between them. Hard to believe that she was five months pregnant, because she was not showing any signs of carrying a child. Anthony Romano's brother, Jack and wife sat behind them, together with the senior Romanos and Officer Romano's family.

Thomas could visually study the crowd with much thanks to the formal hat that was part of the NYPD Class A uniform. All officers were required to wear their hat so that it sat low on the forehead. For Thomas, this gave him the advantage. His shaded blue eyes were given a prime opportunity to study the lovely Miss Sofia Martinez, who was the housekeeper for Anthony and Rebecca Romano. She sat directly behind Trevor Romano, quietly trying not to be noticed. It was evident in the plain dress she wore, how her hair was draped forward to hide the scars she received from an attacker almost twenty years ago to the day. The crowd interrupted his thoughts as a moment of applause grew louder for another award recipient.

The commissioner took his seat next to Thomas as the chief made the next introduction.

"The last commendation will be presented by Captain Thomas Rice, because this officer was under Captain Rice's command and it is fitting to this administration to see this medal presented by this commanding officer." Chief Franks turned and Thomas rose to his feet. Pausing to salute the commissioner, Thomas walked straight and stiffly to the podium. Once he reached the podium, Thomas saluted his chief, as the chief returned the salute before taking his seat next to the commissioner.

Thomas looked out at the audience as he reached into his jacket to remove his speech. He was comfortable at the microphone, as he adjusted it slightly for his height. Very little rattled this veteran officer's cage, except for Sofia. He noticed Sofia straighten in her chair, studying him absorbedly. Thomas refocused his attention on the printed words and began in a deep, loud resounding tone that could probably be heard perfectly even without the microphone. "This next medal may be the last given out today, but it is certainly not the least." Thomas looked up from his speech to view the crowd, his eyes landing on Sofia.

"This officer almost paid the ultimate price to help others in our great city." Thomas paused while he waited for the applause that suddenly started. "This officer is an officer who we should emulate and look up to. This officer is what we all strive to be as we wear our shields and carry our oaths through each shift." Again the applause started anew and Thomas granted the customary pause during his speech. "The medal of valor, which is the highest award the department can give, goes to Officer Rebecca Romano . . ." Although Thomas had a few more words, the crowd went wild with cheers and applause so he left it at that.

Thomas watched Anthony Romano's reaction. The man made no secret of the fact that he did not want his wife working as a New York City police officer and made no secret that he wanted her to quit the department. She nearly gave her life and Thomas could see it in every fiber of Anthony Romano that he did not want her to ever be in that situation again, where she would put a total stranger's life above her own.

Anthony Romano sat quietly while his wife's name was called, still grappling with the image she portrayed in her dress uniform that made their son tremble with excitement. When Rebecca put on her pressed dress blues this morning and attached her heavy belt adding her weapon as the last piece to her uniform, Anthony could only stare at her in awe.

Trevor looked from Anthony to Rebecca, his father and mother. "Mom that's you!" Trevor exclaimed. At close to nine years old, Trevor was knowledgeable far beyond his years.

"I guess it is." Rebecca whispered. "I have to go on stage now."

"Can I go with you?" Trevor asked.

"Of course."

Rebecca stood up and Anthony stood up to let them pass as he leaned down to press a kiss on his precious wife's cheek. It was her decision if she continued to work for the department, but, man, he was not going to like it. *Not one damn bit,* Anthony inwardly decreed.

Rebecca took Trevor's hand and led him up the stage. The crowd went wild. Officers were on their feet whistling, cheering and applauding so loudly that the auditorium shook with exhilaration. Rebecca saluted her captain, as he saluted her back. When Trevor saluted Thomas, the crowd went nuts. Rebecca removed her hat as Thomas slid the award over her head. Rebecca mechanically returned the hat to her head, adjusting the brim slightly above her eyes. Thomas saluted her, as Rebecca and Trevor did the same in return.

It was these moments that motivated a department. These events that officers relived and gleaned from for many years to come. Thomas looked at Rebecca who lifted her son up, as Trevor did a fist pump into the air causing the crowd to go absolutely ballistic. The chief and commissioner joined them at the podium. Thomas laughed and tousled Trevor's hair.

All of them stood before the press and Thomas' eyes were nearly blinded by the barrage of bulbs flashing riotously. The chief stood by Rebecca as she held Trevor while the press took too many pictures to count. That was because she was a Romano. Thomas knew. But she didn't seem to care. She smiled for the cameras and placed a soft kiss on her son's cheek, who anyone could see simply adored her.

After several minutes, the rest of the family came on stage and the press went nearly feral photographing Anthony kissing Rebecca on the cheek and all the Romanos taking turns kissing

Rebecca and congratulating her. Thomas strategically made his way over to Sofia who was standing behind everyone.

"Camera shy?" Thomas teased quietly.

"Yes." Sofia admitted just as quietly.

Thomas laughed. "You look lovely today."

"Thank you." Sofia knew he was lying and said that only to be nice to her, because she purposely picked the ugliest dress she had. She never wanted to stand out in a crowd. "You look pretty lovely yourself today." Sofia let her eyes wander over the intricate uniform.

"Thank you." Thomas said in a deep, rich voice.

"I watched Rebecca get into her uniform this morning and she refused to sit until we left. She wouldn't even let anyone get near her."

"Old habits die hard."

"I guess."

"So Rebecca tells me you might be moving out of the city." Thomas wanted to know.

"I haven't decided yet."

Suddenly Lieutenant Ryan and his fiancée, Jodi, who was once Thomas' fiancée walked over to Thomas to say hello, interrupting his conversation with Sofia.

Sofia looked at the blonde beauty and inwardly cringed. Immediately pulling her hair over her scars, Sofia studied the platinum blonde, who wore a deep V-neck, vibrant red dress and red high heels. She could tell that Thomas wasn't pleased with the interruption, but she watched him act polite and cordial. He made simple introductions and when Jodi finally caught a better view of Sofia's face, she physically recoiled. Sofia encountered this reaction so many times before, but this time, in front of Thomas, it hurt like she had been slashed all over again. Sofia murmured, "Excuse me."

Thomas wasn't as polite glaring at Lieutenant Ryan and Jody standing there. "What's it gonna take to get you two to stay the fuck away from me . . . a restraining order?"

Lieutenant Ryan pounced on Jody. "What the fuck did you say to her?" He was desperately trying to make amends with Thomas since Jody left Thomas for him. It made for some mighty tense situations in the station.

"I didn't say anything to her . . . I saw her face and I was so shocked when I saw all those scars. Why didn't you tell me?" Jody rested her hand on her ample bosom, thanks to the fine work from an acclaimed New York plastic surgeon.

"Not everyone can be fucking beautiful Jody!" Lieutenant Ryan turned and left her standing there alone on the stage.

⬡

Thomas noticed that Rebecca saw what happened with Jody and he gave her a head nod that he was going to check up on Sofia. He went behind the stage and looked for her quietly. Then he heard it, a small cry. Thomas found her behind the curtains that pooled deep into a pocket at the side of the stage.

"Sofia . . . sweetheart?" Thomas approached the curtain finally finding his way into the yards and yards of red velvet.

Sofia turned away from him into the curtain. She didn't want anyone to see her.

"Come here . . ." Thomas turned her around, taking her into his arms feeling her tense up the second he embraced her. *Obviously very uncomfortable around men.* After several minutes, Thomas decided to talk softly to her. "You're much prettier than her." He whispered quietly, cocooned in the red velvet with his dark haired beauty. *So beautiful . . .*

Sofia laughed on a sob.

"It's true." Thomas held her close filling his senses to the brim. Getting lost in her exotic scent, the texture of her raven long hair between his fingertips and the tiny upper torso. *Very delicate,* he reflected silently. It absolutely amazed him how she fought for her life and won against her attacker, even though all the odds were stacked against her. Thomas decided to talk to her while she wept softly. "I used to be engaged to her. Ya know . . . Jody."

Immediately Sofia jerked back and looked up at him. "Figures . . ." Sofia puckered her lips.

"What's that supposed to mean? She dumped me, and for a fellow officer!" Thomas smiled, because it didn't hurt anymore to talk about his pathetic love life. He ran his open hand along the scarred side of her face that still had tears running down it.

"Lieutenant Ryan?" Sofia asked quietly.

"Yeah."

"I can see you and Jody together." Sofia was so out of her league being held in Thomas' arms.

"Really . . . because I can't. Not anymore." Thomas leaned down bringing his lips closer to Sofia's. "I see myself with someone else. Someone that I've had strong feelings for . . . for a long time." Thomas leaned down and kissed her, pressing his lips to hers. He wasn't going to push her, but when she opened her mouth for him, he went in for the taste of her sweet nectar. *My exotic flower . . .*

Go to www.dalyromance.com for more of the
Captain and Sofia's Story in "The Wedding Vow"
The Romano Family Trilogy - Book 3